THE PRICE YOU PAY

A DI KAREN HEATH NOVEL

JAY NADAL

1

A FINE DRIZZLE danced across his windscreen. The wipers cleared his view for a few seconds, only to obscure it moments later. It was May and the start of summer. The weather had been warm for the last few weeks, though the evenings still carried a distinct chill. But the misting rain only helped his cause further.

After driving around for the last hour trying to find the perfect area, he settled on the ideal spot, brimming with street girls looking for business. For him, the poor weather served as an ally. Rain was *their* enemy. The girls didn't want to hang around getting pissed on, which only made them less fussy and more willing to offer a *discount* on the normal rates. Not that their rates were extortionate or anything like that, but the chance of a small reprieve inside the warmth of a punter's car was worth it.

He normally wouldn't be in this part of the city, but with limited pickings tonight, it would have to do. As he watched the girls come and go, he crouched low in his driver's seat. The braver ones leaned in through passenger windows trying to convince punters to part with the tenner for a blowjob, or a score for full sex with a "jacket" on.

With his interest piqued, he spotted one woman wearing a baggy leather jacket, a short black leather skirt, both of which he imagined were cheap tacky synthetic knockoffs, and black clunky ankle boots. *Perfect street gear.* Easy for her to hitch up her skirt without getting undressed, and for escaping with her clothes intact if she got caught.

He'd seen her come and go in several cars over the last two hours. Business had been good for her. She was a regular and well-liked by her punters, much to the annoyance of the other girls who stood around, their arms folded across their chests while they dragged heavily on their sodden fags.

Pulling down on his baseball cap and adjusting his thick-rimmed glasses, he turned the key in the ignition, flicked on the lights and pulled away from the kerb moving in her direction. It was as if the night sky had turned up the notch of misery even further as the fine drizzle became a heavy downpour. Girls scattered in every direction, seeking shelter in doorways. They swore and shouted at their misfortune. Just as the woman was about to turn and dive into the nearest doorway, she glanced up to see the head-lights slowing as the car approached her. She threw a hand over her eyes to shield them from the worst of the rain as she eyed the car with suspicion. Sometimes there weren't punters inside, but cops looking to have a friendly word.

She walked to the passenger side window as it slid down.

With sheets of rain pounding around her, she checked him over. He looked like any other punter. Desperate, fidgety, eyes shifting from her to the surrounding street, alert for any signs of danger, including the police.

"You looking for business?" the woman asked, her tone as gritty as chunks of shattered glass. "Are you sightseeing or browsing?"

He threw her a smile. "I'm definitely looking for business." He eyed her up for a few moments, letting his intentions be known. "And out of all the girls here, you fit the bill the best. I'm ready if you are?"

"Well, I don't wanna be hanging around in this pissing rain any more. What are you after? I can suck you off and spit for a tenner. I'll swallow for fifteen. Twenty quid for full sex."

He nodded and raised a brow. She had fair skin and though he already knew her age, she tried to look younger. Her glazed-over eyes told him she was on something to take away the misery that she felt every day. Her make-up, carelessly applied, now streaked her face. Yet beneath her sloppy presentation, she carried a beauty that had been eroded through a life of drugs and prostitution. "Twenty quid is good for me. Have you got anywhere we can go?"

The woman opened the passenger door and slid into the front seat. "I'm wet through," she moaned as she ran a hand through her dark, wet lank hair. "Go straight ahead, take the second left. Don't hang around here or we will both be in trouble if the Old Bill turns up."

"Okay," he replied, turning in his seat and pulling away.

2

"LISTEN, do you do anything extra on top?" he asked as he drove through the darkened, wet streets.

The woman pulled a face and twisted her lips. "What more do you want? Twenty quid and you get a shag. That's it."

"Well, I was thinking of a bit more. I know a place where we won't get disturbed and even though I've done this loads of times, I fancy something a bit kinky. I'd love to bend you over my bonnet and take you from behind."

"Listen, mate. This is business. I'm not your girlfriend. I'm not your wife, and I'm not your bit on the side. You're wasting my time. If Arthur doesn't find me back here in fifteen minutes, he'll beat us both black and blue. If you're looking for that kind of stuff, there are plenty of incall services that you can find online."

"Hundred quid."

The woman shot him a look as if to suggest, *have you lost the plot?*

She hesitated for a minute which was enough time for him to come in with another tempting offer. "One-hundred-and-fifty quid."

Her eyes widened as she looked at him again and then stared through the windscreen.

"Come on. It's the best offer you'll get all night. You can make more with me in half an hour than you'd make for the entire night. I'll even chuck in a bonus if you're really good."

"How much more?"

"You do well, and you'll find out."

She nodded in consideration. "I could give Arthur fifty quid and keep a hundred for myself. I could tell him that the punter gave me a hundred. He'd be more than happy with a fifty-fifty split. He'd never find out the truth."

The man smiled and nodded before reaching into the pocket of his jacket and pulled out a crisp fifty-pound note. He passed it over to her. "Down payment."

The woman snatched it from his hand and stared at it wide-eyed. "I don't think I've ever seen a fifty-pound note."

"There's a few more of them if you play your cards right," he said with a wry smile. "Deal?"

The woman caved in and nodded. The offer was too good to turn down. "Deal."

Stupid bitch.

"I know somewhere quiet where we won't get disturbed. It's not far from here. There's no police, no CCTV, and no traffic. *Dead* at this time of night. You'll… be… safe," he said, doing his best to offer her a reassuring smile. His pulse throbbed in his neck and pounded in his head as the excitement grew in him. Things were unfolding perfectly.

"I don't want to go too far. Arthur will call me if I'm gone too long." Fear laced her words as she chewed on her bottom lip.

"Drop him a text and tell him you will be back in half an hour. Tell him you've picked up a punter with lots of cash. Sorry, I don't know your name…"

The woman shrugged. "You don't need to know my name. This isn't a date." She retrieved her phone from her handbag and tapped away, pressed send, and tucked it away in her bag again. She pulled out a condom and clutched it in her hand, ready to get on with the deed.

The wipers slowed as the rain eased off. She glanced around at the unfamiliar surroundings. "Where are we going?"

"Not far. It's a few minutes away. By the time I drop you off, you won't have been gone for more than thirty minutes."

Making his way from the area, the streets grew darker, as did his mood. Occasional streetlights illuminated the inside of the car for a few seconds before a cloak of darkness returned. Neither of them offered idle chit-chat. They both had a job to do. Except this would be her last job.

Ever.

3

Mɪsт ʜᴜɴɢ low in the air as he slowed his car, the damp only adding to the chilling gloom that enveloped them. Weeks of searching had led him to this location. It wasn't overlooked, hours could pass without a single vehicle being seen, and there was no CCTV for miles around.

"Where are we?" she asked as nerves tingled her body. She was so far away from her usual patch that she had lost all sense of direction. But the temptation of earning a few hundred pounds proved irresistible. Though she'd forgone a hearty meal for months, her veins craved something far more sinister that stripped her body of all her senses. "It's pitch black out there," she added, trying to focus on the stretch of road ahead illuminated by his headlights.

"I said I want to go somewhere that's safe. I've been wanting to do this for such a long time that I want nothing spoiling it. Besides, in fifteen minutes' time you're going to be a few hundred pounds richer."

With hesitation in her voice, she wriggled in her seat. "I'm not so sure about this now. This place is giving me the heebie-jeebies. Someone could murder us out here and no one would find us for ages."

That's the plan.

"Look. We are going to do this my way, or I'll turn around and drop you back and find someone else to give the money to. Your shout."

The ease with which the words tripped from his tongue and how easy it would be for her to miss this payday alarmed her. "Okay. Okay. Let's get this over and done with. Or Arthur is going to kill me."

He'll have to get in line.

He pulled off on to the side of the road and into a makeshift lay-by before finding the gap in the hedge where the metal gate once used to be. His headlights showed him the way as the grassy verge levelled out on to a concrete path, which revealed a vast expanse of land for as far as the eye could see.

"Here we are," he said, switching off the engine but leaving on his headlights.

He opened his door. The internal lighting in the roof lining flooded the inside of the car. He looked at her. Though her hair had dried out, her pathetic attempt at make-up made her look like a Coco the Clown cast-off as mascara trails snaked down her cheeks and bright red lipstick smudged her chin.

After stepping from the passenger side, a little shiver travelled along her limbs. She stood there like a little lost girl; feet turned inwards; arms pulled in close to her sides.

"Come on. Are we going to do this or not?" he demanded.

She rolled her eyes and swallowed hard as she came around to the front of his car. She handed him the condom. "Safety first."

HE TORE the packet apart and pulled out the greasy rubber. He hated the look and feel of these things. But it was essential that he wore one. He didn't want to leave any evidence.

"Go on then. Turn around and bend over."

The woman obliged. Though his demand was unusual, she was used to sex being a mechanical, unemotional, financial transaction. She would blank the event from her mind and focus on the money. Turning, she took off her jacket and threw it on the ground, bent over and slid her knickers down to her ankles before hoisting her skirt up. The warmth crept into her fingers as she put her hands on the bonnet. She could hear him undoing the zip on his jeans and fiddling with the condom as the elastic rim slapped and snapped on to the skin.

He stepped in behind her and entered her with a hard thrust.

She gasped. "Take it easy!" she yelped through gritted teeth as she waited for the initial shock to subside.

"I told you I wanted it kinky," he replied as he thrust harder.

Her hands struggled to support her as her body rocked back and forth. At one point, she fell forward on to her elbows, unable to move as his hands pressed down on to her shoulders. He clenched his jaws as a surge of adrenaline coursed through his veins.

"Hurry… up!" she urged through ragged breaths.

The power he felt as he dominated her only strengthened his resolve as his hands moved from her shoulders to her neck. Bare arms exposed tattooed sleeves that inked every inch of her flesh. With every inch her top crept upward, he saw the first glimpse of the tattoo across her lower back. His eyes widened in excited anticipation.

His fingers spread around the sides of her neck and tightened.

"What the fuck…?" she yelled as she tried to push herself away from the bonnet and stand up.

With his hands firmly gripped around her neck, he pushed her body back down and squeezed harder and harder until her screams became a guttural, gurgled cry for help. She thrashed, but her legs gave way. Her feet scraped across the ground—desperate for some traction—anything that would give her a fighting chance to push him away.

His grip held firm as his fingers pressed into her soft flesh. The excitement of killing her replaced the eroticism. She thrashed harder as spittle erupted from her lips and peppered the bonnet. Her body weakened. Her lungs burnt, her eyes bulged, and her face flushed red.

It fell quiet as she let out her last breath. He stepped away and watched as her body slid down the bonnet and crumpled to the ground. He pulled up his jeans and zipped up his fly before walking around to the boot and pulling out his gleaming sword. With one hand still holding the sword, he grabbed her by one ankle and dragged her body along the ground to an overgrown grassy area.

He stood over her before placing her body in a crucifix

position with her arms outstretched at her sides. Her body looked broken, like an emaciated mannequin thrown on the tip. He took a few deep breaths before raising the sword above his head and bringing it down in one powerful arc on to the woman's right wrist. The hand separated. Picking up the limb by its bony fingers, he examined it for a few seconds before casting her one last look and heading back to his car.

"Sayonara."

4

It wasn't a straightforward museum all geared around one theme. Instead, it had a smorgasbord of themes to explore, peppered with historical curiosity along the way such as the face mask of Oliver Cromwell next to the opening displays.

Karen glanced across at Summer and wondered if she was enjoying the visit. The teenager's hands were stuffed in the front of her fleece as she shuffled along looking at the various exhibits. Zac trailed a few feet behind them, soaking up the exhibits with intrigue and thought. Karen didn't think it wise to bring Summer with them, but Zac had convinced her it would be a good idea for them to all spend time together whether or not Summer agreed.

"You okay?" Karen asked, as she nudged Summer with her elbow.

Summer nodded and smiled, though Karen remained unconvinced.

"I know you'd rather be at home scrolling through hours of endless TikTok videos, but your dad thought it would be a good idea to get out of the house. I'm more than happy to knock it on the head and we can grab a late lunch?"

Summer pulled a face. "Oh, sorry, Karen. You're right. It's not how I'd like to spend my Saturday, but I know Dad is trying. I don't want to upset him."

"You wouldn't be upsetting him. He's just doing what he thinks is best. I'd be just as happy at home having a Netflix and pizza afternoon."

Summer's eyes lit up at the offer of something far more appealing to while away the hours.

Karen winked. "How about if we wrap up soon and head off? I'll convince your dad that us girls know better."

"What about Dad? He's been looking forward to this..."

Karen put her arm around Summer's shoulder. "Don't worry about your dad. Leave him to me."

Summer's smile grew.

Though Karen enjoyed spending time with Zac, sometimes other things took priority. Summer was part of the package, and spending time with her was important to Karen because if Summer was happy, Zac was happy. Besides, the more time she spent with Summer, the more she enjoyed her company. Cheeky, stroppy, and loud on the outside, Karen had seen the soft and sensitive side that made Summer more endearing to her.

"What are you two ladies whispering about?" Zac asked as he caught up with them.

He flicked his eyes from one exhibit to another then glanced over his shoulder to see a few children gathered around a woman dressed in a Victorian costume. The woman recalled fictional tales of what it was like to live and work in the Victorian street setting as the kids ambled through.

"Nothing, Dad. Sometimes girls need to have *conversations.*"

Zac's eyes widened. "Oh! *Those* kinds of conversations. Don't let me interrupt," he offered, holding up his hands.

Karen and Summer exchanged glances before they burst into laughter.

Zac furrowed his brow in confusion. "What's so funny?"

Karen pursed her lips and blew him a kiss. "It's above your pay grade," she replied as Karen and Summer picked up the pace and scurried off, their laughter still echoing in Zac's ears.

The York Castle Museum was unique. Originally built in the 11th century by William the Conqueror, the present rendition was the culmination of years of expansion, rebuilding and repurchasing. The current structure stemmed from an 18th century debtors' and women's prison that was constructed upon the original castle ruins. It now offered a valuable insight in to everyday Victorian life and was a popular tourist destination.

"Eww…" Summer mumbled as she scrunched up her nose a short while later.

The three of them were now stopped by an old Victorian prison cell. The cell was basic in construction, with a domed brick roof and cream stone walls. A slatted metal-framed bed rested on stone pillars and beside it was a large stone box with an opening in the bottom and topped with a large flat piece of stone with a hole in the middle.

"Is that what I think it is?" Summer asked.

Zac laughed. "No flushing toilets here. They did their business in that hole, and it fell into a bucket below before being removed from the opening in the base."

Summer pretended to gag as she threw a hand over her mouth. "Eww," she said again, "that's so gross, man."

Zac raised a brow in Summer's direction as Karen laughed.

Zac leant forward to read the information board on a wall close to them. "This was the cell of the famous highway man, Dick Turpin. They called it the condemned cell."

Summer chuckled at the name.

"Do they not teach you anything in school?" Zac asked, shaking his head.

Summer shrugged as she stared through the bars and looked around.

"He was a famous thief and robber in the 1700s. For a while he hid out as a fugitive in your neck of the woods," Zac added, looking in Karen's direction.

"I know," Karen replied. "Epping Forest. He shot someone while in hiding before he legged it to East Yorkshire. I used to drive through Epping Forest all the time. It was a well-known dumping ground for bodies during the 50s and 60s, especially during the reign of the Krays."

Zac was about to butt in with more trivia when Karen's phone buzzed in her pocket. She pulled it out to see Jade's number flash on the screen. "Sorry, give me one sec," Karen said, stepping away from Zac and Summer who resumed their inspection of the cell.

"Jade, everything okay?"

"Hi, Karen, sorry to disturb you on your day off. Are you having a good time?"

"Well, I'm looking at where Dick Turpin used to take a crap! What do you think?" Karen could hear Jade laughing at the other end.

"Right… Um… That's gross!"

"Yep. But Zac seems to be loving it. I'll tell you something. If we still had cells like this now, criminals would think twice before committing a crime. They have a cushy life in prison now with duvets, TVs, games consoles, and three meals a day."

"I hate to tear you away from your step back in time, but our team has been called to the discovery of a body. A street worker. She's missing a hand."

5

It took a while for Karen to find the location since Acaster Malbis, a postcode and reference to a former RAF station running close to the River Ouse were all she had to go on. It felt like she spent most of her time travelling to crime scenes that involved driving through quaint country roads lined by hedges, with rolling farmland for as far as the eye could see. She saw nothing wrong with that, because it offered a pleasant contrast to the grimy, bustling, exhaust-filled streets of London that had been her patch for so many years.

Karen spotted a patrol car parked up in the distance as she approached, she saw the lay-by before turning in to a gap hidden among the hedgerows.

After pressing the button to slide down her window, Karen pulled out her warrant card to present it to the officer on duty. "Is it much further?" she asked.

"No, ma'am," the officer replied with a smile. He took a

step back so he could point Karen in the right direction. "Just through here and off to the left."

Karen thanked him and continued through the two metal posts which she imagined once held sturdy metal gates. Once through, she followed his instructions and soon spotted a white forensic tent and a hive of activity around it. Several police cars, a white forensics van, and two unmarked cars were parked to one side.

Switching off her ignition, Karen stepped out of the car and took in the scenery. Grassy fields extended in all directions. She could just about make out the rooftops of what she imagined were industrial or farm buildings far off in the distance. The rumble of a farm vehicle carried on the breeze. She couldn't make out the direction but imagined it to be a few fields away. Other than that, there was nothing else to see and even less to listen to other than the sound of birds in the bushes and trees.

Jade made her way towards the car and met Karen halfway. "You found us then?"

"Of course!" Karen said as if Jade was teasing Karen's ability to find her way out of a wet paper bag. "Don't tell me you didn't find it hard finding this place either? It's in the arse end of nowhere," Karen said, looking around again.

"I found it no problem. I hitched a lift in a squad car."

"Yeah, yeah, show off. What do we have?"

"Sallyanne Faulkner, age thirty. Street brass. It looks like she was strangled to death and had her right hand chopped off."

"Did you get that from her ID?"

Jade shook her head. "No. She doesn't have any possessions on her. One of our uniformed colleagues arrested her for soliciting in a public place."

"Who found her?" Karen asked.

"A vagrant. Some fella who lives in the trees further up the lane. He's in the back of one car. An officer felt sorry for him and gave the old boy his packed lunch and a can of Coke."

"Bless. We'll have a chat with him later. It's bleak here."

Jade nodded. "Out-of-the-way. Locals will know about the place and its history, but I doubt anyone from outside of York and the surrounding areas has heard of it unless you're a military buff. Perfect spot if you think about it."

"Yes, that's what I thought, too. That doesn't mean it was a local person who killed her, even though that would be my first assumption. Could also have been someone passing through the area looking for an isolated spot."

Karen followed Jade towards the inner cordon, where they both signed into the scene log and helped themselves to a set of Tyvek overalls and blue booties, before slipping under the cordon tape and making their way towards a patch of tall grass. Two SOCOs were crouched down outside the tent documenting the evidence. A further area close by was cordoned off with what appeared to be clothing on the ground. The area between the two sites was also cordoned off with police tape.

"Is Izzy here?" Karen asked, looking at the pair.

Before either could reply, Karen heard whistling coming from inside the tent. She nodded in Jade's direction. "Let's see what she has to say."

6

Karen lifted the flap and poked her head in through the gap to see Izzy bent over the body.

Izzy tipped her head back and scrunched her eyes before continuing her high-pitched whistling.

Karen cleared her throat. "I can't see the Eurovision Song Contest begging you to be the main act."

Izzy looked over her shoulder and laughed before shrugging. "They don't know what they'll be missing out on with this raw and unique talent…"

Karen tipped her head to one side. "Um, I'm not so sure I'd agree with that. How are you getting on?"

Izzy sat back on her heels and dropped her hands by her sides as she looked up and down at the figure. "Pretty good. There's not much more for me to do here. I need to let the forensic team back in again."

Karen came from behind and crouched down beside Izzy as Jade appeared through the entrance. The body of the victim was laid out in a crucifix position, with her legs crossed over at the ankles. Her arms were extended by her sides and her dark, matted hair was splayed out in a halo around her head. Karen noticed bruising impressions around the victim's neck. With her skirt gathered around her waist, she was naked from the waist down.

"Other than the bruising to her neck, there doesn't appear to be any other deep trauma injury... Well, apart from the bloody obvious..." Izzy sighed, pointing to the victim's right arm. "Bloody odd, if you ask me."

Karen cast her eye up and down the victim. Sallyanne Faulkner appeared underweight with bony thin legs, protruding hipbones and thin tattooed arms. "Any signs of sexual activity?"

"I believe so. I'll be able to do a more detailed examination when I get her on the table. There are extensive abrasions on the back of her arms and legs. They don't appear to have happened at this spot, but the forensic team believe she was dragged the short distance from where they found her jacket."

Karen stood and looked at Jade, who agreed with the assessment.

"Cause of death?"

"Strangulation," Izzy replied.

Karen stood up and walked around the body before crouching down again as she turned her attention to the victim's arm. "What can you tell us about that?"

Izzy raised a brow. "Done after death. Minimal blood loss. Whatever was used gave a clean cut. Again, I'll be able to give you a better indication of that once we've examined her, but there's only one indentation in the ground at the end of her limb."

"An axe?" Karen speculated.

"Possibly… if it was sharp enough. It's certainly heavy enough to provide the right amount of force… and it would have required a lot of force. Sometimes you need to have a go at these things several times to cut through. Also, if it was a blade or saw with a serrated edge, the damage to the surrounding tissue, bones and blood vessels would have been more extensive."

Karen rose again and thanked Izzy, before stepping outside for a moment with Jade. They walked the short distance between the tent and the other cordoned off area. A black jacket was being bagged up and documented by the forensic officers. The distance between the two sites was only ten or fifteen feet. From where she stood, there was no evidence of blood trails or human tissue.

Jade stood close by with her hands on her hips, looking further afield and attempting to make sense of the situation. "There's nothing around here. Local officers said this used to be an RAF airfield but was decommissioned back in the 60s. There are two small industrial estates on the site, but around the other side." Jade pointed off into the distance. "I've sent officers to make enquiries there already."

"Great. Thanks, Jade." Karen stared at the ground and ran through a series of questions in her own mind. *Why this location? Why did they need to drag Sallyanne's body the short distance from where her jacket was found to where her body was discovered? And what was the significance of her losing her right hand?*

"I'm confused…" Jade said a few minutes later, after she

had walked around the immediate area. "Why here? Was she attacked where we discovered her jacket, before making a run for it, only to be attacked for a second time over there?" Jade asked no one in particular as she looked back towards the white tent.

Karen didn't have the answers as she rejoined Izzy back in the tent. She stood in one corner and crossed her arms over her chest. She noticed a silver pendant hanging from a small thin chain around Sallyanne's neck. Karen made a mental note to remind SOCO to secure the chain and pendant as forensic evidence.

She took a few moments to think about the victim. Sallyanne Faulkner was someone's daughter, perhaps sister. She imagined that there were people out there now waiting to hear from Sallyanne who would never get the chance to hear her voice again. Karen came across a lot of street girls in her career. The majority never sold their bodies intentionally. Many *needed* to feed their drug addictions, sometimes even to put food on the table for their children. Their lives were dangerous and often short-lived.

Karen left the tent feeling melancholy. "Any signs of her possessions or the missing limb?"

Jade shook her head. "No handbag, no phone, not even a packet of cigarettes. We don't know if she came here with any underwear on, because there were no signs of that either. As for the hand, nothing yet. We've have a search team arriving soon with a specialist search dog. If there are human remains close by, the dog should be able to pick it up."

7

KAREN LEFT Jade to oversee the troops while she took a moment to have a chat with the vagrant who had discovered Sallyanne's body. He sat in the back of a patrol car tucking into a sandwich with gusto. Karen paused by the rear window and peered in. The man appeared to be enjoying it so much that he seemed oblivious to Karen's presence. Judging by the speed at which he was attacking the sandwich, pausing to stuff a few more Quavers in his mouth, she guessed he hadn't eaten in a while.

Opening the car door, Karen leant in.

"Whoa." A rush of bile scorched the back of Karen's throat as the smell hit her. Karen coughed and turned away to grab some clean air. "David? David Silva?"

The man nodded in her direction before returning his attention to the food.

"I understand from my colleagues that you discovered the body?"

He nodded again but didn't take his eyes off the food as he looked down into the sandwich box and eyed up the green apple.

"One of my officers informed me you live close by in the woods. Did you hear anything last night? Perhaps the sound of a vehicle driving past or stopping here?"

David cleared his throat. "You hear the odd car, van or tractor, but mostly during the day. I don't remember hearing anything last night. It was pissing down, so I don't wander round when it's like that. I ignore everything, pull the sleeping bag over my head and throw a plastic sheet over me."

"Okay. And what were you doing this morning which led you to the discovery?"

"I was heading off towards the industrial estate. There are a couple of units down the road that are kind enough to knock up a brew and give me a few slices of toast in the morning. That's when I discovered... her. Bloody awful mess."

Karen realised he couldn't offer anything to help her investigation but she'd get one of her officers to take a statement from him anyway. She thanked him for his time before heading back to the crime scene.

Izzy was loading her case back into the boot of her car as Karen approached.

"All done here, Karen. I'll let you know about the postmortem. I have a sixty-two-year-old female to do next. Badly decomposed. Snuffed it at least three weeks ago. Found sitting back in a recliner chair. Bruising to her forehead."

Karen grimaced. "Rather you than me. I can think of better ways to spend my time."

"What like standing in a deserted airfield on a Saturday afternoon with a dead prostitute who's missing a hand, and a vagrant smelling of poo?" Izzy replied, raising a brow.

Karen laughed as she walked away. "Don't we lead glamorous lives!"

"Any more updates from SOCO?" Karen asked as she met up with Jade again.

Jade shook her head. "Nothing at the moment. They've bagged up her leather jacket and her hands." Jade paused, realising her slip. "Her hand, in case there's DNA evidence trapped under her fingernails." Jade looked over towards where the leather jacket was found, "SOCO is going to do a sweep of the area around there. We could assume that's where she was standing to begin with?"

"That makes sense. I can only imagine they took her from that spot and to the long grass to hide her body." Karen was about to continue when she heard the high revs of an engine. She turned to see a blue Mondeo stop close to the other service vehicles. A man in a dark grey suit, white shirt and blue tie stepped out. A hard scowl fixed his features as he glanced around for a brief second before marching towards Karen.

Karen furrowed her brow as she examined the man with curiosity. Overweight, heavy double chin as big as the man's forehead. Jet black, short, curly hair. With a heavy gait and wild swinging arms, he glared at Karen as he closed in.

"Who are you?" he demanded.

"I should ask you that. This is an active crime scene and I'm the SIO. Detective Chief Inspector Karen Heath." His hostility had already annoyed her.

"Bollocks to that. I'm DCI Carl Shield. This is my patch. I'm in charge of the team that deals with sex trafficking gangs and prostitution. I think you'll find this is my case. You and your team can do one," he barked, throwing a thumb over his shoulder before walking off towards the tent.

Karen folded her arms, pulled back her shoulders, and stood her ground. "I don't think so. I'm more than happy to extend professional courtesy to any serving officer but, because you've clearly experienced a frontal lobotomy which has gone wrong, I'm not going to do that for you."

Shield stopped and spun round, striding back towards her and invading her personal space. Karen could almost feel his stale breath on her face. Though she wanted to turn the other way before she choked on his toxic cigarette breath, she held her ground and fixed him with a stare. She had met men like him before. He was straight out of the Skelton charm school.

He snarled through gritted teeth. "I know who you are. Just because you were in the Met, people round here are treating you like royalty. Like they've bagged a top officer." He paused for a moment, his lids flickering just a fraction as tension bristled in his face. "You can't be trusted. Your incompetence led to two officers being killed on your watch. News travels fast. People are already talking about you. No-one wants to join your team. You... are... a poisoned chalice."

Karen's stomach somersaulted. For the first time since

leaving London, memories surfaced of that tragic incident. Her mouth ran dry, and her bowels cramped. She thought she had left that behind her, but it was going to follow her for the rest of her career and beyond. Everyone had been so welcoming towards her... until now.

Karen glanced at his hand, spotted his wedding ring, and jumped at the chance to wind him up. "You clearly didn't get your oats this morning because your wife had one of her *headaches*. There is a change of guard here now. I'll extend professional courtesy to every officer. I'm not looking at sex trafficking rings. I'm investigating a homicide. A brutal one. If you have an issue with that, then take it up the chain."

Shield glared at her as the muscles in his jaw tensed and his eyes narrowed. He took a few steps back and jabbed a finger in her direction. "You haven't heard the last of this," he barked as he marched back towards his car.

Jade moved forward having witnessed the whole altercation. She stood alongside Karen and watched as Shield opened his car door, stared at Karen for a few moments before getting in and slamming his car door so hard that all the officers at the scene paused for a few seconds to stare at the source of the noise.

"What just happened?" Jade asked, incredulity in her voice.

"I don't know." Karen remained rooted to the spot, her body rigid with shock. She didn't enjoy talking to officers like that, especially those carrying the same rank, but her time in the job had taught her there were still ego-driven, macho officers who carried a chip on their shoulder about anyone who undermined their authority.

"I thought you said this was a nice place to work?" Jade said, jabbing an elbow in Karen's side.

"It is. But every force has a few tossers. Dinosaurs like him who thrive on control and domination. I bet he thought I would just buckle soon as he started throwing his weight around and would step aside and let him take over."

"Karen, you scare the crap out of me sometimes. You've got balls to stand up to people like that. I would have crumpled into a heap of fat, steamy turd if he'd spoken to me like that."

Karen shrugged. "Well, I'm not the best role model, but I'll take that as a compliment. I just don't like being pushed around. If there's one thing you need to understand in this job, Jade, there's always someone ready to knock you back down when you least expect it. Some are obvious and blatant with it. Others find subtle ways to erode your confidence, your belief in yourself and your credibility as an officer among your peers."

"Geez, deep for a Saturday afternoon," Jade said, the corners of her mouth tugging upward. "But thanks for the heads-up. For the record, you're a great role model. I can't wait to grow up and be a badass like you who is not scared to kick butt."

Karen shook her head and groaned. "Ple-eease don't grow up like me. You will regret it."

Though Karen felt she had won that confrontation, she sensed it wouldn't be her last. Once the adrenaline had subsided, she questioned whether she'd handled it properly. A part of her felt annoyed that she had let Shield get to her, but a swell of anger swirled within her about the way she had been spoken to. They were both serving police officers, carrying the same rank and knew the boundaries of responsibility and etiquette. In her mind, disagreements among officers were an everyday thing, but Shield had overstepped the mark.

8

SATISFIED WITH HIS RESULTS, the man leant against the kitchen top and stared out of the window. Clusters of white clouds drifted effortlessly across the sky, untouched and unspoilt by mankind. He wondered what it would be like to float and glide on the thermals like the birds that peppered his view.

He needed little in life. His books, along with his deep fascination with ancient Far Eastern cultures and the National Geographic TV channel, kept his mind occupied.

It was the *other* stuff that bothered him more. Them. The tarts that touted their trade. The young women who looked so fresh, vibrant, and innocent. They were all his weakness. Up to this point, his life had been good. He hadn't been one of those who'd had a bad upbringing, or never seen their dad, or lived in ramshackle council housing. He hadn't been fiddled by a pervy uncle or molested by a dodgy teacher. None of that crap.

The plain fact was he loved the darker side of sex.

He'd had a strange fascination with it from an early age. The trigger event remained firmly fixed in his mind. The day that Gary whoever had convinced his older brother to buy a top shelf copy of *Rustler* from the newsagents round the corner. Gary and his mates had huddled in a corner of the playground as they'd flicked through pages of scantily clad women doing all sorts of things with their *bits*.

They may have laughed and giggled, but he was sure that they'd been as curious and turned on as he'd been. As far as he could remember, it was the first time he'd experienced a boner. From that day on, he'd seen women in a different light. He'd hung around after school and headed to the cloakroom where everyone hung up their gym bags containing their PE kit. Adrenaline had coursed through his veins, and his skin had tingled as he'd rummaged through the girls' PE bags. He'd cradled their gym knickers in his hands like they had been precious commodities that he'd feared dropping.

He'd known it was naughty. But that had made it even more exciting. His own little secret. From there, his desires had driven him on. In high school, he'd held his small camera under the desk and taken photographs of the female students who'd sat opposite him. Most of the photos had turned out to be blurred, dark, and hazy. But occasionally he'd got lucky and landed a decent up the skirt opportunity. His fascination with women had become an obsession. The risk of getting caught excited him. He wanted to break all the rules of sensibility and feed the growing urge to explore the female form and its provocative appeal.

At university, he'd come into his own. He'd befriended female students at parties and helped them to stagger to

their student digs or halls of residence before dropping
them on their beds blind drunk and unconscious. He'd
played with them as much as he'd wanted, and they'd never
known they'd been violated when they'd woken the next
morning.

But he'd wanted to take things further. He'd wanted to be
able to do those things when they were awake. And the
only way he could do that was to pay for it.

The timer chimed on his phone, which jogged him out of
his reverie. He turned around and headed to the cooker. His
casserole pot bubbled away, plumes of steam pirouetting
and dancing above it. He grabbed his stirrer and disturbed
the frothy broth. The limb had been simmering for a few
hours now. The skin had loosened and fallen off, the soft
flesh beneath it breaking away from the bone like a tender
lamb shank. Stringy tendons and veins twisted around his
stirrer. *Another few hours.*

Soon, he'd have a new exhibit.

His thoughts turned towards her. She'd been scared, but
willing. He recalled her tattoos. She'd been adding to the
ones he remembered. There was something so wild, aggressive, and taboo about them. Especially the full sleeves. In
his mind, they represented a statement, rebellion, and identity. She'd always been different. Happy to speak out in
front of others, confrontational... but in a good way and
lively. He'd lost count of the number of times she'd turned
up in the morning with a steaming hangover but still firing
on all cylinders.

It had been an instant attraction from the beginning.
Someone who took risks, just like him. After all this time, it
annoyed him that she hadn't remembered him, though it

had worked in his favour. Maybe she would have put up more of a fight if she had. The fact she had turned to working the streets made it easier for him to get closer.

Just another regular punter willing to have sex with her skinny, drug-ridden body.

9

KAREN LEFT Jade at the scene to oversee the forensic operation and the search team. With Jade having the day off tomorrow, it made sense for her to finish a shift at the crime scene and then head home, even if it was a late one.

The hum of activity surrounded her as Karen pushed through the double doors to the incident room. Support officers had set up extra workstations, maps of the area which were pinned to the walls, and a few extra whiteboards to help with the briefings. Karen thanked them as she made her way to the front of the room.

"Okay, team. Can you gather round?" she instructed. She waited a few moments for all available officers to filter down to the front of the room. Some stood. Others shared available desk space, while the rest swivelled in their chairs, notepads, and pens at the ready.

Ed and Tyler jostled for desk space, both keen to be as close to the front as possible.

"Will you two pack it in!" Belinda muttered under her breath. "You can act like a bunch of dickheads sometimes."

Other officers laughed and jeered at the two chastised officers who hunkered down, embarrassed that their antics had drawn the attention of everyone else in the room.

Karen raised a brow and shook her head in their direction. "Thanks, Bel. Right, *when* you're ready, we need to crack on with this briefing. The case involves the murder of a street worker. Sallyanne Faulkner, aged thirty. In this case, we have a name and some history to work on which gives us a head start out of the blocks." Karen turned towards a whiteboard and pinned up mugshots of Sallyanne from the previous times she had been arrested.

"The investigation of the crime scene is still ongoing. I've left Jade in charge. We have a specialist search team on scene. Hopefully, you've all had the chance to look at the bodycam footage. The victim had her right hand chopped off."

"Has it been found yet?" an officer asked.

Karen shook her head. "No. The search team is bringing a dog trained in finding human remains. If it's anywhere within the vicinity, we'll find it."

"It seems a pretty remote area..." Ed added, pointing towards the map and a red pin which marked the crime scene.

"It is. There's a small industrial unit about a mile away. According to officers who visited the site, there wasn't a lot of activity there." Karen circled another group of buildings on the map. "There's a busier larger industrial estate about two miles up the road. Officers are going through the units and making their enquiries. All available CCTV is being secured."

Karen took a moment to inform them of Sallyanne's missing possessions, which would also be the subject of a detailed search of the area.

"Souvenirs?" Ed suggested.

Karen shrugged. "Possibly. The perp may have wanted to remove all evidence, especially if they had touched any of it."

"Who's next of kin?" Belinda asked, looking around the room. A sea of blank faces met her question. "Well, can someone find out for us? We need to know where she lives now and who her next of kin are. Does she have siblings? Parents?"

A support officer raised her pen and confirmed that she would get on to that straightaway as she spun round in her chair and started tapping away on a keyboard.

Karen offered herself a small smile. Belinda had grown on her over the weeks. She was a solid officer, not afraid to speak her mind, nor bark orders. Dependable in Karen's eyes.

Karen flicked through the charge sheet that had been passed to her. Sallyanne had been cautioned more than a dozen times and arrested twice for loitering and soliciting for prostitution. Even the offer of a Drug Interventions Programme hadn't tempted her as a way out of her situation.

"Did she have a pimp?" Karen asked.

"Yes, boss. Arthur Minchin. Well known to us. Complete toerag," an officer replied.

Even with fewer resources, Karen's team performed well. She was pleased with how quickly they were coming back with answers. It was a far cry from the Met MITs where each murder team was at least twenty-six officers strong, led by a detective chief inspector who commanded two detective inspectors, four detective sergeants, eighteen detective constables and one police constable. A further four to six staff members provided support to the team. Her team in York was half that size on a good day.

"I doubt door-to-door enquiries will help us that much because of the remoteness of the location, but we might get lucky and catch a vehicle that has been in the area either before the discovery of the body or scoped the location for several days," Karen said as she turned and stared at the map. "I want a full victim profile built up. Phone logs, who she's been talking to, last known sightings, any grudges, outstanding debts, who she may have pissed off, the works. While we're doing a full trawl, can someone check the sex offenders register? Check to see if we have any local suspects displaying a propensity for violence against women? And check the prison release logs for any local violent offenders."

A murmur of approval rippled around the room as the briefing broke up.

10

KAREN MADE her way towards Detective Superintendent Laura Kelly's office. She was still bristling from her encounter with Shield. His appearance at the crime scene had left an unsettling feeling in her stomach. She thought she had left behind the days of her colleagues and bosses giving her a hard time, but the ugly spectre of jealousy appeared to be rearing its head again.

She nodded as she walked past the other senior officers who shared the same floor as Kelly. There was a distinct atmosphere and vibe in this part of the building with quieter conversations and less busy corridors.

Karen stopped in Kelly's doorway and tapped on the open door. "Ma'am."

Kelly looked up and greeted Karen with a big smile that pressed in dimples on her cheeks. "Karen, I heard you've been rustling a few feathers."

Karen rolled her eyes. *News travels fast*, she thought. "DCI Shield?"

Kelly nodded. "Yep. He's been going around airing his displeasure at you stomping on his patch."

"Ma'am…"

Kelly didn't let her finish as she held up her hand to silence Karen. "It's fine. There's no need for an explanation. Believe it or not, I'm on your side. DCI Shield likes to be in the centre of all the action. Historically yes, he's dealt with a lot of homicides, but his remit more recently has been to identify and break up the sex trafficking rings." Kelly rose from her chair and headed round to her small coffee machine. "Coffee?"

"I'm fine. Thanks, ma'am."

Kelly rustled up a coffee, the machine gurgling and spluttering in the background once she had made her choice. "In fairness, his team would have been deployed to deal with this homicide before the set-up of the Serious Crime Unit. Clearly the message hasn't reached him that major crimes and homicides fall under your remit now."

"Would you like me to have another word with him, ma'am?"

Kelly shook her head and retrieved her coffee from the machine before returning to her desk. "No. Leave it with me. I'll talk to him. If he kicks off again, then come and let me know. I have every intention of reinforcing my commitment to the SCU. And to prove my point, you have two new officers joining your team at some point tomorrow morning."

Karen raised a brow in surprise. Why was she the last to hear about this? "Oh. I didn't know that we were increasing our headcount?"

"Well, we weren't. But the two officers were about to be seconded to another unit, but I made a bid for them. It's only for six months, but if they prove useful, we can put in a case for them to stay with us permanently."

"Who are they?" Karen asked.

Kelly rummaged through her notes, becoming frustrated when she couldn't find what she was looking for. "Ah, here we go. TDC Ned Chambers, aged twenty-five. Keen to please and very enthusiastic. You also have DC Preet Anand, aged thirty-one. I've asked them to find either yourself or Jade."

"Okay, great. Thanks, ma'am." While Karen had Kelly's ear, she provided an update on the victim and the initial stages of the investigation. Kelly didn't object, nor did she have anything further to add before Karen left her to it.

Karen checked in on the team again before she left for the evening and made sure everyone knew their assignments, including an update for the late shift. Officers had confirmed the address for Sallyanne's parents. Karen agreed that the sooner they knew the better, so she planned to stop by on her way home to break the news. Belinda had organised for a family liaison officer to be made available should Sallyanne's parents need one during the investigation.

As soon as she jumped into the car, Karen called Zac and put the phone on Bluetooth. She started the car and drove away while waiting for Zac to answer. When the call rang out, she redialled again. Zac usually answered within the first few rings, so she was puzzled why he hadn't answered. He answered on her second try.

"Hey, you still at the station?" he asked.

"No. I've just left. I wanted to call and apologise for having to cut short our day out."

"No need to apologise. These things happen. What do you have?"

Karen took a few moments to fill him in on the homicide and how she was on the way to break the news to the victim's parents.

"That's a tough one. I hate those kind of house calls."

"Me too," she replied. Before hanging up, Karen promised to update him a little later, if she got the chance.

The address given for the Faulkners was in a quiet location to the west of the city, an average residential street with an array of terraced and semi-detached properties. With the last remnants of sun disappearing behind the clouds and night creeping in, a stillness fell across the neighbourhood. A few cars in nearby streets broke the silence. But other than that, a silence chilled her bones. It was as if the shroud of death had followed her, sucking the atmosphere from the air, and replacing it with grim morbidity.

She walked a few yards until she found the house number. The lights were off. The driveway empty. It was as if her presence wasn't welcome. She took a few deep breaths before walking up the short path and ringing the doorbell. She expected the hallway lights to snap on and the sound of footsteps to thunder down the stairs, but neither of those things happened. Karen crouched down and peered through the letter box. Darkness greeted her. She tried the doorbell again before stepping away from the door and peering up towards the bedroom windows for any signs of the curtains twitching. Nothing.

She tried next door, and even though the neighbours wanted to know why she was looking for the Faulkners, Karen fobbed them off with how the Faulkners had wanted advice from the police about house security. Though still suspicious, they confirmed that the Faulkners were away on holiday and would return tomorrow. Karen got a mobile number for the Faulkners before she thanked the neighbours and returned to her car.

Before heading home, Karen called the number only to be met with a voicemail. She was in two minds whether to leave a message about something so personal and tragic but left one about the need for Mr or Mrs Faulkner to contact Karen on the number that she provided. There was nothing more she could do for this evening and would try again tomorrow.

11

AFTER SUCH A LONG, hard day, Karen crawled through her front door and yawned. Her body ached, her brain felt like mush and her eyes felt as if two hot pokers had been thrust through them. She kicked off her shoes and wiggled her toes. *God, I'm shattered.* She flicked on the light and brushed aside her mail with the side of her foot.

"Manky! Mummy's home," Karen hollered down the hallway. With Manky not making an appearance, she scrunched her face and called again before padding down the hallway. She poked her head around the door to her bedroom and saw the cat curled up in a tight ball on her bed.

"There you are you little monkey. You didn't fancy coming to say hello?" she said as she flopped on to the bed and gave him a kiss. She ran her hand through his soft, warm fur. He purred appreciatively. "Let me make us dinner. Are you hungry?" she whispered as she pushed off the bed and headed off towards the kitchen.

She flicked on the light in the kitchen and stared at the floor. She raised a brow and shook her head. Manky had left her a welcome present slap bang in the middle of the floor. Poo. *That would explain why he's hiding in my bedroom.* "You cheeky bugger. Thanks for the present!" she shouted, grabbing a sheet of kitchen towel and disinfectant spray.

Karen cleared up his mess and then refilled his bowl with fresh food before sticking a lasagna in the microwave. She headed to the fridge and pulled out the opened bottle of Pinot Grigio before proceeding to pour herself a large glass. The first glug tickled her throat as the chilled wine coated the inside of her mouth. She closed her eyes and savoured the taste as it warmed up her empty stomach. Karen stared out the darkened window at the floodlit car park behind her apartment block. Beyond it was a line of trees that stood like silent guardians watching over the cars.

Three beeps from the microwave jolted her from her daze. She took another swig of wine before grabbing a tea towel and extracting the piping hot meal. The instructions said leave it for one minute, but she was too hungry, having hardly eaten anything all day. She turned it out and it fell out with a plop before the cheese sauce spilled over across the plate. A handful of salad as garnish and voilà, a meal in under ten minutes. *Gordon Ramsay, beat that!*

Karen headed through to the lounge and dropped into the sofa before reaching for the remote control and flicking on the TV. She browsed through the channels trying to find something of interest. Nothing seemed to grab her, so she turned to the movie channels and scanned through them until she found *The Bourne Identity. Love a bit of Jason Bourne. What woman wouldn't?* She smiled.

The first few mouthfuls scorched the inside of her mouth. When would she ever learn? She had a knack of being impatient when food was in front of her. She'd lost count of the number of times she had done that with hot pizza, only to find that bits of flesh hung from the roof lining of her mouth the next day.

The meal hit the right spot as she ran her fork around the plate to scoop up every scrap. She was about to pour more wine when her phone buzzed from the hallway. She sighed and closed her eyes. *Please don't let this be work. Please. Please,* she pleaded as she raced down the hall to fish it out of her bag. Her eyes fixed on the screen for a few moments. Dread turned to surprise and then excitement.

"Wainwright, how the devil are you?" she squealed.

"Ah, Karen. I didn't disturb you, did I?"

"Of course not. I always have time for you. I've just finished eating," she replied as she headed back towards the lounge.

"Good. Jolly good. It's been a while since we spoke, so I was just sitting here in the office finishing paperwork, and you popped into my thoughts. Hence why I'm calling you."

"Ah, bless. You're still missing me. I thought you'd be chuffed not to have to deal with me. A thorn in your side and all that."

"Well, I... Well, you see... I guess..." Wainwright struggled to find the right words to convey his thoughts.

"I know what. You've saved yourself a fortune on biscuits because I'm not there, right?" Karen teased.

Karen imagined Wainwright offering one of his thin, tight-lipped smiles at the other end.

"I certainly have a lot more biscuits in my bottom drawer since you've been gone…"

Karen paused for a moment. She thought she heard a tinge of sadness in his voice. Perhaps it wasn't in the words he'd just said, but more so about the words he had missed out. Wainwright was a protective man who guarded his emotions. But the more she had seen of him, the more relaxed he had become around her. There was much more to him than she had first imagined. He was a clever, intellectual man with a dry sense of humour. He took her teasing on the chin and had even been cheeky enough to throw the odd sarcastic comment back in her direction when he felt brave.

They spent the next ten minutes catching up, with Wainwright telling her about the cases he'd been working on and, in return, Karen filling him in on her current case. The conversation flowed. It was as if they were right back in his office sharing a cup of tea and a biscuit… Or several biscuits. Karen missed those times the most. They were poles apart as people, but for some reason they had gelled. Wainwright was a fantastic listener, and she had never felt comfortable enough to talk to anyone in a way that she did with him. For that, she was grateful. She really missed him.

"Any chance of you gracing us with your presence soon?" he asked.

"I hope so. It would be nice to go back and visit the team. How about I give you a bell once I arrange something?"

"Perfect."

Karen agreed to call him and made a mental note to sort something out as soon as possible before hanging up. She stared at her phone and enjoyed the warm glow that settled within. Yes, it had been a tough day, but Wainwright always had a knack for making everything good.

12

KAREN HOVERED outside Ed's house and tapped on the steering wheel. Jade had the day off, so she was flying solo. With Tyler and Belinda tied up on enquiries, she'd sent Ed a text late last night to warn him she planned on dragging him out with her. Ed lived in a tall apartment block in a leafy residential suburb. Wherever she went in York, one thing Karen noticed was the much slower pace. She watched as other residents of the block appeared over the next five minutes, sauntering off to work.

When Ed finally appeared, she looked him up and down. Grey suit, white shirt, and pale blue tie. He was always impeccably dressed and looked far more suited to be working in an investment bank or city law firm. With his legal background, he fitted the bill perfectly. She felt under-dressed in comparison. Black trousers, white blouse and flat pumps.

Ed pulled open the car door, took off his suit jacket and folded it in half before taking a seat beside Karen. "Morning, Karen."

"Morning, Ed." She examined him more closely while he belted up but was caught out when he glanced across at her and smiled. "What?"

"Nothing. I was just thinking about how smartly dressed you always are. I'm always impressed by how well you do your tie. I don't think I could ever do one as well as you."

"I do a full Windsor knot. It's large and symmetrical. It looks the part. I'm not into those scrawny knots that most men do."

Karen nodded. She doubted she could tell the difference between any knot, even though Ed gave her a quick lesson on tie etiquette. She smiled at Ed's detailed descriptions. He could be such a nerd sometimes, but she meant that in the kindest possible way. Everything he spoke about had to have depth, meaning, and logic. His legal training again. "I grabbed us both a coffee," she said, nodding towards the centre console.

"Brilliant. Thanks."

They drove a short distance to the address that they had on the system for Sallyanne Faulkner. Along the way, they made idle chit-chat, sipping on the coffee and throwing around theories about the current case. The address in Clifton wasn't far from the hospital, and the first thing that struck Karen was the narrowness of the street. Double-parked with single file traffic. Small, terraced housing with even smaller front gardens.

Karen drove up and down the road a few times, becoming more impatient with each drive by. There wasn't any parking anywhere, and the odd gap that was available only provided enough space for a smart car or motorbike. She had to settle for parking around the corner and walking the short distance back to the house. It was a quiet street with very few people around.

When Ed pushed open the metal garden gate, it squealed on its hinges. A black bin liner served as a dustbin, overflowing with tied up carrier bags of rubbish. The front door was dusty with chipped paint and a rusty letter flap.

Karen took a step to the side. "I'll let you do the honours…" she said as her eyes darted between the front window and first-floor bedroom window.

Ed knocked on the door and waited. He couldn't see any movement through the frosted glass, so knocked again.

Karen positioned herself against the front window and cupped her hands around her eyes to get a better look through the net curtains. She couldn't see much, but thought she spotted a shadow move across a doorway further into the property. She narrowed her eyes and stared more intently. "I think there might be movement in there."

Ed banged on the door with a fist before crouching down and sticking his fingers through the letter box flap. "Police. Is anyone there?"

Karen wasn't sure if Sallyanne lived with anyone. Back in London, she'd found that prostitutes often lived together, sharing a house among a few of them to spread the cost.

The shadow moved between the back rooms, the dark reflection caught in the light bouncing off the doors. "Someone definitely in there."

Ed listened. He heard footsteps and then what sounded like a door opening, its hinges creaking before the footsteps scurried away. Reality dawned on him. "Someone's just legged it out of the back door!" he yelled as he jumped back and headed back on to the pavement.

Karen followed as he searched up and down the road to check if any entrances led along the back of the houses. She spotted two, one at each end of the road. She figured there must be an alleyway and instructed Ed to race down to the other end while she headed to the nearest one. She hoped that they could trap the runaway in the middle.

Karen charged along the pavement and turned left on to a dirt track with patches of grass that led along the side of the last house in the street. She grabbed the baton from her bag and flicked it to its full length before resting it on her shoulder, ready to strike if someone came towards her. She ran along the full length of the house and then turned left again to be presented with a long alleyway with overgrown grass and a track wide enough for vehicles to squeeze down. About fifty yards ahead of her a man raced away, glancing over his shoulder.

"Stop! Police! Stay where you are!" Karen shouted. Her commands were ignored as the man quickened his pace.

He slid to a stop when he saw Ed turn the corner at the other end and charge towards him. Ed looked like he'd just stepped out of the courtroom, but Karen had to admit she felt relieved at his presence. Ed screamed at the man to stop and get down on his knees.

The man glanced over his shoulder as Karen closed in on him, her baton raised in case he put up a fight. Watching his chance of escape dwindling away, he dropped to his knees and held his hands above his head in surrender.

"Okay. Okay. I give up," he shouted through laboured breaths.

13

ED CUFFED the man and hauled him to his feet, before pinning him up against the wall. Ed searched him, checking to make sure he wasn't carrying anything that could harm them.

"You either have something to hide or you are breaking into that property. Which one is it? Or is it both?" Karen demanded.

The man thrashed his head from side to side. "I wasn't doing anything wrong. I was looking for a mate."

Karen nodded but viewed him with suspicion. He was a thin man with a few days of facial hair and weasel-like features. For whatever reason, he appeared to find it hard to stand in one place and shifted nervously on the spot.

"We don't have all day. You didn't answer when we knocked and then legged it out of the back door. That tells me you have something to hide." Karen gave him a little shake.

The man grimaced for a few moments. "Man, why are you always giving me a hard time?"

"Name!" Karen yelled.

The man rolled his eyes. "Arthur. Arthur Minchin."

Ed and Karen exchanged a glance.

"Did you find your friend?"

Minchin shrugged and shook his head.

"And does your friend have a name?" Karen had already figured out the answer.

He continued squirming. "Sallyanne," he finally blurted out.

"Right, let's put you in the back of the car while I go inside." Karen and Ed each took an arm, and escorted Minchin back to their vehicle until he was safely stowed in the back with Ed beside him.

Karen made her way back along the alley and through the garden gate. With her baton still poised on her shoulder, she glanced around the small space in case she encountered any nasty surprises. She sighed as she glanced around the so-called garden. Litter, discarded boxes, an old tatty chair, and a few plastic crates were strewn across the ground. Karen made her way to the back door, left slightly ajar when Minchin had escaped.

After peering inside, her eyes took in the kitchen, a pokey room with a sink full of dirty plates and mugs. A pot on the stove still had the remnants of breakfast or dinner. She wasn't sure which.

"Hello...? Is anyone there? It's the police." Karen walked through the hallway, peering into the lounge which was just as dirty as the kitchen. An array of footwear lined one wall of the hallway. She repeated her announcement as she took the first few steps to the next floor, listening for any sounds. The house remained silent except for each step creaking underfoot. A faint mustiness lingered in the air. She thought the house could do with a good airing. The first room she came to was the bathroom. A laundry bag in one corner overflowed with dirty washing and underwear. The next room had a single bed and belonged to a man since the smell of men's aftershave lingered in the air. The theme of untidiness continued with a pair of Nike trainers tossed to one side together with a grey tracksuit. Chains, rings and a packet of cigarettes sat on a bedside table.

Karen moved to the next bedroom. Empty again. Judging by the underwear on the floor, the smell of cheap, tacky perfume, and fairy lights along the headboard, this room belonged to a female. Karen took a moment to wander around the room and stopped by a wall mirror with pictures wedged into the wooden frame around it. Photos of two women, one of which appeared to be Sallyanne. She noticed other pictures of Sallyanne being hugged by a man. Sallyanne looked much younger in this strip taken in a photo booth somewhere.

After making it to the end of the hallway, Karen paused in front of a closed door. She turned the handle and pushed open the door a few inches to peer through the crack. She couldn't see much from her position, but she stepped into the room and was taken by surprise when she noticed a woman asleep on top of the bed.

Sensing someone was in the room, the woman opened her eyes and screamed, snaking back along the bed to get away from Karen. Her eyes were wide and disorientated, her mouth a gasp. "What the…?"

Karen held up a hand to pacify the woman. She pulled out her warrant card and held it up for the woman to see. "It's okay, love. I'm a police officer. We've just arrested someone who was escaping from the rear of the property. What's your name?"

The woman cleared her throat. "Alexia."

"Alexia what?"

"Alexia Davies."

"Does anyone else live here?" Karen asked.

The woman with scrawny features yawned and rubbed her eyes until they were red raw. "Me."

Karen tutted. "I gathered that. Anyone else?" she asked as she eyed three large boxes of condoms on a bedside table. It didn't take a genius to figure out Alexia's line of work.

"Just some other woman. I don't know her name. I hardly see her. I've only been here a few weeks."

"Anyone else?"

"Yeah, Arthur."

"Is Arthur a friend?"

Alexia looked at Karen and shook her head. "He's my land-lord and pimp."

Karen asked a few questions about when she had last seen Sallyanne, but the answers were short and unhelpful. Karen went and retrieved the photo of Sallyanne being hugged by another man. She returned a few moments later and showed Alexia. "Is this the other woman who lives here?"

Alexia shrugged. "I guess. I don't go in the other rooms. I'm not allowed to."

14

KAREN LEFT Alexia dozing in her room while searching Sallyanne's bedroom. In fairness, it was cleaner and tidier than the other two bedrooms and Karen sensed that Sallyanne may have once taken a little more pride in herself. A small dressing table contained an array of make-up, powders, face cleaning solutions and wipes, but many remained unused.

Turning her attention to the wardrobe, Karen snapped on a pair of latex gloves and flicked through the various hangers. Jeans, tops, and skirts. A pile of shoes, boots, and a few carrier bags of more clothes sat in a heap at the bottom. They were normal clothes, nothing garish, no bold colours and nothing Karen would class as straight out of the Ann Summers catalogue. Karen moved away and headed towards the bedside table. She perched on the end of the bed and pulled open the drawers. Headphone buds, packets of tissues, odd pieces of jewellery, a few pens. Nothing stood out. She looked around and noticed how average and normal the bedroom looked.

Then she knelt on the floor and looked under the bed, her eyes drawn to the shoebox. Karen wiggled it out of the tight space. It was covered in a fine layer of dust and, not wishing to disturb it, she prised the lid off and placed it to one side. Karen soon realised that the contents would give her a better insight into Sallyanne's personal life.

There were envelopes, a few trinkets and hand bracelets, which, judging by the size, would have fitted a child's hand. Karen assumed they'd belonged to Sallyanne when she was a child. She next picked up a brown envelope full of photographs. Emptying them out on to the bed, Karen ran her finger through them. There were pictures of two girls sitting together enjoying an ice cream while sitting in swimming costumes beside a paddling pool. They smiled back with a squint as the sun shone in their eyes.

Karen soon realised that many of the pictures once belonged in a family album and that the girl in the picture was Sallyanne, the other probably her sister. There were pictures of Sallyanne being held up aloft by her dad. Karen imagined that if it had been a video clip instead of a still photo, Sallyanne would have been squealing with delight. The images reflected happier times and innocent child-hoods. She wondered at what point in Sallyanne's life things went wrong? Karen returned the photographs to the shoebox and tucked it beneath the bed before heading back.

As she neared the car, Karen was on the phone to control when she heard a loud exchange of voices seeping out of a small gap in the rear windows. It seemed Ed had been having a tough time as Minchin protested about being held unnecessarily.

Karen pulled open the rear passenger door. "Right, keep your trap shut or I'm calling a van to take you away now."

"You can't keep me in here forever. It's roasting in here. At least open the bloody windows more," Minchin protested.

"So you're Sallyanne's pimp, right?"

"No," he replied.

"Well, that's a lie for starters. I've had a friendly chat with Alexia. She said you were the pimp for both of them. And by living under the same roof you could keep an eye on them. When was the last time you saw Sallyanne?"

Minchin bowed his head in resignation. "Friday night when she was working."

"What time?"

Minchin shrugged. "Dunno. Late."

"And you tried to contact her?" Karen asked.

Minchin snarled. "Yeah. She's not answering the phone. She's got my money. No one has seen her. I swear, if she's pissed off, I'll kill her."

Too late, mate.

"Well, it looks like someone has beaten you to it, because her body was found yesterday. Where were you on Friday night between ten pm and nine am. Saturday morning?"

Minchin didn't reply.

"What's the matter. Did she make you angry enough to kill her and dispose of the body?" Karen asked.

Minchin shook his head. "I swear. I didn't even know she was dead, and I swear I had nothing to do with it. All I know is that she went off with a punter. I got a text from her saying that he was promising big money, so she was going off grid for a bit."

"Did you get a look at the punter?"

"No. I was two streets away looking after that dumb bitch upstairs. She's new to this. She spends too much time off her face, which isn't good for business."

"We are taking you down to the station for questioning. We're also seizing your phone as evidence while we try to build up a picture of Sallyanne's last known movements. And you may have been one of the last people to see her."

Minchin threw his head back and bounced it off the rear headrest. "You can't do this. I've done nothing wrong. You can't take my phone. People need to find me. I have rights."

"I've been on to our control. It turns out that we needed to find you anyway. There's an outstanding warrant for your arrest." Karen smiled.

"For what?" Minchin spat back.

"Inciting and controlling prostitution for gain, under Section 52 and Section 53 of the Sexual Offences Act 2003."

Minchin leant forward and buried his head in his hands.

Karen winked at Ed before she jumped into the driver's seat and took them back to the station.

15

WHILE MINCHIN WAS BEING BOOKED into custody and handed over to the right team, Karen and Ed raced off to the canteen to grab a quick lunch. Officers were filtering in and out, a few grabbing a quick sandwich before heading out on patrol, while others used the opportunity to catch up with their colleagues. Karen spotted a few officers tucked away in the corners, preferring quiet time as they read a few chapters of their book. With their roles being so fast-paced and frenetic, officers needed the downtime to unwind and reduce their stress levels.

Karen opted for a jacket potato and salad, boring and bland, but it would give her the energy she needed to last throughout the day. Ed, meanwhile, went for a gut-busting lasagna and chips, which Karen eyed with envy as he sat down opposite her.

A background noise of murmured conversations punctured by the occasional laugh filtered through to her awareness as Karen's mind processed the events of this morning. She thought back to the box of personal effects that she had found under the bed, Sallyanne's only connection with a normal life that she'd once led. She wondered what happened in Sallyanne's life that had led her to sell her body for sex?

"Ed, are you familiar with all the popular spots where we can find street girls?" Karen asked, forking food into her mouth.

Ed nodded as his eyes rolled up to the ceiling, his mind tracking back to past conversations, investigations, and arrests. "There are a fair number, but much less than there used to be. With active police initiatives, the force has clamped down on it quite a lot. Belinda knows more than me. There used to be a lot of activity around key areas where university students live."

Karen pursed her lips with interest.

"Yeah, it was intense and easy pickings for the street girls. Believe it or not, students had a lot of money to burn, and it was an easy twenty or thirty quid for quick sex. They'd go to student houses where they could pick up three or four customers and walk out an hour later with a hundred quid."

Karen grabbed her phone and called Belinda.

"Hi, Karen."

"Bel, I'm just in the other building having a bite to eat with Ed. We've been talking about any intel on where the hotspots are for street girls to hang out. Ed reckons you know more than him?"

"I can get a list together for you, but they move on quickly. A popular spot this week could be dead next week. They do it to keep us on our toes. It's common for the girls to head over to an area behind the rail station. Cinder Lane is quite popular after dark."

"Thanks, Bel. That would be helpful."

Karen hung up and returned to her lunch.

"Why one hand?" Ed asked.

"Sorry?"

"The victim. Why was only one hand cut off and not both?"

Karen lifted one shoulder and let it drop. "Perhaps he was disturbed? Or heard something?"

"Silva?"

The thought had already crossed her mind. *Perhaps the killer heard David Silva in the bushes. Perhaps Silva knows more than he's letting on. Maybe he did witness it but is too scared to admit it.* "It's a possibility. I'll send officers to track him down again. They can have another word with him."

As Ed speculated, he threw around loads of theories. It was as if his mind never stopped analysing the evidence, but Karen admired that quality about him. His analytical brain had an eye for detail and for identifying connections, solutions, and answers.

"It could be a trophy," he surmised as he stabbed his last remaining chips and used them as an improvised shovel to scoop up the remaining sauce on his plate.

"Yes, certainly a possibility. She may have scratched or injured him which could offer vital DNA evidence beneath her fingernails. If he was forensically aware, then perhaps he removed her hand rather than try to clean it."

Karen's phone rang with a call from a member of her team. The vibration sent the device rattling across the table.

"Dave, what's up?"

"Karen, Sallyanne's personal effects have been found by Bootham Bar."

The location was vaguely familiar to Karen since Zac had mentioned it a few times. Though she hadn't been there herself, she knew it was one of the four gates into the city, or something like that.

"What was discovered?"

"Her handbag was discarded by the road and handed in late last night. Her keys were inside along with her purse, lipstick, condoms, and a packet of fruit pastilles."

"No phone?"

"No, Karen. No phone and no underwear."

"Okay, get it off to forensics. It's probably already been compromised by whoever picked it up and whoever else might have handled it between the time that it was taken and discovered. If our killer wasn't wearing gloves, then his prints will be on that too."

Karen hung up and updated Ed before grabbing their stuff and heading off.

16

HE LEANT FORWARD in his chair and adjusted the lamp on his table to give him more brightness on his clean and dust-free work surface. It provided plenty of space to move his hands around. He blinked a few times and stared at the exhibits. The first bit was easy, but the next step would sap his concentration.

His mind drifted back to his younger years. He'd spend hours watching his father build the most ornate wooden pieces. Kumiko was the delicate and sophisticated Japanese technique of assembling small wooden pieces without nails. His father had toiled for hours using wooden pieces which he'd grooved, punched, and mortised before fitting them using all his tools.

He'd marvelled at and admired his father's patience. Whenever his father had involved him, he'd tried to copy him, but his efforts had always ended in vain and he'd skulked off crying.

"Success in any endeavour requires single-minded attention

to detail and total concentration," his dad had reminded him.

He'd never understood at that age. But his dad had kept repeating the statement with what he'd thought were words of encouragement. They'd never felt like that though. In his mind, he'd been a failure compared to his father.

"It's not what's happening to you now or what has happened to you in the past that determines who you become. Rather, it's your decision about what you focus on, what things mean to you and what you're going to do about them that will decide your ultimate success."

"Yeah, yeah," he muttered as he examined each bone. Each one had been slow boiled to strip it clean. Dried and left to rest, they were ready to be worked on.

He took his craft electric drill and made tiny holes in the first bone. His hand trembled. The pieces felt so small. One slip and the bone could break, leaving shattered pieces which were of no use to him. He took a deep breath and exhaled to calm the nerves that rattled in him. He repeated the process again. It felt like he'd held his breath for the whole time as he sat back in his chair and took an almighty gulp of air.

He rearranged all the pieces to fit. It reminded him of a skeletal hand that you might find in a lecture theatre of the medical school, or on the shelf in a supermarket beside all the other gimmicky toys that they stocked for Halloween.

Moving to his utility box, he rifled through a few drawers before he found a reel of thin wire. He carefully threaded the wire through the end of one bone before connecting it to the next. One by one, the bones took shape until all four fingers and thumb looked like a ghoulish artefact ready to come alive after being buried in an Egyptian tomb for thousands of years.

He took a moment to examine his craftsmanship. If he'd been alive, his dad would have offered nothing more than a suitable nod of acceptance, before returning to enjoy another chapter from his favourite book of Japanese cultural history.

Bending over, he took the box he'd left on the floor beside him and placed it on the table. He took the lid off and examined the soft burgundy velvet cushioned pad that nestled in the bottom. This was the bit he hated the most. The risk was that all his hard work could end in disaster if the bones broke or were held for too long. He licked his lips and focused. Carefully levering his fingers underneath the bones, he lifted the exhibit as if lifting a newborn baby for the first time. His eyes travelled from the hand to the box just a few inches away, but it felt like a mile.

Holding his breath, he placed the hand inside before closing the lid. Heading into the hallway, he opened the cupboard door beneath the stairs to reveal a flight of stairs leading to a gloomy basement. His hand patted the walls, searching for the small switch. Either the switch was broken, or the bulb gone. Each old wooden step creaked as he descended into the darkness that lay beyond.

The space beneath the house was dark, musty, and claustrophobic. Smaller than an average size room, he had made it into a liveable space, with an old armchair, table, Japanese prints on the wall and a CD player which sat on a floating shelf towards the far end of the room. He grabbed the pull cord and tugged on it. A small bulb in the middle of the room shed a brilliant light that brought the room alive. The gentle tones of Japanese music filled the space as he switched on the CD player.

For a moment, he closed his eyes and let the music in. Stillness filled him. He couldn't remember how long he'd been standing there cradling the box but opened his eyes and turned to his right where a cabinet with glass doors sat against one wall. He opened one door and slid the box into the place that he left for it.

It looked so perfect there. Right alongside all the others.

17

MOMENTS before she left the station, Ted Faulkner returned Karen's call to say that they were on their way back from the airport. Concern tinged his tone as he pushed Karen for a reason she needed to see them. Not wishing to upset them while they were driving, Karen said she'd like to meet them in person within the hour.

Karen grabbed Belinda before taking one of the pool cars and heading off to the Faulkners.

"It's going to be horrible breaking the news to them," Belinda said as she tapped her pen on the notepad.

"To be fair, I'm not looking forward to it myself. I've already contacted an FLO and put them on standby in case we need them."

They drove in silence for the rest of the way, Karen's eyes firmly fixed ahead as pictures of Sallyanne's body flashed through her mind. It was never easy breaking the news to parents that they had lost a son or daughter. She had done it many times while in uniform. The number of road traffic accidents she had attended that had resulted in young fatalities meant many visits to parents, and it never got easier.

Karen arrived at the address and felt that feeling of dread wash over her again.

A Volvo estate was parked diagonally across the front drive as Karen and Belinda approached the front door. Before Karen pressed on the doorbell, the door flew open as if Sallyanne's dad had been waiting impatiently behind it.

Karen and Belinda presented their warrant cards.

"Mr Ted Faulkner?" Karen asked.

Ted nodded with wide eyes, a mixture of curiosity and concern etched in his features. A woman came up behind him and hovered over his shoulder, her arms wrapped across her chest.

"This is my wife, Helen."

Karen offered the smallest of smiles before they were invited in. She followed Ted into the lounge where he offered the officers a seat on the sofa. Ted took one armchair, while his wife grabbed the other and tucked her hands between her thighs.

Belinda opened up her notepad and glanced around. It was a warm and inviting room with grey sofas and wooden floors. The walls were sparsely decorated to give a minimalistic effect, and a cabinet to the other end of the room housed an array of what appeared to be family photographs.

"What's this about?" Ted asked.

Karen cleared her throat. Her mouth had become tinder dry. "We're here about your daughter Sallyanne."

The Faulkners exchanged a brief glance before Ted shrugged. "Um… our relationship with our daughter is a bit fractured. We haven't actually seen her in a long time. Six months, perhaps longer. I guess you must know what she does…?"

Karen nodded. "Yes, we do. There isn't an easy way to say this, but we discovered a body yesterday morning which we believe is your daughter. Officers who attended identified her from earlier interactions that she'd had with the police for soliciting."

Ted's eyes widened as he gasped. He glanced across at his wife.

"Sallyanne?"

"We believe so."

"Um… what… happened to her?" he asked, his voice soft and broken.

"She was attacked and murdered."

"Murdered!" came a scream from behind them.

Karen and Belinda swivelled in their seats to see a young woman standing in the doorway, her body trembling, her hands pinned to her cheeks, her eyes already filling with tears.

Ted jumped from his chair and strode towards the woman. "Esme, sorry darling. I'm so sorry." He pulled her head into his chest as she sobbed. He stroked her hair. "This is Esme, our younger daughter," he said in Karen's direction.

Karen waited a few moments while Ted consoled his daughter. She glanced across to Helen who stayed rooted in her chair, her head bowed. There were no tears, no hysterical crying, not looking up to see the pain her young daughter felt.

"Who found her?" he asked.

"Someone living rough spotted her at the abandoned airfield."

"Is he a suspect?"

Karen shook her head. "It's unlikely. But we are following up all lines of enquiry."

"Can… can we see her?" Ted asked.

"You can do that later. Perhaps you need time as a family to come to terms with the shock and your loss."

Ted shook his head. "No, we'd like to see her. Now," he said, looking towards his wife who didn't look up.

"We can take you there now. She's at the hospital mortuary awaiting a post-mortem."

Esme wriggled out of her father's embrace and went over and knelt in front of her mum, wrapping her hands around her mum's. Helen looked up for a moment before looking down again.

Karen retrieved the strip of photographs recovered from Sallyanne's bedroom, holding them aloft for Ted to see. "I found these in her bedroom. Do you know the male hugging her?"

Ted stepped over in Karen's direction and leant over, narrowing his eyes. He grimaced and shook his head before wiping the tears from his cheeks.

"Esme, could you look?" Karen asked.

Esme glanced over her shoulder but remained kneeling in front of her mum. She took a few moments before nodding. "Roberto Joseph. Sal and him used to be an item back in the day. I can't remember when. I just remember her talking about him a lot."

Belinda scribbled down the name.

"Do you know if she was still in contact with him?"

Esme shrugged a shoulder and shook her head.

"Have you spoken to Sallyanne recently?"

Esme sighed. "About six weeks ago. I visited her to make sure she was okay."

"And how did she appear to you?"

"Same old Sallyanne. Didn't say much. Asked if she could borrow money from me because she was skint. Asked how mum and dad were. When I asked her to come back with me so she could say hi to them, she refused."

Karen and Belinda left not long after, heading to the hospital mortuary with Ted Faulkner.

18

KAREN AND BELINDA parked up back at the station and trudged through their building towards the CSU. The trip to the mortuary had been as painful as Karen had expected. When he'd seen Sallyanne's face, Ted Faulkner had broken down. She'd lain there looking peaceful, as if asleep.

"I felt so sorry for him," Belinda said, letting out a deep sigh. Seeing Ted sob had moved Belinda. She'd stood back with a lump in her throat to give him the space he needed. Her eyes had misted over as she'd blinked hard to clear her vision.

Karen squeezed Belinda's arm. "I guess it's one thing that we never get used to as police officers. Members of the public always see us in a frontline policing role, making arrests on the street, seeing our patrol cars and attending crime scenes. But very few realise there's another sharp end to our policing like discovering bodies and dealing with bereaved families."

Belinda nodded. She knew what Karen meant. "Yep. I was

a mess in there. I looked across at you and it didn't seem to affect you as much?"

Karen stopped in the corridor and stepped to one side with Belinda. "It does still affect me. Especially with children. I guess I've been in that situation so many times that I've developed a thicker skin. It's not like I don't care, it's just that I've become better at handling it. If we let every death touch us, it would affect our ability to stay impartial."

"I guess you're right. It gets to me though."

"It will do from time to time. It means you're still in touch with your emotions and that human tragedy still means something to you. Don't let that go. I think we get better at hiding it from the victims' families because they're looking to us for strength and compassion."

"Thanks, Karen."

"Any time. If these things get to you and you need someone to talk to, I'm always here."

"You might regret that," Belinda replied with a weak smile.

"I already am," Karen shot back with a wink before pushing through the doors on to the main floor.

"Good news, Karen. Forensics picked up a few prints off the pendant. Most are partials. But we have a hit on one," Tyler said.

That was great news and the first breakthrough in the case. The news lifted her spirits a bit as she headed to his desk.

Tyler handed her the report from forensics. "Henry Warnock aged fifty-one. Former GP. Cautioned for kerb-crawling eighteen months ago."

"Do we have a current address?"

"Yes."

"Okay, we need to have a word. Pull him in."

"As a suspect or a witness?" Tyler asked.

"Both," Karen replied as she headed back towards her office.

In the corridor, Belinda hovered with two individuals that Karen hadn't seen before. They turned to look as Karen approached.

"Karen, this is TDC Ned Chambers and DC Preet Anand. They're joining our team today."

Karen smiled and extended a hand. "Ah, great. The super said you'd arrive today. Come in and grab a seat."

Karen dropped into her chair. Belinda stood at the back of the room with her arms folded, while Ned and Preet took two chairs opposite Karen. Both officers looked nervous as if it was their first day on the job.

"I'm glad to have you on our team. You've met Belinda, and she'll introduce you to everyone else. I'll schedule time with each of you to find out a bit more about your career to date, along with your aspirations and strengths so that we can deploy you in the best possible way."

"Thanks, guv, I'm looking forward to getting stuck in," Ned replied as he interlocked his fingers in his lap and sat up straight. He had short, dark brown hair, bushy eyebrows, and a couple of days' worth of stubble. He wore a navy suit, pale blue shirt, and red tie.

Karen nodded. He sounded enthusiastic and genuine,

though he appeared a little nervous. "Call me Karen. We keep it friendly here."

Karen turned towards DC Preet Anand. She had a fair, smooth complexion, thick pencilled eyebrows, full lips and dark brown eyes that matched her hair. *She's attractive*, Karen thought. "It's good to have you here, Preet. I understand from the super that you spent two years in robbery. Enjoy that?"

Preet gave off a warm smile. "I did, Karen. Challenging, but very rewarding. Belinda spoke highly of you earlier," Preet said as she glanced over her shoulder in Belinda's direction.

Belinda smiled.

"I paid her to say that." Karen laughed off the compliment. "I think you'll find that we are an easy-going team and I'm not into airs and graces. We work hard and play hard. I'm hoping to organise a night out for the entire team once we have this current case out of the way. That would be a great opportunity for you to get to know the rest of the team away from the office."

"That would be great," Preet replied.

"Okay, let's crack on with it. Belinda can get you up to speed with our current case and if you have any issues, find myself or Belinda. But to be honest, anyone else in the team will be more than happy to help too."

19

A SURPRISE CALL from reception informing Karen she had an unannounced visitor sent her straight to the visitors block. She skirted through the buildings and headed towards the central block that was off the main road. Pushing through the doors, Karen approached the reception staff.

"DCI Karen Heath, I understand you have a visitor for me?"

The man behind reception nodded and peered over the top of his glasses in the direction of the interview rooms. "Yes, a young lady. She's in interview room three."

Karen glanced over her shoulder and thanked the man before heading for the room. She slid the sign to occupied before stepping through the door.

Esme sat cradling a plastic glass of water. With elbows tucked into her sides, the young woman sat upright, taut, and unflinching as Karen appeared.

"Hi, Esme. This is unexpected," Karen said, pulling out a chair and sitting opposite her. She glanced down at the water and nodded. "Can I get you a tea or coffee instead?"

Esme shook her head. She had similar features to her elder sister. Dark, long hair, the same eyes and nose. But the similarities ended there. Esme had a much rounder, fuller face, unlike her sister who appeared to be undernourished, thinner and paler in comparison.

"I'm fine, thanks. Sorry. Perhaps I should have called first. I know you're busy dealing with my sister's d..." Esme stared down at her water.

"No, it's fine. I'm here to help in any way I can. I know your family is going through a tough time. Do you mind if I record this conversation?"

Esme stiffened. "Why?"

"Because everything you say may help us build a better picture of Sallyanne. You and your family know a lot more about her than we do. Every shred of information could help. You can say no if you want to?"

"No. It's fine."

Karen took out her phone and did the introductions before continuing. "Is there anything you wanted to talk about?"

It took a few moments before Esme spoke again.

"Sorry about my mum. I suppose she appeared somewhat distant... as well as upset. It wasn't the reaction you might have expected. But I thought I'd try and tell you a bit more about what's been going on at home and... well, give you a better insight into Sallyanne's life. There are things about Sal that Mum and Dad don't know. I don't know if it will help, but I guess…" Esme's voice trailed off.

Karen pursed her lips and nodded. "That would be helpful. Don't worry about your parents' reaction. It's fine. Everyone has their own way of dealing with tragic news like that. We're not here to judge."

"My parents had a difficult time with Sallyanne. Especially my mum. Sal was clever but hung around with a lot of bad people in her teens. Small gangs, string of bad relationships and… drugs. It's like you're not part of the gang unless you take drugs. Sal went along with that and, when she was in, she couldn't get out."

Karen asked if her parents knew about it. Esme replied that Sallyanne kept a lot from their parents, so they never understood how deeply she had got into trouble.

"Sallyanne drifted apart from Mum and Dad, which upset Mum. But she did find a way to break free. She confided in me a lot. I tried to give her all the support and help I could. She got clean and went to university."

"Can you remember when that was?"

"2015. She was twenty-three."

"That's good to hear. I'm sure she appreciated everything you did for her," Karen said.

"Yep, I guess so. Then history repeated itself again. She fell in with another bad crowd. Not as bad as the first lot, but there were still drugs involved. Late-night drinking. A bit of casual sex. I don't know the exact details or when it happened, but she got drunk one night in her final year." Esme looked towards the ceiling, pulling more thoughts from her mind. "2018. Sal thought her drink had been spiked. She didn't tell me exactly what happened because she couldn't remember much, but Sal changed after that."

"Did she give any other details? Perhaps a name? A location? Did she mention the name of any friends who were around when she believed her drink was spiked?"

Esme shook her head. "No. Not that I can remember. She didn't say who it was or what happened. Sal was never the same after that..." Esme wiped her wet eyes with the back of her hand. "Just as she'd pulled her life back together."

"Did you tell your parents?"

"No, Sallyanne didn't want any fuss. She said she was fine."

"When you say she was never the same again, what do you mean?" Karen asked, probing deeper.

Esme shrugged. "I dunno. She was never the same. We used to talk about everything, but she started holding back a lot more. Sal began taking more drugs and sleeping around. Then she started asking for money when guys wanted to sleep with her. I think that was the start of that horrible relationship between money and sex."

Karen opened her case file and pulled out a photocopy of the strip of photos she had shown Esme before. "You mentioned that Roberto and Sallyanne were an item. Was he the one that introduced her to drugs?"

"I don't know. He drifted in and out of her life for a few years. I think they started hanging around together in high school when they were fifteen or sixteen. He was a bit of a bad boy back then, but she was attracted to that. Then I didn't hear Sal mention his name for a few years until she was nearly twenty."

"Does he live in York?"

"He did. He's Italian. I heard that his family moved back to Italy, but he stayed on for a little longer. He was working the coffee shop circuit for quite a while. The last time I heard his name being mentioned was over a year ago."

"Where did Sallyanne go to university?"

"Here in York. I don't think she could let go of her friendship circle."

"And was Roberto still part of that friendship circle while she was at university?"

Esme nodded. "As far as I'm aware. Sal said that he came to visit her in halls a few times, then stopped coming when she started spending more time on the piss with her university friends."

"Was he angry or jealous?"

Esme shrugged. "I don't know. I wish I could help more. But if I think of anything else, can I phone you?"

Esme glanced at the strip of photos which sat on the table between them. She smiled and tapped the images. "Do you know Sal loved that green suede miniskirt," she said, staring at the images of Sallyanne wearing that skirt with black tights and a white top. "It was her favourite. Wore it everywhere. Like it was glued to her. I swear she had it on *every* time we chatted over video. Sal said she'd wear it on most nights out. It was a running joke between us that they'd have to bury her in it…" Esme fell silent, lost in her thoughts. "After university I never saw her wear it again. She must have thrown it away."

Karen smiled and then furrowed her brow. An image flashed through her mind.

"Of course." Karen slid her business card across the table and stood up. "You can get me on this number any time. I really appreciate you taking the time to come in. It wasn't an easy thing for you to do. I'll show you out."

20

FIVE BOXES. Five victims. With two empty shelves, there was plenty of space for more. His collection was taking shape.

He'd spent the last few hours cleaning the blade on his sword. Every millimetre polished and restored to its former glory. With the dried blood and small tissue traces washed away, nothing but his pin sharp reflection stared back at him. He didn't want to damage, chip or scratch the blade when he brought it down to bear. As he returned it to the ceremonial rack, it would be hard for anyone to determine which of the blades had been used.

He turned and headed for his chair, lowering himself in before tipping his head back and closing his eyes.

His fingers tapped on the armrests as he listened to the soft sounds of another of his favourite traditional Japanese songs, "Glow of the Moon". *Soothing serenity in a fast-paced world. Pureness among a den of filth, violence, and vice.* But who was he to judge after everything he'd done? He'd become obsessed with women who traded their self-respect for money. An obsession that had sent him on a power-hungry quest of revenge. *Listen to the music. Relax. Don't let those thoughts invade now.*

The track faded and silence prevailed once again. Opening his tired eyes, he reached for the fabric beside him. Cheap, faded Marks & Spencer's knickers. They were hardly what he imagined Sallyanne would wear. He scrunched them into the palm of his hand. His senses swirled as he closed his eyes. Intoxicated, dizzy, light-headed. *Sallyanne. Sallyanne.* His thoughts turned to that night when he'd taken her. *Sallyanne. Sallyanne.* Powerless to stop him. Taken for his own pleasure.

He stood and smiled at his collection of samurai swords. Hours of craftsmanship had gone into making every single one of them. Finely balanced and sharp enough to cut through raw flesh with minimal effort, the swords were the ultimate fighting weapon for the samurai.

He paused by the handmade black blade Japanese samurai Wakizashi sword. A magnificent object with an eight-inch handle and a thirty-inch blade that sat in its own ceremonial stand. He hadn't used this one yet, but no doubt knew that one day it would serve its purpose. For the time being, he knew which one to employ next, his handmade Katana samurai sword, with similar proportions to his Wakizashi sword.

With his whole upbringing centered around Japanese culture, this room carried so much significance to him. Instilled in him at a very early age, the folklore, traditions, and the power of the samurai coursed through his veins.

Along from the rack of swords, an impressive display of samurai helmets sat beside a bookshelf stacked with Bushido books.

Soon it would be time again to take another hand.

21

As KAREN LEFT the office for the evening, she checked the time on her phone. She needed to visit a few of the locations Belinda had identified as hotspots for soliciting, but first, she had to visit Sallyanne's address. Following Esme's visit, an image had tugged on her memories. Theories and questions swarmed her thoughts as she made the brief journey and parked.

Having snapped on a pair of latex gloves, Karen removed Sallyanne's keys from the evidence bag and let herself in through the front door.

"Police! Show yourselves!" Karen shouted. Standing in the darkened hallway, Karen listened for any signs of noise or movement. She assumed that Minchin and Alexia Davies were out *working*. Her assumptions were confirmed as she walked around the ground floor before making her way to the bedrooms.

Karen walked into Sallyanne's bedroom and flicked on the

light. A dull glow brought the room to life. She headed to the wardrobe and knelt before rummaging among the pile of shoes, boots, and carrier bags.

I knew it, Karen thought as she pulled out a Sainsbury's bag and lifted a green suede miniskirt that poked from the top of it. It was the one from the photos. Sallyanne hadn't thrown it away and though it was a long shot, she wondered if this might be the vital bit of evidence she'd been looking for. Karen placed the skirt in a brown paper evidence bag and then placed the Sainsbury's bag containing other items of clothing in another evidence bag.

———

PERHAPS IT WAS TOO EARLY in the evening. It had just gone eight pm, but there were very few girls around. They viewed Karen's car with suspicion before darting into doorways and alleyways. It was as if they had a sixth sense.

The streets were as dark as the surrounding vibe. The warmth of the summer sun had slipped away as a cool night followed. It was dry, and that offered Karen a better chance of talking to as many women as possible.

"I'm not the enemy. I'm trying to save your lives," she muttered, turning down another street. The glare of headlights blinded her for a few moments as a car slowed, inching forward past two women who stood on the corner.

I'm going to have to do this on foot, she thought.

Dressed in jeans, T-shirt and a denim jacket, she felt overdressed compared to some women she'd seen during the last half an hour. Stepping from her car, Karen made her way back to where the two women stood.

"We're not your cup of tea, luv," one woman shouted from across the other side of the road.

"You're not mine either," Karen replied, pulling out her warrant card. She put both women in their late thirties, possibly forties. The first had blonde peroxide hair, the smallest purple boob tube, and a denim skirt that barely covered anything. It wasn't the most flattering look for a chubby, short woman. Her scrawny, thin friend would hardly win any prizes in Milan Fashion Week either. She wore chunky black boots, spray-on faded denim jeans and a green fleece that appeared several sizes too large for her. Karen wondered what men would be driven to pay little and large for sex!

Scrawny rolled her eyes. "Give us a break. We're trying to earn a living, and you're bad for business. You'll scare away the punters," Scrawny added, glancing over Karen's shoulder towards another car that slowly cruised down the street towards them.

Karen pulled out a picture of Sallyanne. "Have you seen her?"

The women narrowed their eyes and stared through the gloomy darkness at the pictures. They looked at each other before shaking their heads. *A little too quickly*, in Karen's opinion.

"Nah, not seen her. Why?" Chubby replied.

"Because she's dead. She worked the streets like you," Karen glanced around, "probably stood on this very corner looking for business, but she was murdered."

Chubby sneered and shrugged. "Shit happens. Hazards of the job."

"Have you seen anyone lurking around here? Perhaps not looking like your average punter? Maybe someone that troubled you a bit?"

The women laughed. "Average punter? They're all weird, desperate and needy. Does that qualify?"

"Look, we have a grieving family who want answers, and I need to get the toerag off the streets before he hurts any more girls. Even you."

Scrawny took a long draw on a cigarette and blew the smoke in Karen's direction. "We'll take our chances, luv."

"You don't get it, do you…? The next punter that you pick up could be your last." Karen was just about to continue when a dark Audi pulled up.

Chubby and Scrawny took a few steps back, concern on their faces as they stared at the well-built man behind the wheel.

"Move!" he yelled through the open passenger's window.

Karen pulled out her warrant card and held it up. "Police, what's your problem?"

The passenger window went up and the Audi tyres screeched on the tarmac as the car sped up down the road, its red taillights disappearing into the distance before it took a sharp left and roared out of view.

"A friend of yours?" Karen asked, turning towards the women. On first impressions, Karen assumed that he may have been their pimp, or hired muscle paid to drive around to keep an eye out for trouble or rival crime gangs looking to take control of the area.

Scrawny jabbed a bony finger in Karen's direction as she moved away. "You're bad for business. You're going to get us in trouble. Piss off out of here."

Karen tried to catch up with her. "I'm trying to get some information. That's all."

Scrawny stopped and stared as several other cars loomed into view, stopping at various corners and further up the street, their car engines revving. Her anger turned to fear as she looked back at chubby, who looked scared and worried.

"Shit is going to go down if you hang around here. Get out while you can still walk," Scrawny whispered as she scuttled off down the street.

The atmosphere changed as a dark veil of menace descended. Tension bristled in the air. These weren't punters, they were the men who controlled the girls. She counted five cars with their engines revving. They heavily outnumbered her. Karen knew her life would be at risk if she stayed much longer. The gangs weren't scared of the police and a lone female officer stood little chance of protecting herself.

Karen reached for her phone and unlocked the screen ready to call for help as she hurried back to her car. She checked over her shoulder every few yards and noticed the cars had moved position and were trailing her. As they approached, she quickened her footsteps and put her hand into her handbag to retrieve her keys. Karen jumped in and started the car, glancing in her rear-view mirror to see the ominous bright orbs of light stationary in the middle of the street about fifty yards behind. Pulling away, Karen checked again.

The orbs hadn't moved. She let out a deep breath as her heart hammered in her chest. If their intention was to scare her off, then they had achieved that.

22

HAVING DROPPED off the two evidence bags with forensics first thing, Karen grabbed her morning coffee and a croissant while heading through town. The events of the night before had taken her by surprise. She hadn't expected simple enquiries to turn ugly so quickly. Not long after getting home, she'd called Zac to tell him about it. After a bollocking about the dangers of heading out into the streets at night without support, he'd filled her in on his observations.

Through that conversation, she'd discovered a recent escalation in turf wars between rival gangs fighting for domination over the streets in the supply of drugs. A spate of tit-for-tat knife attacks and shootings had led to a menacing rise in intimidation. That information explained so many cars last night. Though no one had threatened her, the intention and warnings had still been there.

The journey out of town proved slower than normal, the morning rush hour in full swing. Though it was nothing like the hectic, smoky and congested rush-hour experience in London. It was more like a slow meander, which quickened as she left the outskirts of the town behind her.

She pulled through the opening to the abandoned airfield and parked. Stepping out of the car, serenity surrounded her. Birds chirped in the trees and a gentle breeze stroked her face. It was hard to imagine the horrors that had taken place here just a few days ago. She walked the area again, beginning where Sallyanne's jacket was found, and then towards where her body had lain. Karen processed the scene, visualising in her mind that fateful night when Sallyanne's body was dragged the short distance between those two spots. *How much of that did Sallyanne experience? Was she already unconscious by then? Or worse, dead?* She hoped those answers would be revealed at the PM.

The PolSA search had revealed nothing of significance. Other than a small-bladed knife discovered in an area close by, they'd found nothing. No clothing fragments, personal effects, new bloodstains, or even a discarded piece of chewing gum.

Karen wrapped her arms across her chest as she set off. She wandered deeper into the airfield to take in the enormity of the site. A few buildings appeared in the distance, but they'd been checked by officers. This made little sense. If he'd wanted to discard her body in such a remote spot, why hadn't he taken her into the woods and buried her? As it was, her body was anything but concealed. *Did he want her to be discovered?*

The removal of the hand plagued her. Sallyanne wasn't the first prostitute to be murdered. It was a sad occurrence that happened up and down the country. But from the many case files she had come across in her career, most prostitutes died through strangulation or a violent beating. The removal of her hand took this up to a whole new level. *Did it signify something? Did the killer like collecting hands?* Karen almost laughed at her own thoughts.

Many serial killers collected trophies. A lock of hair. An item of clothing. In many cases documented around the world, serial killers had removed a part of their victims' bodies as souvenirs.

Karen remembered a serial killer in the US who'd removed his victims' eyeballs and pickled them in jars before leaving them in his pantry. Another case involved a serial killer who'd sliced off his victim's ears and attached them together using string to create a macabre necklace.

A hand seemed a bit different. Perhaps he wanted the fingers? Then why one hand? Why not both?

A member of her team with Iranian roots had mentioned how Islamic authorities in Iran punished the first offence committed by thieves with the amputation of four fingers of the right hand. The Saudi and Somalian authorities went one step further by chopping off the hands of thieves.

Is that it? Karen thought. *Did Sallyanne steal something? And got her hand sliced off as punishment?*

23

KAREN PARKED up at the hospital and made her way through the large reception area on her way to the mortuary. Throngs of visitors and outpatients filtered through in all directions, appearing from side corridors and criss-crossing her path as they headed to visit patients and attend clinics. The smell of coffee from a small shop off to her left drew Karen's attention. She'd only had the one this morning, prepared at home and taken with her in a travel thermos cup. She'd sipped on it while walking around the abandoned airfield.

God, I could do with another, she thought. But the smell of coffee would be more useful once she had left the post-mortem. A good way for her to flush out the smell of death and disinfectant from her senses.

"Morning, Karen," Jade said as she stood to meet her.

"Morning. Been waiting long?"

"Not really. Ten minutes. Been watching a steady stream of patients in their pyjamas and dressing gowns shuffle out towards the main entrance for a fag. It cracks me up how they still feel the need to get their nicotine fix."

They continued the short distance in silence, the corridors teeming with hospital staff, people being pushed around in wheelchairs and the sound of their shoes echoing around them.

By the time a mortuary technician let them in and showed them through to the main examination room, Izzy was in full flow. Another technician stood beside her, assisting, while silence prevailed around them. Karen wondered why there wasn't the familiar sound of Izzy's radio playing in the background.

"Morning, Izzy. Sorry we're late," Karen said.

"Morning. Deliberate on your part no doubt." Izzy teasingly raised a brow in Karen's direction.

"Well, it's not the highlight of my day, so yeah, I thought I'd let you get started," Karen replied.

Both Karen and Jade took a moment to examine the thin, bony cadaver in front of them. The post-mortem was in its advanced stages. Sallyanne's body had already come under Izzy's scrutiny. Her internal organs had been removed, weighed and documented for completeness.

Jade stood a few feet back, keeping her distance. She was as close as she wanted to be and would stay rooted to the spot unless needed.

"What do we have?" Karen asked as she took a moment to examine the cadaver from the head down to the feet. Sallyanne's skin was almost translucent in places. It clung to her bones, particularly around her hips, shoulders and collarbones. "She's certainly undernourished," Karen commented as she stared at Sallyanne's pitted and pallid complexion. The broken body in front of her presented a marked contrast to the images that she had seen of Sallyanne in her early twenties. Healthy looking, large-breasted, shapely, and attractive.

"Drugs. They've ravaged her body," Izzy replied, lifting Sallyanne's left arm and pointing to the needle tracks that peppered the inside of her arm. "There are just as many of these behind her kneecaps. Her lungs are in an advanced state of disease. I've taken the blood and toxin samples. But whatever she was pumping into her body had a significant impact on her liver, too. This is the organ disease that I would associate with someone twenty years her senior."

Karen glanced over her shoulder at Jade who jotted down a few notes. Jade looked up and grimaced, appreciating the weight of the feedback.

"There's significant damage to her GI tract as well. We found evidence of blood in her faeces," Izzy added, before assessing the condition of the cadaver. She pointed out that Sallyanne had experienced hardship and suffering in recent years. Her toenails were long and dirty, as were her finger-nails on the one remaining hand. Izzy had taken scrapings from beneath all of them for forensic analysis. The general health of her skin was poor, with noticeable scabs along her arms and legs.

"Is there evidence of sexual activity?" Karen asked.

Izzy nodded. "Yes, there is evidence of vaginal penetration. There is also slight bruising to her upper thighs at the rear. My assessment would be that the sex was forceful. There is no evidence of anal penetration. Again, I've taken a vaginal swab to look for secondary DNA."

Karen paid attention to the abrasions to Sallyanne's skin, noticeably on the back of her arms, tops of the shoulders and her upper back. Izzy pointed out that they were in line with the injuries caused if a body was dragged along the concrete.

"Okay, and the missing hand. Any ideas of the kind of weapon or tool used?" Jade interrupted; her pen poised above her notepad.

"Something very sharp, and I mean *sharp*! For it to cut through flesh, bone and muscle tissue, with no damage to the surrounding area, means that you're looking for a weapon that isn't serrated, hasn't got a large surface area and isn't heavy."

Karen took a sharp intake of breath and puffed out her cheeks. "So not a saw and not a hunting knife with a serrated edge?"

Izzy shook her head.

"An axe?" Jade offered.

Izzy shook her head again. "Far too heavy and a much larger surface area. Even though it's sharp, we'd witness fragmentation to the bone. We don't have that in this case."

"Okay, that's helpful. I need to get back to the team. I'll await your full report. Thanks for your time, Izzy."

"No problem. I'll speak to you later."

24

WITH JADE out on enquiries following their visit to the hospital, Karen was back in the office and moving among the team getting updates on the various lines of enquiry. With the release of an update for the press, it would only be a matter of time before the team started fielding questions, suspicious sightings, and concerns from members of the public. Parents and loved ones of those who were still missing would call in to ask if the police could renew their efforts to track down their nearest and dearest.

This type of thing happened in every investigation. The job of the officers was to decide what information was relevant and act on it.

"We need to find out as much as we can about Roberto Joseph," Karen said to the team. She gave them an update on Roberto and his relationship with Sallyanne. "We need to find out if he's still in York, or even in the country. He may already have left. We need to track him down to determine whether he's a suspect."

Officers around the room nodded and added that to the list
of things to do.

Karen took a few moments to highlight the key points from
her conversation with Esme and the insights into her
sister's turbulent life.

"Are we increasing police patrols in the hotspots where
street girls hang out?" someone asked.

Karen turned to the officer. "It's something that we're
looking at. I think the problem we face is that if we
increase patrols in the area, the girls are going to think
we're clamping down on their business though we're trying
to save them from harm. It's a fine balance and resources
that we don't have."

Tyler got off the phone and made a beeline for Karen.
"Karen, officers have pulled in Henry Warnock. He's being
held at another station. Do you want him brought
over here?"

"No. Can you give Jade a buzz and ask her to meet me
there in an hour? Is there a forensic update on Sallyanne's
possessions?"

"There's a bit of a backlog. I chased them up this morning,
but they said they're working on evidence DCI Shield
requested they work on first."

Karen stiffened and gritted her teeth. "Oh, really? We'll see
about that."

At pace, she headed from the building towards an adjoining
block, where she yanked open the door and strode through
the corridors, her stern look attracting curious stares from
officers she passed.

"Karen," came a voice.

Karen turned on her heels to see Kelly appear in a doorway having concluded a meeting.

Oh no. "Ma'am."

"Is everything okay?"

"Yes, ma'am. I just need to have a quick word with DCI Shield."

"Good. I'm glad that you're able to work together."

"Yes, ma'am," Karen replied before heading off.

She had a rough idea of where his office was and headed in that direction, scanning the door plates as she walked. Her blood boiled when she found his office with the door open. DCI Shield sat behind his desk, his fingers interlocked behind his head, rocking back and forth in his chair as he stared at his monitor.

Shield smiled as Karen entered his room and let out the slightest of laughs. "DCI. So you've come to your senses and decided to hand the case over to me?"

Karen glared at the man and planted both of her hands on his desk and leant across it. "Don't DCI me. I just found out that my evidence with forensics has been delayed at your request. What gives you the right to interfere with my investigation?"

Shield shook his head. "Don't take it personally. I've been here longer, and I have a better relationship with forensics. If I need something done, they'll pull out all the stops for me."

"That's crap and you know it. You're still pissed at my team taking over the homicide."

"DCI… Heath. You're handling this badly. Word on the street is that you found yourself into a bit of a bother last night. You don't have a clue about the mess that you're creating."

Karen folded her arms across her chest and stared him down. "I know what I'm doing. I'm investigating a homicide. This is nothing compared to the cases I've dealt with in London. You might be a DCI up here, but you wouldn't last five minutes on the streets in London."

Shield bristled with anger. His eyes narrowed as his lids twitched. "Let me tell you something… DCI. If you'd had the decency to ask me, I could have given you the intel. You're undoing all of my work," he spat, slapping his hand on the desk. "I have an undercover officer who has infiltrated an OCG that is involved in drugs and prostitution. You turning up last night only made the OCG more twitchy."

"So screwing around with my forensic request is your way of asserting your authority? How petty! You know what… DCI? If you'd had the decency to act in a professional manner at the crime scene instead of storming in like a complete idiot, I might have asked for your lofty opinion about *my* case. We could have helped each other like colleagues do. What is it? Can't you handle the competition?" Karen asked in a steely voice. "All you're doing is trying to make me look incompetent. And the only person looking foolish here is you."

"You're already incompetent. I don't think you need me helping you to do that."

Karen seethed as she took a step forward to plant her hands on the desk again.

"Enough," boomed a voice from behind them.

Karen looked over her shoulder to see Superintendent Kelly filling the doorway, her face reddened with anger. "This is not how I expect senior officers to act. Karen, you head back to the team. Shield, I want a word with you."

Karen stood her ground for a few moments, casting an eye between Kelly and Shield. Shield stared back, the corner of his mouth curled up.

"Of course, ma'am."

Adrenaline stiffened her muscles. With a shudder, her chest tightened as her breath caught in her throat. She headed to the nearest ladies' toilets and barged in. A mixture of anger and shock paralysed her. She stared at the twisted face in the mirror before splashing copious amounts of water on her face.

"Bastard," she whispered.

Her phone bleeped. Pulling it from her pocket and checking the screen, she read a text from Zac asking if she fancied a glass of wine and a catch-up this evening. Karen fired back a quick reply.

Yes, and make it a bloody big bottle.

25

KAREN STILL BRISTLED with anger as she returned to her office. Shield had overstepped the mark, in her opinion. Not only had he interfered with her investigation, but from their first meeting he hadn't shown her an ounce of mutual respect as an officer of the same rank. Yes, she knew she'd overstepped the mark herself by storming into his office, but she was sick of being treated like a second-rate officer.

Resting her elbows on the desk, she dropped her head into her hands and groaned. "When will someone give me a break?" She knew that losing two officers in London had tarnished her career and would continue to haunt her, despite making a fresh start in York.

"Karen."

The sound of Kelly appearing in a doorway made Karen jump and sent a spasm of pain through her stomach. "Ma'am... I'm..."

Kelly cut her off in mid-flow. "Listen to me, Karen. I will support my officers one hundred per cent *if* I believe they're right. What you did back there was not only disre-spectful to a fellow officer, but to me as well."

"I know… but."

"Karen, there are no buts. As I said to you earlier, if you have an issue with Shield, then you come and speak to me. I'll deal with him. You two haven't got off to a good start and I can't see that situation improving. I suggest you both find a way of working together. I've said the same to him." Kelly closed her eyes for a moment and sighed. "Look, he's an excellent officer, as you are, but he has his head so far up his own arse that I'm surprised he can breathe. You're better than him. Don't let him get to you."

"Yes, ma'am. I agree."

Kelly smiled. "About being a better officer than him, or finding a better way to work together?"

Karen laughed. "Both."

"He was out of order to push your forensic request out of the way so his was processed first. I'll pull him up on that. That's not acceptable."

"Thanks, ma'am."

Kelly nodded before leaving the room.

Karen took a deep breath to control the palpitations in her chest. She sat there questioning how much of the situation was her own doing and how much was down to others still poking a stick at her. She planted her hands on the desk and rose, widening her eyes and blowing out her cheeks before joining the team.

"How are we getting on?" she asked, making her way to Belinda's desk.

"We have some progress. Forensics have come back with their report on evidence recovered from the body and clothing Sallyanne was wearing on the night of her murder. They identified three different DNA profiles from several strands of pubic hair found on her inner thigh. Two are unknown. There was only one DNA match. Grant Rowling. No fixed abode, cautioned for kerb-crawling and an alleged assault on a female. They charged him with committing an indecent act with a female in a public place, but he didn't show up at court."

"Grant Rowling had sex with Sallyanne Faulkner in the hours before her death," Karen murmured.

"I've checked with the council to see if he's been assigned housing, but no one has located him for the past two years."

"Well, he's still in York and doing his best to stay under the radar," Karen replied.

"They discovered two different strands of hair on her clothing. Neither belonged to her," Belinda offered.

"Cross-match them against Minchin's and her scrawny flatmate's," Karen said, before pulling up a chair to scan through the report. The analysis of the cut on Sallyanne's right wrist alarmed her. Microscopic analysis confirmed an absence of serrations or cut marks to the ulna or radius bones. There was no blunt force trauma or chop marks.

The report threw up more questions than answers for Karen as she continued to read it with intrigue. Under microscopic analysis, there was no compression or fragmentation of the underlying bone structure. Again, under detailed analysis, there was negligible soft tissue damage.

Their conclusion was that a non-serrated and light to

middleweight weapon had been used. They suggested that the most likely blades would belong to a machete, meat cleaver or sword.

Karen sat back in her chair, her mind swimming in a quagmire of detail. "Did you read all of this?"

Belinda nodded and raised a brow. "Pretty savage if you ask me. You only have to look at those expensive meat cleavers used in Japanese restaurants. They slide through slabs of fresh tuna like they're paper thin."

Karen stood and paused for a moment while she rubbed her temples trying to figure out what to do next. "Bel, can you look at the sale of swords in this area? Check with martial arts schools, exhibitions, and antique stores. Have any been burgled recently?"

"Will do. Shall I look at the meat cleaver angle? Places like industrial kitchen suppliers?"

"Yes, that would be good. I'm not expecting much. Maybe the sale of swords in antique stores and specialist retailers is more regulated with a stronger paper trail." Karen didn't feel hopeful. "But from my experience in London, swords, machetes, and meat cleavers are freely available."

Karen remembered how colleagues in north London had been called to the scene of a murder in Waltham Cross, where two victims had been brutally attacked by a madman wielding a two-foot-long samurai sword. The brutal attacker had been seeking revenge after a group of white men had racially abused him one night in a pub. It was just one of many cases she could recall. The escalation in violence between gangs of youths wielding foot-long machetes, swords and axes had spiralled out of control on London streets.

26

Outside a police station to the west of the city centre, Karen pulled up alongside Jade's car. It was a smaller hub with an older-looking building set down a side road away from the hustle and bustle of the local high road.

"Sorry I'm late. It's been bloody manic." Karen sighed as she stepped out of her car and headed towards the front door with Jade.

Jade was fine with it. She'd been sitting in her car for about ten minutes with her eyes closed, listening to music and enjoying a bit of downtime.

Karen and Jade presented their warrant cards to the main desk and informed the officer on duty that they were there to interview Henry Warnock. The officer showed them to an interview room where they set up, awaiting Warnock's arrival from another part of the building.

Jade took a few moments to scan through Karen's file and the details on Warnock. "Former GP. He'd certainly be forensically aware. Cautioned several times after being caught in prostitution hotspots. He's been a bit of a naughty boy, which would explain why they struck him off for malpractice."

Karen nodded. Warnock had been struck off after being found guilty of illegally supplying painkillers. Discovering that he'd become sexually involved with his patients during appointments and had carried on a seven-year relationship with a vulnerable patient only exacerbated his case. Evidence had surfaced about a string of sexually explicit messages and pictures between Warnock and three other women. The GMC tribunal had found his actions predatory and manipulative, showing a disgraceful pattern of misconduct lasting over a decade.

"He's certainly a nasty piece of work. He preyed on the vulnerable but was also vile towards his colleagues. He called one receptionist 'a steaming fat blob' and another 'thick as shit'." Karen tutted in disgust. "I can't believe he described patients as 'moany fuckers'. I'm not surprised that they kicked him out."

Warnock was shaping up to be a character whose moral compass had broken a long time ago. With little respect for others, it was no wonder he had turned to street girls to satisfy his depraved needs.

Jade's examination of the file was interrupted when the door opened and an officer escorted Warnock in. Karen thanked him and shut the door after he left.

"Mr Warnock, would you take a seat please?" Karen began, pointing to the seat opposite them.

Warnock was fifty-one, short, with a large receding forehead. His dark bushy eyebrows were in marked contrast to his salt and pepper hair.

"Would someone mind telling me what I'm here for?" he asked, staring back at them with flared nostrils.

Jade read the formal caution and reminded him he was free to go at any point, but his cooperation would be appreciated. She started the recorder and glanced across at Karen.

"Mr Warnock, I'm the SIO dealing with the brutal slaying and homicide of a young lady called Sallyanne Faulkner. She was a street girl, and your name has popped up on our radar following a forensic examination of her personal effects."

Warnock's eyes narrowed as they danced between Karen and Jade. He began sliding his tongue along his bottom lip as he studied them with suspicion.

"I'm not familiar with that name. I certainly can't recall someone by that name as a patient."

Karen opened her file and took out a picture of Sallyanne before sliding it across the desk in Warnock's direction. He slowly lowered his gaze and stared at the image for a few seconds before looking up again. It was long enough for Karen to know that Warnock recognised Sallyanne's face.

"We found your print on the pendant that was hanging around her neck. Could you begin by telling us how that may have ended up there?" Karen asked.

Warnock stiffened and pulled his shoulders back but remained silent.

Karen raised a brow. "You know how this works. I'm sure you've liaised with the police frequently. We can sit here all day if you want to. You're not keeping me from my job. I have a whole team working in the background. If you choose to remain silent, then that's your choice, but it won't slow down our investigation."

Warnock rolled his eyes and tipped his head back for a few seconds before shifting it from ear-to-ear, the bones in his neck cracking. "I picked her up Friday night and drove somewhere where we had sex. You won't find semen traces, as I wore a condom." Warnock sneered. "I'd hate to imagine what I'd catch if I didn't."

"And what time was this?"

Warnock shrugged. "I can't be certain. Just after nine pm."

Warnock explained that Sallyanne was one of the regular girls that he picked up. They drove a short distance to a neighbouring street where they had sex in the back seat of his car for twenty pounds.

"And then what?" Karen probed.

Warnock shrugged again. "And then I dropped her off at the same spot she had been standing at earlier."

"Why did you pick Sallyanne?"

"I've used her several times, so I guess I'm used to her. She knows what I enjoy."

Karen offered a small smile. *Easily pleased. If she knew you liked the sound of drums, she would have got out her drum kit if it meant getting paid.*

"You could be one of the last people to have seen her alive. Did you have any arguments with her?"

Warnock furrowed his brow. "Certainly not."

"Did she ever refuse to have sex with you?"

This time when he flared his nostrils, Karen could see he needed to trim his nose hairs. "No."

"Did anyone see you dropping off Sallyanne?"

Warnock massaged his temples and closed his eyes. "I'm not sure. I can't remember."

Karen was just about to continue when Warnock interrupted her.

"Wait! Yes. There was another girl close by. I don't know her name, but I've seen her once or twice. She's asked me for business before. Flame-red hair, squinty eye, walks with a limp."

Karen bit her lip, desperate to hold back a laugh. The picture that Warnock painted hardly suggested that the woman ranked highly in the hottie stakes.

Jade made a note of the description and stared wide-eyed at Karen.

"Where did you go afterwards?" Karen asked.

"I went home and showered. Well, you know. You feel dirty after being with women like that."

This bloke is a real piece of work.

"And where did you stay for the rest of the night?"

Warnock pressed his lips into a thin, white line. "At home. Before you ask, I live alone."

Karen released him not long after, while they continued their enquiries. Warnock, despite initial objections, agreed to having his house searched later and his phone and GPS records examined.

27

HE SAT SLUMPED in his armchair channel surfing. Nothing seemed to grab his interest. He checked the time on his phone. The countdown timer confirmed he still had ninety-three minutes left. As the smells wafted from the kitchen and through to his room his nose tickled. The aroma of a gently simmering pot of human remains excited him. It smelt like a meaty casserole which made his stomach growl.

Inhaling deeply, he let the smell fill every tiny sac in his airways. There was something quite comforting in the aromas. It reminded him of cold winter days when a big bowl of lamb and vegetable casserole would warm his insides.

He paused and flicked back to the previous channel, featuring a news segment with the presenter recapping on the death of Sallyanne Faulkner. The newscaster turned in a chair and looked at the monitor beside her where a reporter was coming live from a street he knew well.

She spoke about how some girls were terrified for their own safety, but none of them wanted to appear on air and show their faces, so they were interviewed from behind, their identities kept private.

"It terrifies me to walk the streets alone. I don't want to do this, but I don't have any other way of making money," one prostitute explained.

"We take our lives in our own hands each time we get into a car with a stranger," her friend added.

He smiled to himself as he listened to their concerns. "You shouldn't have been so greedy in the first place," he growled.

He increased the volume on the remote control, enjoying the fear that laced their words. He had driven past this spot frequently and knew the area well.

The reporter turned towards the camera and stared at the lens. "Police sources have confirmed that the investigation is ongoing and that they are following several lines of enquiry. The police have proactively been speaking to as many of the girls as possible to reassure them of their safety." The reporter glanced up and down the street, following the camera as it took a wide shot before returning to her face. "Police have talked about increasing patrols in the area and hope that their visible presence will reassure the women who congregate here. It's hoped that proactive policing will address concerns from residents who are outraged that prostitution has led to a violent killing."

"Are you stupid?" he shouted as he laughed at the TV screen. "More police patrols and prostitutes don't really go hand in hand. You'll have them running into the darkest alleyways the minute they see a police car. You lot clearly haven't thought it through. You'll just drive the girls away."

He tossed the control to one side, slipped deeper into his armchair, and closed his eyes. This could go two ways as far as he was concerned. It would either make them harder to find, or more willing to jump into a punter's car before they were seen. He smiled to himself as an idea formed in his mind.

28

"I'M SO SORRY it's late," Karen said as Zac opened the door and smiled. "It's all I seem to have been saying today to everyone. It's been a crazy and very long day."

"Hey, it's not a problem," Zac replied, pulling her into his arms and giving her a long hug.

Karen welcomed the warmth and security that his embrace offered. It felt soothing and comforting. So much of her wanted to stay in that embrace and not move.

"It's the nature of the beast. Unsociable hours, missed meals, and partners who are left watching the clock," Zac added.

"Now you're making me feel bad," Karen replied, her voice muffled in his chest.

"I'm pulling your leg. Come on. I'll pour you a glass of wine."

Karen followed Zac into the kitchen and stopped in her tracks. On the kitchen counter was a large platter of dried cured meats, olives, slices of crusty bread and sun-blushed tomatoes.

She threw a hand over her mouth, her eyes wide in surprise. Zac held out a glass of chilled white wine.

"Oh my God… Seriously?" she squealed, taking the wine from him, her eyes not knowing what to focus on.

"Well, I figured you probably hadn't eaten much, so I threw a few bits together for us. Is that okay?"

Karen stepped in towards Zac and placed a hand on his cheek before leaning in to kiss him. "Are you kidding me? I'm blown away… You're so thoughtful. Wow, I don't know what to say. Thank you doesn't seem enough."

"You don't have to say anything. You can thank me later," he said as he shot her a sly grin. "Now tuck in."

Karen didn't need telling twice as she eyed up all the goodies, not knowing what to start with first.

They spent the next hour picking at their food, working their way through a bottle of wine and catching up on their day. Karen laughed as she explained the interview with Warnock and his description of the prostitute who had seen him dropping off Sallyanne. She wondered who would be so desperate to go with a prostitute with a dodgy, squinty eye and a limp. A woman who, according to Warnock, also talked so loudly he wondered if she had a hearing impediment.

"I don't suppose you have a number for this attractive woman? She sounds like a catch. I wouldn't mind looking her up," Zac teased.

Karen punched him in the arm and harder than she'd

intended, but the wine was making her head spin. "You crack on, mate; I'll drop you off at the nearest STD clinic afterwards."

Karen felt at ease. This felt normal to her. Coming home from work and letting off steam with her partner. A simple pleasure and something she had experienced little of.

They settled on the sofa in the lounge, and Karen cuddled into Zac as they stretched out along its full length. She explained her run-in with Shield, which only irritated her again. "What's the deal with him?"

Zac popped an olive in his mouth and washed it down with a hefty glug of his wine. "He has a chip on his shoulder about being overlooked for the DCI role in my team. He feels like he's being side-lined a bit."

"That figures. He just comes across as an A1 macho prick with a small dick," Karen fumed.

"Don't worry about it. He's pissed off a lot of people. Shield has a lot on his plate already and senior management wants him to get results. It's high-profile stuff. There's been an increasing number of attacks on street workers and those working in massage parlours. It's mainly aimed at British women and there's been an influx of Eastern European girls muscling in on their territories." Zac shifted his position to get more comfortable. "Shield is trying to figure who's behind it. He's been liaising with our European partners, and they believe a Polish OCG is active in the North of England, targeting York, Leeds, and Manchester specifically. They've deliberately steered clear of London."

"I bet it inflated his ego to Elton John levels!" Karen laughed.

Zac agreed as he placed his wine glass on the floor and pulled Karen in closer. He kissed her for a few moments, both welcoming the connection as the intensity grew.

"How about if we continue further testing out this kissing lark upstairs?" he whispered.

"I thought you'd never ask."

29

KAREN PUT the key in her door and smiled as Manky bounded down the hallway meowing his happiness at her return. A neighbour had fed him late last night, but the cat's pleasure at seeing her was clear as he wrapped himself around her ankles and followed her every move.

"Aw, you missed me?" Karen asked, bending down to pick up her moggy and hugging him tight. She held on to him in the kitchen while flicking on the kettle and popping two slices of bread into the toaster.

She'd left Zac's early as he was due in for a meeting, which gave her the chance to come home and grab a shower before heading off into work later that morning. He didn't live too far away, so it wasn't out of her way to take a short diversion back to hers.

Having enjoyed her breakfast on the couch with Manky curled up in a tight ball beside her, she stripped off, stepped into the shower and enjoyed the intense pulse of water that prickled her skin. Even though she didn't smell of it, she could swear the musty odour of sweaty sex still lingered on her body from the night before. With her eyes closed, Karen allowed her mind to drift back to those few hours she'd spent with Zac.

She almost pinched herself over how her life had changed in just the space of a few months. For much of her adult-hood, she had focused on the job and accepted the chances of experiencing a normal happy relationship and a contented life hovered just out of reach. And then Zac happened. Along with a fresh start and a new job in York.

Karen turned off the shower, grabbed her towel, and patted herself dry as she headed to her bedroom. With a fresh set of clothes, fresh smelling hair and a bit of slap on her face, she felt human again.

Dropping into a chair at her dining table, Karen fired up her laptop. With another cup of coffee beside her, she scanned through her emails. The search of Henry Warnock's place last night had resulted in his laptop, mobile phone, and car being seized, along with several items of clothing. Karen wondered what they might discover. As yet, she was unde-cided if Warnock had anything to do with Sallyanne's murder. He'd not come across as being unbalanced during their interview, nor did he have a motive. But then again, he was a former doctor who'd interacted with the police professionally, so was used to remaining calm under pres-sure and cross-examination.

The team would use cell site data analysis to track his movements on the night of Sallyanne's murder. Karen figured it would at least show if he was in the area. The question was whether the analysis would pick him up closer to the abandoned airfield or not.

Karen logged into the national database. Something bothered her about how Sallyanne's body was left after her murder. In every other homicide case that she'd either investigated or seen, no victim had ever had a hand removed. She was used to seeing victims of strangulation, stabbings, drownings and even being mowed down by a car. Finding out why Sallyanne had her limb sliced off was what Karen believed would help her crack the case. As a result, she needed to start there.

She typed in a few search terms around sword attacks, but that generated a list far too long. Karen scanned through them and soon realised that many of the cases involved knife-related incidents in a much younger population, mainly in male teens. Karen tightened up her search terms and changed the age ranges. This helped to narrow the list of search results that the database generated.

The next hour left her rubbing her eyes as she went through line by line searching for anything that stood out. A few random murder cases popped up across the country involving swords or machetes. That still wasn't what she was looking for. The locations weren't close enough either. Leicester, Sheffield, Bristol, Derby, Norwich.

Karen sat back in her chair. *Am I wasting my time?* she thought but was determined to keep looking. As soon as she arrived in the office, she would task a couple of research assistants to begin a wider search of the database using different parameters. But not willing to give up, Karen sat up again, blinked hard, and continued scrolling.

"What. Whoa… back up," she muttered as something caught her eye. Scrolling back a few lines searching for the entry, Karen paused and clicked open the record before scanning the details. "Bingo!" Her heart rate accelerated as she read about a case of a prostitute being murdered in Dorset and her right hand being severed.

30

WITH A RENEWED ENERGY and a new line of investigation, Karen made the quick trip to another street that Belinda had identified as a known area for prostitution. This area was slightly different as women brazenly touted for business in broad daylight. Her earlier research had identified reports of working girls being intimidated with threats to cut them up into pieces.

Karen grabbed a takeaway coffee from a local café and slowly sauntered up and down the street. As she watched carefully, things appeared no different from any other busy road. Shoppers went about their business, women scuttled past pushing prams on the nursery run, and delivery drivers unloaded their goods.

She needed time to think. There was still no certainty to confirm whether Sallyanne's murder was targeted, deliberate, or a random attack.

It didn't take long for Karen to spot a few street girls scattered along the street. Their garish outfits of minidresses and stilettos looked out of place for so early in the morning. She watched as they stopped men who were walking past. Brief interactions. The shaking of many heads and polite declines.

Karen crossed the road and headed towards the closest female.

"As much as I want to nick you for solicitation, I need information," Karen said as she approached, holding out her warrant card.

"Come on. I'm only looking for a fag," the woman replied, her voice hoarse.

"Of course you are. I need some information at the moment," Karen repeated. It was hard to tell her age, but Karen put her in her late forties. Thin, sunken cheekbones and dry cracked lips. Her bottle blonde hair was a little untidy but pulled back in a ponytail.

"Do you always hang around here touting for business?" Karen asked.

The woman smiled, revealing brown stained teeth. "I do. It's rush hour, babe, the best time. Easy to pick up a few of the school run dads. I'm a bit late today, but seven am to nine am is peak for us. I can get twenty quid for oral, or thirty quid for sex. There's an alley around the corner."

Belinda had given her the heads-up about the area. With half a dozen primary schools within a mile radius of the road, it offered rich pickings for the girls. Cheap prices for quick sex. Many of the girls took their customers to an open car park behind the shops which was littered with condoms, cigarette butts, empty beer cans and smashed spirits bottles. Belinda explained they would disappear altogether for a few weeks to try a different area but would always come back. Often fights broke out among the girls as they argued about pitches and where they should stand.

"Have you heard of any women being threatened or attacked with large, bladed weapons? Maybe a machete or sword?" Karen asked.

The woman nodded. "I've not seen it myself, but I've heard from other girls being picked up about some of the punters turning violent."

"Were a machete or sword involved?"

"As far as I know, yeah. I don't think anyone's been hurt. A few girls have been raped and others have had their earnings nicked off them."

"Where can I find these girls?"

"No idea, luv. As I said, I've never met any of them. You hear things when you're on the streets."

Karen pushed for more information. "I get that. But you must have heard of where some of these things have been taking place?"

The woman let out a long sigh. "Listen, I don't want to get involved. All I know is that it happened in and around the station."

"Any descriptions? What the men looked like? What vehicles were involved?" Karen asked.

"No, luv. I've got to go now. You're losing me money," the woman moaned as she trotted off, looking unsteady on her feet.

Karen was about to head off towards the rail station when her phone rang. Officers needed Karen back at the station because they had tracked down the red-headed prostitute based off Warnock's detailed description.

31

"THIS SHOULD BE INTERESTING," Jade said as she followed Karen along the corridor to the interview room.

"Promise you'll keep a straight face?" Karen smiled as she glanced back over her shoulder.

Jade's grin split her face wide. "I can't promise!"

Karen rolled her eyes as they stopped outside the door, sliding the door notice to engaged. "I'm kicking you out of the room if you misbehave."

As Karen stepped through, she spotted the first sign that this interview was going to be challenging for all the wrong reasons. Courtney, the flame-haired prostitute, looked up with one eye fixed on them, the other staring off at an angle towards the wall.

Karen shot a look of consternation in Jade's direction who glanced up for a second before returning her gaze to her notepad.

"Courtney, I'm Detective Chief Inspector Heath, and I'm

the senior investigating officer in the homicide of a street worker by the name of Sallyanne Faulkner. Does the name ring a bell with you?" Karen asked, sliding a picture of Sallyanne across the desk.

Courtney continued to stare at them with one eye. "No, the name doesn't ring a bell, but I recognise the photo," she bellowed in a strong Scottish accent, the tone of her voice so loud, that it took both Karen and Jade by surprise.

"It's okay, Courtney, you don't have to shout. I'm sitting across the desk to you."

Courtney shrugged. "Aye, I'm not shouting. I'm replying to your wee question!" she replied in a loud and forceful voice.

Maybe she does have a hearing problem, Karen thought. She examined the woman for a moment. Her flame-red hair was vibrant and out of the bottle, which only made it stand out more against her pale complexion. Karen noticed Courtney scratching her arms, the reason becoming clear when she spotted track marks on the inside of both elbows.

"I'm desperate for a wee ciggy," Courtney moaned as she looked around the room, her dodgy eye remaining on them.

Jade cleared her throat after looking in Karen's direction and noticing a hint of amusement on Karen's face as the corners of her mouth curled up.

"You can have one later," Karen said. "We need to ask you a few questions about your movements on Friday night. We understand you were on Coombe Road?"

"I was in a lot of places, but aye, I was there."

"We're trying to build a picture of Sallyanne's last known

movements, and we understand that she may have been dropped off close to you after seeing a punter." Karen opened her folder and removed a picture of Warnock's grey BMW along with a picture of Warnock. "Do you recognise the car or the individual in the pictures?" Karen asked, tapping both items.

Courtney leant forward and stared at the photographs, her head only a few inches off the table. From Karen's vantage point, it looked like the woman was praying. Courtney twisted her head from left to right as she examined the photographs. Karen figured the only explanation was that Courtney was using her good eye to look at the photographs, but her jerky head twitching reminded her of a pigeon.

Karen straightened up and stared at the wall beyond Courtney, desperate to push the image of Courtney's head superimposed on a pigeon from her mind.

"Aye, I kinda recognise the car and the fella." She shrugged. "One punter is no different from another. The quicker they finish, the quicker I get my money," Courtney replied in a matter-of-fact way. "I've asked him for business before, but he said he was looking for a particular woman."

"How did he appear to you? Did you notice anything suspicious about him?"

"It doesn't get more suspicious than driving along a street at five miles an hour, with the passenger window down, staring at women... Does it?"

Karen nodded, agreeing with the observation. "Can you remember him dropping off Sallyanne?" Karen asked, tapping Sallyanne's picture again.

Courtney continued to scratch her arms to where spots of blood were breaking on to the surface. She grimaced. "I remember her getting out of a grey BMW car. I can't be certain it was him, perhaps it was. Listen, I don't hang around on the streets to people-watch. It's getting tough out there. The pimps, gangs and punters are using us like punchbags. We get pushed out by Eastern European street girls who charge less, are more aggressive and more willing to have sex with anyone because they're so scared."

"Scared? Of whom?"

Courtney rolled her good eye, but the other didn't blink as it skewed off in a different direction. "Everyone. You don't know how hard it is to make money these days. I've been desperate for money because I'm rattling for the heroin. Some days it's even hard to make sixty quid. I've been on the game for fifteen years," she replied as if referring to the takings in the shop. "The punters are coming asking for lower prices and we're saying no. But this lot are agreeing and doing it."

Karen wondered, *is this what desperation and addiction do to these women?*

"How am I supposed to compete against that?" Courtney said, her booming voice bouncing around the room. "Some girls give it away for four quid. They're battling for the business because they're desperate to get crack." Courtney took a sip of water and licked her dry lips. "There's a rivalry between the local girls and Eastern European ones and it lowers prices. It's a competition. The cheapest I've ever heard is two quid for sex."

Karen knew that most street girls sold sex to pay for their habits. A few she'd come across did it to buy Christmas presents for their kids. Others did it to pay the rent after getting their benefits cut. It wasn't a black-and-white picture of them being involved because of the drugs. She had seen first-hand evidence of the abuse and physical violence that street girls experienced. *No wonder Shield is so tetchy about my case.*

Karen changed tactics. "Have you heard of any women trying to rob their clients?"

Courtney nodded. "It happens. These younger lasses fancy their chances and rip off their punters. That increases the risk of violence against us even more."

Karen closed her folder and ended the interview after asking a few more questions. "Okay, Courtney, you've been helpful. Thank you for taking the time to come in."

She also gave the woman the contact details of the local support group that helped street girls like her to tackle their addictions and get them some place safe.

Once outside the station, Karen and Jade watched in bewilderment as Courtney hobbled away to a waiting taxi. Though she struggled, Karen admired her grit and perseverance to earn a living.

32

KAREN SAT down in her chair and fired up her computer. Her efforts so far had yielded little in the way of results. Her attempts to speak to street girls had proved fruitless and put her in danger. She thought that by talking to them, she might have been able to build a picture of the violence they were experiencing, and who was behind it, especially if the aggressors were using large, bladed weapons.

But the crime in Dorset piqued her interest, and though she had previously only glanced at the case file, she accessed the database to study it in greater detail. Karen sat back in shock minutes after opening the file. The name of the SIO jumped out at her. DI Tom Nugent. She grabbed her phone and dialled his number. She tapped her fingers while waiting for it to connect, a sense of excitement rising in her.

"DI Tom Nugent," came the reply.

"Tommy… Guess who?"

There was a pause at the other end. "Um... Who is this?" Nugent replied.

Karen rolled her eyes and laughed. It felt like years since they'd spoken. "Tommy, it's Karen Heath, Kaz! Remember me?"

A loud chuckle of laughter raced down the line. "Oh my God. Seriously? What the hell, Kaz. I can't believe it, you old slapper."

The roar of laughter continued much to Karen's amusement. She rocked back in her chair as tears squeezed from the corners of her eyes. "Polite as ever!"

Karen and Tom Nugent had joined the Met at the same time and were best buddies at Hendon. They'd spent the first few years based at stations a few miles apart, which had given them the opportunity to hang out together after work. Occasionally, they'd both attended disturbances and crime scenes. Their paths had taken them both through the CID route, starting as TDCs, trainee detective constables. Despite a strong sense of friendship, they would sometimes end up on the same promotion boards, much to their dismay.

"Where are you now, Kaz? Are you still in the Met?" Nugent asked.

Karen laughed. "Long story. I took a new post in York and got reinstated as a DCI. I see you're still a DI," Karen teased.

"York? What on earth are you doing up there? Couldn't you handle it in the Met?"

"You cheeky git. You can talk. Dorset? Bet you only deal with sheep rustling and mobility scooter theft."

Nugent took in a sharp intake of breath. "Ooooh, that hurt. You could be a right nasty bitch when you wanted to be."

"I still am. How's the family? Still putting up with you?"

Nugent laughed. "Yep, not sure why. Perhaps Erin knows she won't get another man as good-looking as me!"

Now it was Karen's turn to crack into laughter. She remembered seeing pictures of Erin many years ago. She was stunning back then. Every officer on his shift had ribbed Nugent about how she'd only agreed to go on a date with him out of pity.

"What is she up to now?" Karen asked.

"Primary school teacher in a small village. Fourteen kids in the entire school. Gossip central."

"I bet. Does she enjoy it?"

"Loves it," Nugent replied.

"And what about... Um..." Karen struggled to remember his daughter's name. Rolling her eyes in annoyance.

"Fran is doing good. Sixteen going on twenty-one. I can't keep up with her life, mood swings, and dramas."

"Oooh, difficult time. I can relate to that," Karen said, thinking about Summer.

They spent the next few minutes catching up before Karen moved on to the reason for her call. "Tommy, I have a case that involves a street girl being strangled and her right hand being chopped off."

"Sounds nasty. Shall I lend you a hand?"

"I can see that you still need to work on your jokes.

Anyway, I searched the database and found that you had a similar case back in November 2019? What can you remember about it?"

Nugent fell silent for a few moments as he tapped away on his keyboard. "A Romanian prostitute. Twenty-four years old. Raduca Bogdan. Pretty sad case to be fair. She came to the UK with her mum when she was twelve years old. Left home at sixteen to live in a hostel and fell into drugs. Heroin and cocaine. She started engaging in sex work and worked in massage parlours but was then asked to leave when she stole to feed her addiction."

Karen tutted. She'd heard similar stories over the years.

Nugent continued. "Her mother was unaware she was a sex worker and thought her daughter worked in a bar or hair-dressers. She was working the streets one night and disappeared. Her body was later discovered on waste ground with her right hand sliced off."

"Any leads?"

"Nothing. We did a trawl of CCTV and fingertip search of the crime scene and her squat. We did a door to door around her pitch, and we put out several press appeals. The result…? A big fat zero."

"Any intel from the Romanian authorities?" Karen asked.

"Yes, we spoke to them as well. They were less than help-ful. They said it was a common problem with young Romanian girls being promised better paid jobs in London. Once here, the trafficking gangs take their passports and keep them in organised brothels, or move them around the place, taking them from hotel to hotel. It's quite hard to track them down."

"What can you tell me about the weapon used?"

"Not much more than we already have on the system. I can send over anything else that we have, but the case remains open. Forensic services believe that a large sharp bladed weapon was used, possibly a machete, but more likely a sword. Has your vic suffered the same fate?"

Karen confirmed the similarities between the two cases. What interested her more than anything else was the method used to sever just the right hand.

"Kaz, I'm going to have to dash. I have a briefing."

"Oh dear, another ice-cream van been stolen?"

Nugent laughed. "One of these days, I'm going to sit you down and give you an insight into proper policing. Let's catch up soon, yeah?"

Karen ended the call, thanking him for his time and looked forward to the next catch-up.

33

FRUSTRATION AND IMPATIENCE gnawed away at him. His efforts to find his next victim had proved fruitless. He had driven around last night searching the same streets he had covered for days, but women had seemed to be thin on the ground. Of course, there were women, but not his type. He loved those with dark, long hair and a full-on passion for tattoos, but all he'd found were smackheads desperate for their next fix, or ones with so much make-up on they probably looked like Quasimodo's twin sister beneath it all.

Maybe business was slow at the start of the week, but like him other customers had been cruising the streets looking for casual sex. As he'd driven past slow-moving oncoming vehicles, drivers had exchanged brief glances with him.

The press appeals and increased police presence didn't help his cause. Prostitutes wondered who'd be next. They asked more questions and appeared hesitant to get into a punter's car. Only the jittery, desperate ones didn't care. Scoring the next hit was the only thing on their minds.

He closed his eyes for a moment and let the music calm his mind. His basement was his sanctuary. A place that offered enrichment, and yet, each time he collected a new specimen, he rarely looked at it again. Tucked away in their velvet boxes, they were delicate pieces of artwork. Never to be touched, only to be admired.

Thoughts cascaded through his mind about cornering a woman and the thrill and excitement that came with it. Seeing them helplessly fight to survive until he had squeezed the last drop of air from their body. The fact that he could be discovered or caught any minute made it even better.

"Why do I do this?" he questioned. Holding their naked flesh felt so good. The softness of their skin on his fingertips. It was only when he moved his hands to their necks that an overwhelming rush of power permeated every cell of his being. Once his fingers tightened around their delicate throats, he couldn't stop himself. At the images, his fingers tightened and squeezed as if on autopilot. Just like a one-way ticket, once he started, he couldn't stop. It was like his hands took on a mind of their own.

Another one of his Japanese songs filled the room, its soft tones stroking his skin. Relaxing, his mind drifted in and out of sleep. In a few hours, he would be back out there again on the hunt for his next victim.

34

With a new thrust to their investigation, Karen mulled over the current evidence. She wondered if she was dealing with two different cases. One was the murder of Sallyanne. The second was the increasing threats and violence from gangs peddling prostitution and drugs. For the gangs, it was a marriage made in heaven, but for the police, it was a complex web which often had them chasing their tails. Karen wondered how the cases were connected, or if they were connected at all?

Karen checked the system to review police records on recent arrests and cautions for soliciting and controlling prostitution. She found seven cases in the last five weeks where street girls had ended up in hospital. Though she wasn't surprised, it worried Karen how they were unwilling to give statements or press charges. She stopped on one case and noticed that DI Anita Rani had been the SIO. Karen grabbed her phone.

"Anita, it's Karen. How's things with you?"

"Hi, ma'am," Anita replied.

"It's fine, Anita. You can call me Karen. I know Zac isn't into titles and frankly I agree with him most of the time."

Anita laughed. "It works for me, Karen. I hear you have a tough case on at the moment?"

"I do. That's why I'm calling. I'm interested in your case involving Debbie Langley. What else can you tell me about it?"

"There's not a lot to say. The case remains open. She was violently assaulted. Refused to give a statement. But from what we can gather she was pulled off the streets, bundled into a van and threatened by who we believe to be Romanian men into working for them. And if she refused, they would chop off one of her arms."

Karen took a sharp intake of breath. "I assume she refused?"

"She did to begin with, but they slashed her across the face as a marker and said they would come back for her. They threw her out of the van outside the hospital and drove off. Their intention was to put her in one of their brothels. She needed eleven stitches."

"Where is she now?"

"One sec," Anita replied, checking for the latest information on the system. "A charity has her at an undisclosed location. They're hoping to get her out of the area."

"I'm wondering if Sallyanne Faulkner ever crossed paths with these gangs, and her refusals led to her death? A lot of these attacks seemed to involve large, bladed weapons," Karen said, referring to the cases on the system.

"It might be worth having a chat with DCI Shield. He has the intel on this," Anita suggested.

Karen closed her eyes as that sinking feeling hit the bottom of her stomach. There he was again, his name seeming to pop up everywhere she turned. She noticed Anita's faltering words. "Don't tell me you've heard about my run-ins with him already?"

Anita laughed. "Sorry, Karen. Word gets around fast. Off the record?"

"Off the record, I promise," Karen reassured her.

"I don't blame you for sticking to your guns. He's a right chauvinistic sod sometimes. I know he's senior to me, but he struts around here acting like he owns the place. No doubt you'll end up on a night out in one of the local pubs. Trust me, he's even worse after a few drinks. If you think he's loud, bossy, and arrogant now, it's just the tip of the iceberg."

Karen smiled. "Thanks for the heads-up, Anita. I've dealt with his kind before." Her mind drifted back to Skelton, her former DCI. "You might have to drag me kicking and screaming to talk to DCI Shield!" She laughed before thanking Anita and ending the call.

The email from DI Tom Nugent arrived in her inbox not long after her call with him. She smiled as she remembered the conversation.

Karen opened the attachments and read his message.

Kaz, I hope you find this useful. Give me a shout if there's anything further. It was great catching up with you and look forward to our next call. T

She looked forward to it as well.

Karen scanned the attachments. Tom's photos differed from the photos taken by SOCO. They depicted the surrounding area, which appeared to be desolate with evidence of fly-tipping. Both dump sites appeared to have been chosen for their remoteness. That was one connection in Karen's mind.

The savageness of the attack disturbed her even more. Karen examined the blood trails that followed the path along which the body had been dragged about thirty feet to a patch of overgrown waste ground where she had been covered by a discarded piece of tarpaulin.

The killer had also beaten his victim around the head post-mortem resulting in a broken jaw, five missing teeth, a fractured eye socket and fractured skull. Sallyanne didn't have any of those injuries. Perhaps the killer had refined his technique, which was something that often happened when the killer committed more crimes.

Karen rubbed her eyes. It was getting late, and it would be another night where she'd have to rely on a neighbour to feed Manky. But after reading the closing remarks from the forensic science laboratory, she was certain that the two cases were connected. Following detailed sharp force trauma microscopic analysis, they'd concluded that with no evidence of bone compression, fragmentation, splintering of fractures, or stress lines, it was likely that the weapon used was a high-strength steel blade, such as a sword.

35

IT AMUSED him to see the mundane life that most people experienced as they pushed their trolleys around his local Tescos.

After waking from his slumber, he'd wanted to pick up provisions before heading out again for the evening. This was a larger Tesco supermarket, which had an upstairs floor for a large electrical and clothing department. Curious more than anything else, he took the escalator up to the first floor and wandered around.

Parents with screaming kids in tow jostled down the aisles looking for cheap bargains in the clothing department. One or two couples hovered around the bank of flashy TVs admiring the sharpness of the pictures and deciding which large monstrosity would fit on the wall above the fireplace.

He slowed and watched them before his eyes were drawn to a piece that popped up on many of the screens. With the local news in full swing, the reporter was talking about *his* case. The reporter cut to what appeared to be another impromptu press conference held outside one of the local police stations. Residents had gathered, expressing their concerns about the fact that a maniac was still roaming the streets and the police were no further along with their investigation.

A member of the North Yorkshire police force press department stood beside a senior officer. Wearing her smart uniform, she was an overweight lady with dimpled cheeks who gesticulated flamboyantly and offered words of support and encouragement about safety and your day-to-day activities. He paused for a moment and listened. He couldn't make out all the words, so moved closer to the nearest TV and listened with one ear while he scanned his surroundings. The officer, a superintendent of some sort, offered words of advice about travelling alone at night and assured the presence of increased patrols in certain areas of the city.

His skin prickled with excitement. They were talking about him. The same thrill he experienced when killing women caused a wave of concern among everyday citizens. He had already whipped them up into a frenzy of fear, something he would enjoy playing on.

After all, spaces on his shelf still needed to be filled.

Several residents booed and heckled the senior officer, demanding action. As the crowd ratcheted up their vitriol, the superintendent and her press buddy got hit from all angles, a verbal volley that neither one of them could control. The continuous tirade of abuse forced them to retreat into the building.

He smiled to himself and laughed. The idea of going to the press with renewed pleas for information and vigilance had backfired on them this time.

The game of cat and mouse just got a lot more interesting.

36

"HOW COME YOU'RE STILL HERE?" Jade asked as she poked her head through the open doorway to Karen's office.

Karen let out a deep sigh and tipped back in her chair, throwing her arms up in the air to stretch her aching muscles. "That's a question I ask myself all the time."

"This case is bothering you, isn't it?"

Karen sighed again and nodded. "I hate it when we don't have tangible leads to follow up on. At first, I thought Warnock could be a prime suspect, but he could have an alibi."

"Unless he came back to find her again?" Jade suggested.

That was a possibility. For the time being, she wasn't prepared to let Warnock slip away. The results weren't in yet on the forensic search of his car or his laptop and phone. Everything seemed to take much longer than normal. Even the cell site data analysis that she had requested seemed to take forever.

"You want a coffee?" Jade asked.

"That sounds like a great idea," Karen said as she rose from her chair. They both headed to the small kitchenette where Jade rustled up two coffees, neither one in a hurry to head home.

"Why are you're still here?"

Jade shrugged. "I had a few loose ends to tie up."

Karen noticed a slight hesitation in Jade's voice. She furrowed her brow, wondering if something was getting to her professionally… or personally. "Is everything okay? You still good with the job up here?"

Jade took a sip from her coffee and cursed for burning her lips. "Of course. I love the job. I don't like the long days or the long hours that creep into the night, but I love it when we get a good result."

"Me too."

Karen still sensed hesitation. She couldn't be certain what it was but wanted to push. "Go on then, spill the beans. I think I've known you long enough to know when there's something bothering you."

Jade stared at her coffee before looking to Karen with a wry smile. "James sent me a text message. He wants to know if I'd fancy going for a bite to eat next week?"

Karen's eyes widened as a grin broke across her face. "That's fantastic. I assume you said yes?"

Jade shrugged. "I guess. But I haven't replied yet. I don't know whether he's being friendly, or whether there's more to it?"

"Does it matter? It's just nice to make new friends while we are here. Besides, you never know where it might lead."

"That's what worries me. I'm not sure I want it to go anywhere."

"You're kidding, right?"

Jade smiled but remained tight-lipped.

"Listen, have a night out. Enjoy nice food and a bit of a laugh. Decide after that. If it goes well, you could suggest going out for a drink, or to the cinema, or for a walk around the city."

"I guess."

"Are you nervous?"

Jade shuffled on the spot. "A little. Not used to dating that much," she admitted, staring down at the floor.

Karen noticed a change in Jade's personality as she transformed from being a strong, confident, and often loud-mouthed person to someone who in a heartbeat had become shy.

Needing to change the conversation, Karen gave an update on her conversation with DI Anita Rani.

"It's a tricky one, Karen. I think this is more than just fighting for control of the streets. There was serious intent behind this attack. This wasn't a warning sign, a marker, or anything like that. You would have seen this in the Mafia, or modern-day Japanese Yakuza. They mete out similar punishment and carry out savage killings to send a clear message."

Karen folded her arms across her chest and leaned back on

to the kitchen worktop. Jade had a point. But something still bothered her about the case. Yes, it might have been someone sending a clear message. But would a fight for control of the streets end up with a prostitute being strangled and having her hand sliced off. She wasn't so sure about that. The thought of speaking to DCI Shield came rushing back to haunt her. It was getting to the stage where she might have to pull up her granny knickers and speak to him.

"What are you thinking?" Jade asked.

Karen shrugged. "Nothing in particular. I'm trying to figure out what to do next. I need more information or intelligence about how the sex trafficking gangs are operating in York and if they are connected to my case."

"Can DI Anita Rani help you with that?"

"Possibly. But I think there's one or two others I need to speak to first."

37

THE DARKNESS OFFERED him his own form of camouflage as he cruised the streets hoping for better luck. Each street-light illuminated his face and the inside of his car for just a brief second before he faded into blackness.

He was pleased to see more girls on the streets. Those brave enough to lurk on the edge of pavements, eyed up every car that passed with their biggest smile. He had spotted one potential woman a few days ago when he'd picked up Sallyanne. It had been a close call between the two of them, but he'd already been fixated on taking Sallyanne first. Now he needed to track down Grace again. Yes, she had foolishly let her name slip. It wasn't her fault. As she had made her way towards his open window, one of her friends had called out her name. Now Grace was the one he wanted.

His impatience grew as he drove up and down the streets. He tutted as he saw the same women. "Where are you?" he whispered to himself as his gaze searched the darkness, darting from left to right, keen not to miss her. A few false sightings raised his hopes only for them to be dashed as he neared the wrong girl.

"Come on. Are you looking for business or not?" a woman shouted as he passed her for the third time.

It was almost an hour later when he spotted her white chunky thighs and short black miniskirt. Grace was a little on the heavy side. Even her calf-length black boots strained at the zip. She had a brown, fake fur, waist-length jacket, short blonde hair and a fag dangling from her fingers. He slowed to a crawl, his interest causing girls to step from the shadows towards the road, hoping that one of them would be picked.

"You looking for business, luv?" Grace asked, peering in through the open passenger window. She blew out a plume of cigarette smoke that invaded the inside of his car. She offered a half-smile and wink.

"It depends on what you're offering," he asked.

"Tenner for a blowjob. Twenty for full sex with a jacket."

"Any extras?"

"What did you have in mind? If you fancy going to a room, I know one around the corner. That will cost mind you," she offered, trying her luck.

He took his wallet out and thumbed through a thick pile of notes. "I want something more than that. I fancy doing it outdoors. We won't be long. I know somewhere close by where we won't be disturbed. What do you say?" *Carrot dangled.*

The woman's eyes lit up, and she licked her lips in anticipation before glancing over her shoulder to make sure none of the other girls had heard him. If this was going to be a decent earner, she didn't want other girls muscling in on the business. She paused for a moment as if pretending to have a long think about it. If she held out, she could earn enough to go home straight after. "A hundred quid," she said, chancing her luck.

"Deal," he replied at once.

The woman cursed under her breath at how quickly he had agreed. Maybe she should have started higher and negotiated down.

"Well? Are you going to get in or not?" he demanded.

"Okay, keep your shit together," she yelled, opening the car door and dropping into the passenger seat.

He pulled away from the kerb, glancing in all directions to see how many others had spotted him. Several of the women he had seen when he'd first pulled up had scurried off towards two other cars behind him that had slowed.

She ran her fingers through her hair to tidy herself up and flipped down the visor in front of her so she could apply some lipstick.

He smiled to himself. *Making an effort for me. I'll have to make sure I make an effort for you, too.*

He headed south-west out of the city centre, sticking to the smaller roads, keen to avoid the A roads which had a greater chance of catching him on CCTV or ANPR cameras.

"Where are we going?" she asked, narrowing her eyes as she stared through the windscreen at the short stretch of road in front of them lit up by the headlights.

"I fancy having sex against a tree. It's always been one of my fantasies. Don't worry, you'll be back before you know it."

She furrowed her brow. "It's far. I don't fancy being this far away from my patch."

He reached into his pocket and pulled out a crisp fifty-pound note. "A down payment for you."

The woman shot him a look of surprise before snatching the money from his hand and holding it up in the dim light to examine it. "This is a fake."

"Trust me. It's not. I've got loads of twenties in my wallet. When we get there, I'll take the fifty back off you and replace it with five twenty-pound notes."

The woman's greedy eyes widened as she studied the man. "Um, when you say you've got a load of twenties, how many have you got?"

The man laughed. "A couple of hundred pounds. If you do the job well enough, I'll throw in a forty quid tip."

"Oh, don't you worry, sugar. I'll do the job how you want it, satisfaction guaranteed."

"I hoped you were going to say that," he said, looking ahead.

His thoughts fixed on the image forming in his mind.

38

LESS THAN FIFTEEN minutes later he snaked through the single lane track with short hedges either side of him, searching for the spot that he had discovered on an earlier visit.

"Are you sure you know where you are?" she asked, staring into the blackness that surrounded her.

He nodded. "I've driven through the area a few times for work," he lied. "Ah, here it is." His headlights swept a big, illuminated arc as he turned off and followed the track for a hundred yards, the rough ground throwing them around before he came to a stop. He had chosen this spot carefully. Farming fields and a nature reserve meant the chances of her being heard were slim.

He killed the ignition, left the lights on, stepped out of his car and waited for her to exit. She slowly opened her passenger door and pulled herself out into the eerie silence. "I'm not sure about this."

He laughed to himself.

"We are not going any further. This tree looks perfect," he said, stepping towards a tree a few feet from the car and still within its headlights.

She remained rooted to the spot.

"Think of the money. In ten minutes, you'll be a hundred pounds better off. If you don't want to do it, that's fine. You've just wasted both of our time. We can get back in the car and turn round and I'll find someone else. It's the quickest hundred pounds you'll ever earn… plus tip."

The temptation of money seemed too irresistible to ignore as she threw caution to the wind and came round the other side of the car to join him. "Okay, let's get this over and done with," she said, opening her handbag and tearing off a condom from a strip that she always carried with her. "How do you want to do this?"

He watched her take small steps towards the tree. Grace stared at the ground to make sure she didn't stumble. The urge to take her now caught his breath. But this one needed to be done differently. Once beside the tree, he waited for her to tear the wrapper and thrust the condom in his direction.

The slimy oiliness coated his fingertips. He hated that sensation. "I want you bent over so that I can take you from behind while you're leaning against the tree," he said, unzipping the fly on his jeans.

Unfazed by the request, she turned round, hoisted up her black miniskirt and pulled down her knickers which dropped to her ankles. Then she bent over and rested the palms of her hands against the rough woody bark.

With the condom in place, and one hand on her hips, he

entered her with a heavy thrust. She remained silent as her body jerked forward, shutting down all emotional and physical responses. His breath came in raspy grunts as he leaned forward and placed his hands on her shoulders. When his hands slid towards her neck, he enjoyed her soft skin beneath his fingertips. An overwhelming urge swamped his senses as he imagined her skin oozing through his fingers as it disintegrated.

"Hold on a minute! You're hurting me!" She tried to shout, but the pressure cut off the airflow she needed. The pain grew. "I said you're hurting me!"

Ignoring her pleas, he tightened his grip until he felt her windpipe beneath his fingertips. *Be careful*, he thought. He didn't want her dying straightaway. Releasing his grip, he drew his fist back and sent it crashing into the side of her head, swiftly followed by another. The second blow rendered her unconscious as she slumped to the ground with a heavy thud, her body in a crumpled heap.

He zipped himself up and went to the boot of his car to get his sword, rope and whip before returning. He stripped her naked and took a moment. She had big breasts. Bigger than he had imagined. But she still looked rough. With a saggy arse and flabby tummy, she was mutton dressed up as lamb. Perhaps he should have kept her clothed. He grabbed her under the armpits and hoisted up her limp body, propping it to face the tree. He tied one end of the rope around one of her wrists before tossing the rope around the trunk and tying her other wrist in place.

A faint murmur escaped her lips as she regained consciousness. *Just in time*, he thought.

Grace groaned again as she coughed and spluttered.

"Please, what are you doing?" she moaned through heavy breaths.

He ignored her as he pulled out his phone and shone the torch app on her body. He examined the tattoos on her upper forearms. Snakes, angels, butterflies. He stood back and admired the elaborate tattoo that covered the back of her shoulders. She had gone to a lot of effort to ink her body. He ran his fingers along her skin following the outline of one particular tattoo. It was a picture of a wolf. His eyes widened in pleasure.

Grace didn't know what hit her when he brought the whip down on her back. Searing pain tore through her body. She screamed. Another lash cut into her skin, leaving another red welt which felt like fire as her body stiffened, and her hands curled into fists. "Please! Stop!" she screamed as she cried, pulling at the rope that held her captive.

Her pleas only fuelled his desire to punish her even more. He whipped her harder. The more she screamed, the more he continued. He threw every ounce of energy into drawing the whip back and bringing it down across her back and buttocks. Five times, ten times, twenty times. Her screams, high-pitched at first, turned into groans and then into soft murmurs as the pain racked her body, before she slipped into unconsciousness again and slumped against the rough bark.

With sweat beading on his forehead, he dropped the whip to the ground and picked up the sword before pulling her head back and running the blade across her neck. Warm liquid spewed from the open wound and ran down the front of her chest. Her breath caught in gurgling spurts as the life drained from her.

He waited for a few moments until her body became still. Silence descended around him. The throbbing in his temples subsided. He walked round to the other side of the trunk and raised the sword above his head before bringing it down on her right wrist severing her hand. Her wrist slipped through the knot and freed her body before it fell to the ground.

He retrieved a pack of disinfectant wet wipes from his car and took out a few sheets before wiping down the sides of her body where he'd touched her, including her private regions.

Then he picked up his whip, her possessions, and her right hand by its thumb before taking one last look at her. He scanned the scene, making sure he had left nothing.

"Sayonara."

39

THE CONVERSATION with Jade still played on her mind as Karen got an early start the next morning. She knew there was some inevitability in having to confront Shield. Whether doing so would help her to get the answers she needed, she wasn't sure. Having made herself a cup of coffee, she wandered around the main floor and checked the incident board before returning to her office. A few officers were in bright and early. Most of those on the night shift had updated the system and headed home to catch up on sleep before doing it all again later today.

The feedback on the system was less than encouraging. Various entries followed the most recent press release. There seemed to be a growing concern among residents that the police were dragging their heels. This led to the Police and Crime Commissioner intervening at the highest levels, which only heaped more pressure on her team.

Several leads from anonymous callers claimed to have seen a grey BMW 3 Series matching the description on the night of Sallyanne's murder. That didn't surprise Karen. Based on her interview with Warnock, he'd been in the area frequently.

She turned her attention towards updates from the forensic team. A swab analysis of vaginal fluids taken from Sallyanne during the post-mortem had revealed no semen traces. They had, however, identified several unknown DNA samples from the inside of her thighs which suggested Sallyanne had had sex with several men prior to her death.

There wasn't much good news as Karen continued to pore over the report, tutting in annoyance. An extensive analysis of Warnock's BMW had found no blood, skin tissue, or clothing fibres belonging to Sallyanne Faulkner. Karen sat back in her chair and considered the reasons. Yes, Warnock would have been forensically aware because of his medical background. Had he cleaned his car to remove any traces, whether human or synthetic, other than his own?

Karen took a sip of her coffee and welcomed the caffeine hit. She grimaced at the thick, sour taste. Even though she'd collapsed into bed at night, sleep had been restless and fitful. She'd woken several times and had wandered around the flat hoping to silence her mind.

The teams' efforts to trace down Roberto had proved fruitless. So far, enquiries with HMRC revealed no tax deductions. The man had no current mobile phone contract. His account with the NatWest showed no withdrawals or deposits in over six months, and he didn't appear to be on the council tax register either. Karen concluded in all likelihood that Roberto had returned to Italy. She made a mental note to remind her team to see if they could locate him by checking with Italian authorities, UK airport and airline passenger logs.

Karen tapped her pen on the table while she thought about Sallyanne and her relationship with Roberto. Had it been based on love, lust, or something more sinister? He'd spent a considerable amount of time coming in and out of her life. Was it because they were in love, or was he supplying her with drugs? She recalled a conversation about how Roberto had been visiting Sallyanne while at university. Was that because he was trying to keep tabs on her? Or did he have a more controlling nature he kept well hidden?

"Karen."

Karen looked up to see her boss, Kelly, appear in the doorway, a welcoming smile on her face.

"Ma'am."

"Nothing major," Kelly replied. "I wanted an update to see how things were going. I know we've had a few press appeals, and I got a battering when I dealt with concerns from members of the public. Not my finest hour!"

Karen grimaced. "Yes, ma'am. I heard that didn't go down too well."

Kelly shrugged. "I think that's an understatement."

Karen took a few moments to update Kelly based on the information from the system. Kelly listened and nodded; her expression remained pensive.

"We have a lot of loose ends at the moment that we're trying to tie up. It's chaotic and feels like we're lurching from one side to another. But I'm confident we'll get the clarity soon. I still have Warnock in the frame, but it's proving difficult to find any physical connection between him and Sallyanne Faulkner other than they'd had sex hours before she died. We're doing a wider CCTV trawl to see if we can spot Warnock and Sallyanne in his car after he claimed to drop her off. We've sent his clothes away for analysis to see if Sallyanne's DNA is on them."

Kelly nodded appreciatively. "Well, let me know if there are any other further updates. It will be nice to release another statement with positive news... Oh, DCI Shield is still bending my ear. He's like a dog with a bone. He's insisting that the case get handed over to him because he believes that it may have strong connections to the organised sex trafficking investigation that he is running at the moment."

"Understood, ma'am. I'm not sure. It's a possibility, but we have no evidence at the moment to suggest that. We're keeping an open mind." Karen sighed. She dreaded what she was about to say. "Ma'am, with your permission, I'm going to speak to DCI Shield."

When Kelly narrowed her eyes, Karen held up her hands in surrender. "I'm not looking for a slanging match with him. I want to share the intelligence we have. If there's a connection between what he's investigating, and the death of Sallyanne Faulkner, then it's in our interest as a force to share that information. There is the potential that Sallyanne refused to bow to the pressures of being part of a prostitution ring."

Kelly remained silent.

"I know DCI Shield is looking at how Eastern European crime gangs are trying to muscle in so they can bring in their own girls. I'm wondering whether Sallyanne was approached by those gangs, and when she refused, she was attacked and killed in a horrific way as a warning to others who didn't play along?"

Kelly raised a brow. "That's a possibility. I think it's a good idea that you have a word with DCI Shield. And to be honest, I don't want two senior officers having handbag fights all the time. Once you've had a word with him, let me know how it went. Just in case he kicks off again."

"I will do, ma'am. Thank you."

40

WHILE KAREN HAD a few moments in her office, she called in her latest recruits. She felt bad for not having sat with them so far. Karen always wanted to be a hands-on senior officer and take a keen interest in every member of the team, both personally and professionally. Often both were intertwined, causing stress and difficulties in both parts of their lives. She had lost count of the number of home welfare visits undertaken to officers off with stress during her career. Not only did that take her away from work, but it also meant that it added to the pressures of being under-staffed.

Preet and Ned appeared in her doorway, clutching their notepads and pens.

"Come in guys. Grab a seat," Karen offered with a smile.

Ned and Preet planted themselves in the seats across the desk to Karen.

"Sorry it's taken me so long to get round to sitting down

with both of you, but as you can imagine we need to be focusing on the case."

Her officers smiled.

"How are you both settling in?"

"Very well, Karen," they replied in unison.

"How have you found the transition into the team, Preet?"

Preet nodded. "It's been pretty easy to be honest. The investigation is the same, it's just the crime that is more challenging."

Karen turned to Ned, who sat bolt upright. Karen couldn't help but smile. It was as if he was waiting to be interviewed whenever he was spoken to. "Ned, how about you?"

"There's a lot to take in if I'm honest. It can be over-whelming sometimes, but I love the challenge."

Karen nodded, appreciating his honesty. "It can be. I'm going to assign Jade as your mentor. Jade will be your first port of call whenever you have a question. If she is not around, come and find me, and there are other qualified officers like Belinda who would be more than happy to step in if you need the extra guidance."

Ned nodded and broke into a small smile. "Thanks."

"How is the studying going?" Karen asked, knowing that Ned would need to be sitting for the national investigators' exam and his crime investigation development programme, often known as the CIDP, as part of his journey to becoming a qualified and nationally accredited PIP 2 detective. The training that officers went through now was more advanced than when she'd joined CID. The CIDP was a fantastic grounding for officers which gave them a solid understanding of investigative police skills, law and crime leadership, and management.

Ned's eyes lit up. "Pretty good. I love studying anyway, so I find it quite rewarding."

"What made you decide to go into the police?" Karen asked, noting from his records that he had studied history at Exeter.

He pursed his lips and glanced up towards the ceiling for a few moments before replying. "A sense of responsibility, I guess. I wanted to do something that made an impact on everyone's lives. So I applied to be a research assistant in Parliament and the police. I decided to go with whoever responded first. And... Well, here I am."

Karen laughed. "I think you picked the right choice. Politics... hmm. I'm not sure about that. How about you, Preet? What made you join the police?"

Preet offered a small smile. "My parents."

Karen raised a brow. "Oh, right. Were your parents serving officers?"

Preet shook her head. "Quite the opposite. When I told them I wanted to join the police, they thought it was an abhorrent idea, and I'd bring shame to my family. It isn't the kind of thing that Asian parents expect their children to go in to. If you ask most of the parents of that generation, they'll tell you they want their children to go to university to study to become doctors, lawyers, dentists, opticians, pharmacists, or accountants. In their eyes, those are worthy careers and increase your chances of marrying into a good family. They also want you to find a husband from one of those professions."

Karen had heard stories like this before from when she'd worked in London. Asian families always wanted their children to go into professions, knowing that arranged marriages would be easier to secure.

"Ah, I see. So this was an act of rebellion?"

Preet shook her head. "Not at all, Karen. I guess my generation is much more liberal and we speak our minds. The traditional ways are dying out now. It used to be all about arranged marriages. Not long ago you may have met your future husband just a handful of times to see if there was some compatibility before the families took over and arranged everything."

Karen noticed a hint of annoyance and frustration in Preet's voice.

Preet continued. "Now a lot of other young people of my culture are finding their own partners and falling in love first before breaking the news to their parents, which often goes down like a ton of bricks. So, I guess I'm saying that I wanted to do what felt right to me. Joining the police felt like a rewarding career where I could be treated as an equal and gain promotion based on merit." She paused for a moment. "I hope I'm not stepping out of line, but I know there are pockets of sexism and racism in police forces up and down the country. You've probably heard of many cases in the Met considering it's the biggest in the country."

Karen sighed. "I have. It's hard to root out when it's believed to be institutionalised."

Preet sat up and leant forward. "Plenty of my friends warned me about this, but I was determined to not let that stand in my way. Thankfully, I have experienced no sexism or racism so far, but I might during my career. I'm trying to prepare for that as best I can."

"I apologise in advance if you do, but I won't allow any officer on my team to be a complete arsehole. If they're sexist or racist, I'll kick them out myself and you can have a front row seat and I'll provide the popcorn!" Karen laughed to lighten the mood. "I admire you for your frankness and your determination. It can sometimes be hard for women to progress in the force, especially the higher up you get. At least that was my experience in the Met. I think if you're female and from the BAME community, it can be more challenging. I want you to know that I will support you and treat you as I do any other member of staff, regardless of your gender or your ethnicity."

"Thank you, Karen. That means a lot."

"Right, let's get back to work," Karen said, rising from her chair, Preet and Ned joining her. "It's been really helpful to sit down and get to know a bit more about both of you. If there's anything you need, please don't hesitate. My door is always open."

41

HE SAT at the dining table reflecting on his work from the night before. He was pleased with the outcome. Though she had put up a little bit of resistance, the feelings he'd experienced while taking her at the time sent waves of ecstasy through him once again. He curled his fingers as his body stiffened.

The smell of her hand simmering in the casserole pot wafted towards him. There were still a few hours to go until the flesh, muscles and tendons dissolved and fell off the bone.

"Soran Bushi", a favourite song of his, played in the background.

His mind drifted back to Grace. A chunky girl. Big busted, saggy tits, with an arse heading south.

So many questions raced through his mind. He wondered how many prostitutes looked like a sack of potatoes under their clothes. He hated them. It was all about greed. They were only interested in money. Money to feed their habits.

Money for their rent. Money to feed their kids. Were they nothing more than sob stories to reel in the punters? How far would ten or twenty pounds go? It wouldn't be enough to pay the rent in a dingy squat.

Thieving bitches.

That's all they are.

Thieving bitches.

All they want is money, drugs, money, drugs.

He felt sorry for the men who kept falling for it, because not long ago, he was one of them. He would cruise the streets nightly looking for someone to pick up. There was no love, no physical or emotional connection. Just sex. But sex that he hated himself for afterwards. Now, he channelled that hatred towards the women. They made him feel like that.

But he couldn't help himself. He was addicted. They were nothing more than dirty shag bags. He wondered how many of them were really clean. The thought made him shiver as he screwed up his face. The filthy women had sex with five to ten men in one night without cleaning themselves or having a shower. Not a wet wipe in sight. His lips stretched back as he gritted his teeth.

But his urge for sex had turned to anger and the need for revenge after that night in Dorset.

His mind flashed back to an evening when he'd picked up Claire. Probably one of the most attractive prostitutes that he'd ever seen. He'd met her in a bar frequented by ladies of the night. They'd shared a few drinks before agreeing to continue the night back at his hotel. They'd carried on drinking into the evening. She was in no hurry to leave, and he was in no hurry to let her go, whatever the cost.

After that, he couldn't remember much. He remembered waking up the next morning with a thumping headache and no recollection of the night before. He'd reached for his phone only to realise that it was missing from his bedside table along with his wallet.

The bitch had robbed him. Not only that, but he was convinced she had slipped something into his drink because, as hard as he'd tried, he couldn't remember anything after they returned from the off-licence. He'd vividly remembered the bar, and the fact she'd kept putting out her right hand and saying, "show me the money."

From that point onwards, he had hated street girls. Never would he allow another to take advantage of him. They needed to be taught a lesson.

But perhaps he had been naïve yet again and taken for a ride by Claire and the European woman Raduca, who'd both promised so much. Raduca was the first one he'd used his sword on, and the thrill he'd experienced had set him on a path searching for more victims.

42

KAREN MADE her way over to an adjoining building and headed towards Shield's office. The last time she had been here, their meeting hadn't ended well. The man was fast becoming her least favourite person. She found him arrogant, rude and not befitting of the rank he held. Too bad there were plenty of others like him in law enforcement. And though she felt sorry for those who worked underneath him, she felt especially sorry for female officers who had the misfortune of calling Shield their boss.

When Karen arrived, she found Shield reclining back in his chair. Deciding to be polite from the onset, she tapped on his open door instead of marching in and waited in the doorway.

Shield remained still, only moving his eyes in her direction. "What can I do for you, DCI?" he said with a sigh as if muttering those few words had exhausted him.

"Listen, I appreciate we've got off on a bad footing, and we're both to blame for that," she began, but noticed Shield roll his eyes. Undeterred, she carried on. "We're on the same side here, and I think it's important that we work together. This won't be the last time that our paths cross while conducting our separate investigations. I thought by sharing information we could help each other out?"

Shield studied her for a moment, his eyes narrowing.

"Why would we do that? I'm doing fine without your help or intervention."

What a pig.

She tried another tactic. "I know you're looking at how Eastern European crime gangs are trying to muscle in and push the English girls out of the way so they can bring their own girls in. I'm wondering whether my victim might have been approached by any one of those gangs, and when she refused to work for them, she was attacked and killed as a warning to others who didn't play along?"

Shield rocked back and forth in his chair as he locked his fingers behind his head. "I've had no intelligence to suggest that, but it's possible. As I've said, we have an undercover officer and the information coming back to us is that the criminals are using intimidation and violence, but not to that extreme. They put frighteners on the girls and tell them that they will end up in hospital and not be able to work. If the girls ignore those threats, then they turn to violence, but it means a bit of a beating, getting slapped about a bit… That kind of stuff. Nothing serious."

Nothing serious? If getting a beating or getting slapped about isn't serious in his mind, then what is?

"From the system, we haven't discovered any local prostitutes found dead in suspicious circumstances. So, I doubt my case is linked to your investigation." Karen said.

Shield shrugged. "There's always a first time. If the OCGs aren't getting their way, they may have upped their game and carried out their threats." Shield thought for a moment as he averted his gaze and stared up at the ceiling. "I can think of at least half a dozen prostitutes who've gone missing in the last eighteen months. We are not sure why. Perhaps they moved to escape the violence. Others, especially the European girls, may have headed back home. And then…" he returned his gaze in Karen's direction and shrugged, "a few might be at the bottom of a lake or buried in the woods."

"Okay. Well, if you hear anything else, would you let me know? And if my investigation uncovers something I think might be useful to you, I'll get in touch. How does that sound?"

Shield raised a brow and considered the offer for a few moments. "Works for me."

Karen walked out of his room and blew out her cheeks. She felt a sense of accomplishment. Though he had still come across as a tosser, they had at least had a half decent civil conversation.

43

"HEY, YOU," Karen announced as she answered her phone and headed outside.

"Kaz… It's Tommy. Do you have a moment?"

Karen smiled, enjoying the familiarity of his voice as she headed over to a grassy area to enjoy the softness beneath her shoes, and the dappled shade from branches that parted to tickle her face with warm rays. "Tommy, good to hear from you. This is unexpected. Is everything okay?"

"Yeah, all good here. I've been thinking about your case and another case sprung to mind."

"Oh, right. What do you have?" Karen asked.

A rustle of paper from the other end.

"Another team dealt with a case in September 2019, which involved a violent assault on a lone female inside her house. Denise Carr, aged forty-two. Some fella called Geoff, no surname given, chatted her up in a bar. We can't be certain it's his real name either. He bought her a few drinks, there was a bit of flirting between them, they seemed to get on okay, but Geoff propositioned her thinking she was a prostitute. He asked how much she charged for sex."

"Oh, crikey. Don't tell me she wasn't a prostitute?"

"No. She was a businesswoman, letting off steam after a heavy meeting in town and went to the nearest bar for a few drinks. He got the wrong end of the stick. There was a bit of an angry confrontation between them. You can imagine how offended she was. Anyway, he apologised, and they parted ways. He grabbed his jacket and scarpered."

Karen wondered where this was leading, but an opinion was already forming in her mind.

"Less than a week later, Denise answered a knock at her door. The minute she opened it, a man came flying through and sent her sprawling to the ground. He beat the living daylights out of her. She only survived because her screams alerted her neighbours who came to her rescue. The bloke legged it."

"The same man?" Karen asked.

"She seems to think so. We believe he followed her home that night and discovered where she lived. He had a very similar voice and had this habit of running his tongue along his lips to moisten them. The male in the bar did that, and her assailant did too. But here's the interesting thing about it. The man who attacked her in her house disguised his face behind a Japanese wrestling mask."

"Beats a balaclava! Any other description?"

Nugent paused for a moment while he scanned his records and the reports. "One sec. Yes. She said that the man in the bar was very sinister looking. Angular features. Beady eyes. It was very unnerving when he stared at her. He had highlighted hair, cut short, clean-shaven and a smoker. She could also smell cigarettes on the man's breath who attacked her."

Karen nodded and stared at the ground, walking in circles across the grass. She wondered how this might be connected to her case.

"Here's the interesting thing. Geoff told Denise that he was on holiday from Yorkshire. Claimed to be a university lecturer in Japanese studies. He didn't mention which university though. Denise said that a lot of the conversation flowed around his interests and his love for Japanese ancient traditions."

Karen perked up as a shiver of interest rippled through her.

"And to cap it off, he said he wanted to be a samurai warrior from the 1700s. Weird, I know." Nugent laughed. "He told Denise that it was a shame they weren't back in his hometown because he would have shown off his collection of samurai swords, helmets, and memorabilia."

"I don't suppose you have any other leads for this suspect?"

"I'm afraid not, Kaz. The case remains open, but we've not had any further sightings, leads or forensics to help us. I have an E-fit that Denise helped us to create. I'll get that over to you in a sec."

Karen thanked Tommy and hung up, her mind awash with lots of questions.

44

KAREN FIRED off another thank you text to Tommy as she dropped back in her chair and switched on her computer. Something in what Tommy had said piqued her interest, a few similarities which couldn't be ignored. First, Tommy had referred to the case involving the prostitute with a severed hand. There was now this case of a man propositioning a woman in a bar before committing a violent assault on her. And to top it off, this individual showed a keen interest in Japanese culture and samurai swords.

She began typing away on Google and searched for degree disciplines to do with Japanese studies at universities. There were eleven higher education institutions in Yorkshire, with eight being universities and the remaining three being higher education colleges. The search produced more data than she'd expected, so she spent the next hour searching all of them to find out which ones offered degrees in Japanese studies. That effort narrowed the field to three, Leeds, Sheffield, and York, which offered sixteen undergraduate Japanese-related courses. An excitement grew within Karen as her eyes scanned the screen. She wasn't sure why. Something spurred her on to keep digging. A quick call to all three led to her eliminating the University of Leeds, which left Sheffield and York.

The closer she looked at both universities and their courses, the more interest it raised. She found courses at York that linked to the last days of the samurai and the invention of modern Japan, 1853 to 1912. Karen sat up, even more intrigued now. She scanned through the course modules and made a few notes as she went along. Karen then turned her attention to her case file to cross-reference it with the search they had undertaken to find retailers or exhibitions that included samurai swords. A few entries from her team had identified online retailers, but she found no evidence of exhibitions that focused on ancient weapons or anything of Japanese historical interest.

She wasn't surprised, but it was something that still needed to be done. There were three retailers within the whole of Yorkshire that specifically sold military memorabilia, including swords and bayonets from across the globe. Enquiries with each of them confirmed no sales of samurai swords or long-bladed battle swords within the last year.

Karen tapped her fingers on the table while thinking this through.

She opened another Google search page and entered an enquiry to do with Japanese torture and punishment. Karen found a Wiki page linked to the Japanese Edo period. She scanned through the details relating to the death penalty, which highlighted decapitation by sword. But she wasn't dealing with a decapitation. Close, but not exact. There were references to being boiled to death, crucifixion, and execution by burning. This still wasn't what she was looking for.

Karen continued to scroll down the page until she came to corporal punishment. She ran her eyes along the page. Amputation of the nose or ears replaced flogging. As she scanned the page her fascination grew stronger. They could sentence both men and women to flogging or amputation. This got Karen thinking. She wondered if the suspect had taken the notion of amputation one step further by combining it with the punishment meted out in places like Iran and Saudi Arabia, where hands were chopped off for theft.

This came down to theft again in Karen's eyes. What had Sallyanne stolen?

She continued her search both online and on the police databases. As more evidence came to light, she knew she was on the right track. A pair of human traffickers in Spain had been captured and sentenced. The crimes not only extended to human trafficking and pimping out prostitutes, which netted the pair on average ten thousand euros a night, but to the attempted murder of several of their prostitutes. When one woman tried to flee with her savings, the traffickers sliced off her whole arm as a punishment. On another occasion, when another one of their girls tried to break free, they threatened they would set her mum and grandmother on fire back at home and rape her little sister.

Could Sallyanne's pimp, Arthur, be callous enough to do this? She wasn't sure. A search of his property had revealed no evidence of a large, bladed weapon. His description didn't match the one Tommy had given her, either.

Karen sat back in her chair and yawned before rubbing her tired eyes. A part of her felt she had made progress, but something was missing.

45

FOLLOWING her call with DI Tom Nugent and her own research, Karen gathered her team around her for a quick briefing and update. She began by explaining the outcome of her conversation with Nugent in Dorset, both in terms of the incident in the bar with Denise Carr and the violent assault in her home.

"It seems a bit of a tenuous link," Tyler suggested after Karen had finished.

"I agree," Karen replied. "But it's certainly worth us exploring further." Karen tapped out the key points on her fingers as she recited them back to her team. "The post-mortems on our victim and the one in Dorset suggested a sword or machete of some sort. We have a suspect in Dorset who has links to Yorkshire and boasts about his interest in Japanese samurais and has a collection. DI Nugent believes that Geoff from the bar, and her home invader could be one and the same. That being the case, Geoff has no qualms about using violence against women.

The key point for me is that it happened two months before the Romanian prostitute Raduca Bogdan was strangled to death and her right hand chopped off." Karen added information to the incident board before turning back to face her team. "This kind of thing doesn't happen in Dorset and the fact that both incidents happened within a short space of each other makes it worth paying attention to."

Karen looked around her team. "Preet, can you reach out to the University of York and set up a meeting for me? While you're on the phone, can you find out as much as you can about their degree in Japanese studies? Find out who their lecturers are and see if any match the description given by Denise Carr."

Preet made a note of it and confirmed it will be the next thing on her to do list.

The team spent a few moments going through their list of suspects and people that they were still keen to speak to. Grant Rowling hadn't been located despite an extensive search. Several of the officers had reached out to some of their contacts on the streets, but as yet, they hadn't been able to find anything relating to Rowling's recent movements. With that information, Karen concluded that the man was doing his hardest to stay in the shadows. Since that worried her, while she was in the briefing, she contacted the press office to put out an appeal for information or sightings of Grant Rowling.

The team hadn't been able to progress with their enquiries about Roberto Joseph with the Italian authorities. Going through the correct channels was taking longer than Karen had expected. With only his parents' address to go on, it was taking forever to get local officers to attend.

Karen was just about to throw open the floor to further questions when the call came in.

Another victim.

46

Not long after being alerted, Karen scrambled the team. They made the short journey in convoy and arrived at the scene fifteen minutes later. Karen was in the second car as it snaked along a small single-track road to the remote location. Questions buzzed in Karen's mind as she took in her surroundings. Farmers' fields and outcrops of woods surrounded her. It wasn't the kind of location you would stumble upon, so in Karen's mind it added weight to her theory that the killer had local knowledge.

The cars pulled up on the verge and as Karen stepped out, a swarm of people surrounded her. White scientific services vans were parked further up the lane along with half a dozen other police vehicles. They had already thrown a cordon round the scene to keep curious onlookers at bay, with more officers deployed to set up roadblocks.

Karen spotted several scenes of crime officers in their white Tyvek suits busying themselves beyond the hedge line and under a tree. A blue tent stood beneath its branches.

"What do we have?" Karen asked one of the officers on scene guard duty.

"Ma'am. The call came in about an hour ago. A couple of trail cyclists were coming down this lane and took a left to go off-road. That's when they spotted the victim slumped against the tree."

"Injuries?"

"White female. Naked. Large laceration across her throat. Right hand missing and she's been whipped multiple times across her back and buttocks."

Karen glanced wide-eyed across to Jade, who blew out her cheeks and raised a brow. "Any other witnesses?"

"No, ma'am. We've already taken initial statements from the cyclists, but we've asked them to remain here in case you needed to talk to them?"

"That's helpful." Karen glanced over her shoulder. "Jade, can you get Tyler and Belinda to have a word with the cyclists? Get their account of the events and anything else that might be of use to us. And then get back here."

Jade nodded before hurrying off to assign the tasks.

"Has anyone called the pathologist?" Karen asked, signing into the scene log and grabbing a pack of overalls and booties.

The officer confirmed that Izzy Armitage was on her way.

"Thank you, officer," Karen replied with a smile, before ducking under the tape and making her way towards the scene. There really wasn't much around. Bog Lane was a small track. One path led straight ahead, and a second to her right had a small metal turnstile tucked away in dense shrubbery which led to a farmer's field. She retraced her steps and followed the main path a few more metres before she came to the tent. Before entering, she took a moment to consider her location. The nearest housing was a few hundred metres to her north, and hard to see from her current vantage point because of the tall hedge line. She doubted if any of the residents could see her from her position, and if that was the case, it was unlikely that they would have seen a vehicle travelling along this track. Nevertheless, she would assign a team of officers to conduct door-to-door enquiries for completeness.

By now, Jade had caught up with her, zipping up her overalls. "At least it's dry," Jade commented, kicking the dry dirt with her feet.

"Yes and no. If it had been wet, there would be tyre impressions and footprints. The fact it's dry makes it harder for us."

Forensic officers were darting in and out of the tent. Several others were beginning a preliminary search of the area around it.

"Ready?" Karen asked. When Jade nodded, Karen lifted the flap and stepped through. The first thing she saw was a naked woman slumped forward around the base of a tree. Her shoulder butted up against it, which left the victim in a slouched position.

"Someone's done a right number on her," Jade whispered in shock.

From where she stood, Karen could see the red welt marks, many of which were tinted with dried blood. She counted over a dozen that criss-crossed the victim's back and buttocks. Not wishing to contaminate the scene too much,

Karen skirted around the edge of the tent to the other side of the tree. She noticed how the victim's left hand was still attached to the rope binding. But the evidence of the missing right hand confirmed in Karen's mind that it was the work of their killer.

Karen and Jade removed themselves from the scene and stepped outside of the tent, where Karen noticed no evidence of the drag marks that were identified at the scene of Sallyanne's murder. Did that mean this victim had come willingly? To her left, a crime scene officer picked through a pile of clothes. "What items do we have?" Karen asked.

The SOCO sat back on her heels. "Not much. Skirt, T-shirt, jacket, scarf."

"No underwear?"

The SOCO shook her head.

"Souvenirs?" Jade suggested.

Karen shrugged. "Possibly, but don't forget, not everyone wears underwear. But there's no handbag or personal possessions either. We have no way of confirming her identity at the moment. I think the killer took all of that to cover his tracks."

Karen was deep in thought as she stared at the victim's clothing, unaware of Jade calling her name. It was only when Jade nudged her with her elbow that Karen snapped back into the present moment. "What?"

Jade nodded towards their original direction. Karen spotted DCI Shield arriving, flashing his warrant card to the scene guard before heading up the track, hastily donning his white Tyvek suit.

Great. I could really do without him getting on my case again.

"DCI," Shield uttered. "Do we have an ID on the victim?"

"No, all her belongings are missing. She's a Jane Doe at the moment."

"Mind if I take a quick look?"

Karen shook her head and stepped aside, before rolling her eyes in Jade's direction once Shield had passed them. He returned just a minute later.

"Your victim's Grace Abbott, aged thirty-two. A prostitute," he said curtly.

Maybe he has his uses. "You've crossed paths with her?"

Shield nodded. "Several times. She is well known on the streets. She's on the system. Our covert officer bumped into her a few times as well. I'll be back at the office if you need anything," he said with very little tact or diplomacy before striding back to the cordon.

47

KAREN and her team remained on scene for the next few hours, documenting the evidence and working out theories. The farmer, whose fields surrounded the crime scene, was horrified at the discovery. He confirmed with Karen that he only visited the area once every few days while checking for any damage to the hedgerows.

Karen tutted when she saw superintendent Kelly's car arrive.

"Jesus, that's all I need."

"Karen, I've heard it's a nasty one, which is why I needed to come and have a look for myself," Kelly said as she approached.

"It is, ma'am."

"Same MO?" she asked.

"Yes and no. Missing right hand. Except this victim appears to have taken a severe beating and was struck multiple times across her back and buttocks. She also had her throat slit."

The escalation in violence concerned Kelly, who furrowed her brow and rested her hands on her hips as she gazed around as if looking around the area would help her find the answers she needed. "Let me look," Kelly said as she headed to the tent, returning a few minutes later. "You definitely think it's the same perp?"

"I think so, ma'am. It's not uncommon for killers to intensify the level of violence they inflict on their victims."

"This is both shocking and concerning. I heard it over the radio. And the bloody press already has wind of it," Kelly growled as she flicked her head back in the direction from where she'd come.

That was all Karen needed. It wasn't uncommon for freelance journalists and reporters to hover close to police stations, and then follow police vehicles towards a crime scene in the hope of picking up a juicy story.

"I've told officers on scene guard to keep those vultures as far back as possible. They may need to move the cordon back even further if it becomes too intense," Kelly said.

"Understood, ma'am."

"What's the plan of action?" Kelly asked, walking with Karen back towards the road.

"The pathologist has been already. Cause of death is blood loss. Forensics are completing their investigation. DCI Shield confirmed the identity of the victim. Grace Abbott, aged thirty-two."

Kelly nodded approvingly. "The DCI?"

"Yes, ma'am. The DCI arrived not long after we did. He had a quick look and confirmed the identity of the victim. She is known to us and his team. That gives us something to begin with."

"Excellent. I'll head back now and liaise with our press department and prepare a statement that we can release first thing tomorrow morning," Kelly added, looking up towards the now darkened sky.

"Thank you, ma'am. That would be helpful. I'll be returning to the station, where I'll brief the rest of the team and get the late shift to make enquiries and trace her next of kin."

"I'll be heading off, Karen. I'm meeting friends for dinner in town. But if there are any major developments, you have my mobile. Call me with any important updates. I'll see you tomorrow morning," Kelly added, before heading back to her car.

Thanks for dropping by. You head off to your cosy meal while I stand in this field for a bit longer.

48

AFTER GRABBING a few hours of fitful sleep, Karen headed back into the office for an early briefing on the latest case. Alone in the kitchenette, she made herself a strong black coffee and threw in a couple of teaspoons of sugar for an instant energy rush. She zoned out deep in thought while stirring her drink.

"The coffee won't drink itself," came a voice from behind.

Karen turned to see Belinda arriving with her own mug and flicking on the kettle.

"I was away with the fairies. I could easily go back to sleep."

"Me too. I hung around last night to help the late shift for a bit before calling it a day," Belinda said, letting an enormous yawn escape her lips, which left her eyes watering.

"You shouldn't have done that, Bel. There were plenty of others here to handle the workload."

Belinda shrugged. "It's fine. I didn't have much to go home

to. I think I was too wired to wind down anyway."

Karen noticed a hint of frustration in Belinda's voice. It was always hard for officers to strike that balance between having a life outside of work and focusing on the job. In cases such as this, it was often hard to switch off when you walked out of the door. It wasn't like a normal nine to five in a corporate environment where you could clock off at five pm, head home and not think about work until you returned at nine am the next morning.

"Make sure you take some leave when we've wrapped up this case. Understand?" Karen asked.

"Oh, trust me. I will. I have an old school friend in Suffolk who's been nagging me to come and see her, so I was thinking of going down for a long weekend."

Karen smiled and agreed that would be a great idea. "Listen, Izzy is doing the post-mortem on Grace later today. Would you be able to liaise with her and attend on my behalf?"

"Sure, no problem. Should I take Ned with me?"

Karen laughed. "Yes, that sounds like a good idea. As long as he thinks he's up to it. From my conversation with him, I don't think he's attended a post-mortem before. He might bail out at the very last minute. Can you attend solo if that's the case?"

Bel nodded. "I'll get the tub of Vicks ready."

Karen gathered the team around a new incident board added at the front of the room.

"Even though most of them are not here, I want to start by saying thank you to the late shift who pushed on with the investigation following the discovery of a second victim. Grace Abbott. Prostitute aged thirty-two. If you haven't watched the bodycam footage from yesterday, please do so as soon as possible. She was beaten and flogged, throat cut, and her right hand removed. From my observations at the scene, seems to be another clean cut in much the same way that Sallyanne's hand was removed. What do we know about her?" Karen asked, taking a sip from her coffee and placing it down beside her.

Tyler handed out a brief report on Grace. "A prostitute for over ten years. Has a boyfriend who's on benefits. A work injury. Sadly, she has a three-year-old boy, Charlie."

"Bollocks," Karen muttered with a shake of her head. She took a sheet and passed the pile on. "Right, can we find out where her usual haunts are and get down there to make some enquiries? See if anyone saw anything suspicious. Maybe the other girls saw Grace talking to a potential punter, or getting picked up?"

Preet stuck a hand up. "Karen, I would like to be one of those who are assigned that job, if that's okay?"

Karen nodded. She liked Preet's keenness and enthusiasm. "Sounds good to me. Liaise with Jade, who'll organise a team to head there. Jade, while I think of it," Karen said, turning in Jade's direction, "can you organise officers to begin door-to-door enquiries in the housing development close to where Grace was discovered? It's a bit of a long shot considering the scene is shrouded by a hedgerow and treeline, but we may get lucky."

Jade signalled her understanding and jotted down a few notes.

One task Karen had assigned for the late shift was to carry

out a cell site triangulation on Henry Warnock's phone to identify if he was in the frame. She turned to another officer for that update, but the result was less than encouraging. Though Warnock's signal had been close to where Sallyanne Faulkner was discovered, this time the location of his phone appeared to be at his home address for the last twenty-four hours. That meant little in Karen's eyes. He could have left it at home. The problem she faced was proving that. Karen assigned officers to visit Warnock to confirm his whereabouts over the last twenty-four hours.

Officers had already carried out a sweep where Grace was discovered but hadn't located any CCTV cameras to help with their investigation.

Another officer provided Karen with an update on how they had traced the owners of six vehicles seen on the night of Sallyanne's murder. The officer confirmed that all the drivers had now been visited and cleared as potential suspects.

"Karen, we've heard from the Italian authorities. Roberto Joseph has been back in Italy for over seven months. They visited his parent's address and met him there. EasyJet passenger flight data confirmed he boarded and left the country."

"Great, we can cross him off," Karen replied, turning to the whiteboard, picking up a red marker and running a line through his name.

The team then spent the next thirty minutes discussing motives and how the cases were linked before Karen concluded the meeting, knowing that the next visit would be a difficult one as she notified Donovan, Grace's boyfriend.

49

THE ADDRESS that Karen had for Grace Abbott took her and Ed to the north of the city. A small cul-de-sac with low two-storey apartment blocks. Karen squeezed in between two cars and killed the ignition. The parking space was so tight, she barely had enough room to squeeze out of her open door. "I'm sure they didn't design the spaces for modern cars…" Karen fumed as she sucked in her stomach and shuffled through the tight space.

"Cars have increased in size through the generations. I bet they were designed for the old Morris Minor and Ford Anglia," Ed replied.

Karen looked at him, wondering where Ed had conjured up those names. The Morris Minor was around before he was even born. He always appeared to be a fountain of knowledge.

She rang the buzzer to the ground-floor apartment and waited a few moments. Static on the intercom brought the speaker alive. "Who is it?" a man's voice answered.

"It's York police. May we come in?" Karen asked.

The man hesitated for a few moments before clearing his throat. "Um… sure."

A few seconds later, the electronic buzzer sounded on the door to signal that it was open.

Ed and Karen stepped through and were greeted by a man in a scruffy T-shirt and shorts who stood in the open doorway of the address. Karen pulled out her warrant card. "Donovan Jacobs?" she asked.

Donovan nodded and swallowed hard as he gazed at Karen's ID. "Yes."

"May we come in for a few moments?"

Donovan nodded before guiding the officers through to a compact lounge which had a small sofa, a single armchair and very few personal effects. Small toys littered the floor. He made no effort to clean up behind him as he turned to face them, nerves twitching his facial features.

"We understand that Grace Abbott is your partner?" Karen asked, studying the man. Other than his crumpled clothes, nothing else stood out.

He offered a small nod. "Is she in trouble? Has she been arrested? Grace went out last night and didn't come back. I've tried her phone, but she's not answering. I'm going out of my mind," he said, playing with his fingers.

"There isn't an easy way to say this, but we discovered a body yesterday morning. We believe it to be Grace. An officer at the scene confirmed her identity."

Donovan staggered back, his eyes wide and wild. He drew in ragged gasps of breath. "No. There must be a mistake."

"Can you confirm what she was wearing when she left?"

Donovan ran a hand through his hair as he paced the room. "Um… black boots, black miniskirt, and a brown fur jacket. It can't be her."

Karen exchanged a knowing glance with Ed. Donovan's description matched the items of clothing recovered from the scene. "Based on that description and the identification by an officer, we're certain it's Grace Abbott. But we'd like you to confirm that by attending a viewing at the hospital mortuary. I'm sorry for your loss."

Donovan slumped into a chair and held his head in his hands. "What am I gonna tell Charlie? I knew what Grace did when I met her. But there was something about her I really liked. She was desperate to get out of the game. I was a lorry driver when I met her," Donovan began. "Then we got together. I promised she could quit and that we could live on my salary. She could start a new life," he whispered, searching their eyes for understanding. "A pallet collapsed, and the load crushed my leg. Broken in seven places. I have nerve damage and can hardly feel anything most days. I gave up work and claimed benefits."

Karen remained quiet, giving Donovan time to process his thoughts and offer a further insight into Grace.

"I knew it devastated Grace after I was injured, and I begged her to go get a job in a supermarket or something like that, but she was adamant she wouldn't get anything. All she had ever known was working on the streets. Grace said that she would carry on doing that to bring in money for the three of us." Donovan wiped his eyes on the back of his hand.

Karen was about to speak when a child's whimper filtered

into the room. Donovan leapt up from his seat and disappeared through the lounge door, returning a few moments later clutching a boy, half asleep, his head resting on Donovan's shoulder. Donovan rocked from side to side as the boy drifted back off to sleep.

Karen and Ed exchanged glances for a few minutes. Karen saw a different side to Grace's personal life. There was no drug or alcohol addiction. There was no pimp controlling her and forcing her to work. Grace was a woman doing the only thing she knew to pay the bills and put food on the table for her small family. A meagre income to supplement her boyfriend's disability and social benefits.

"Sorry about that. He's been unsettled ever since Grace left the house. We didn't sleep very well last night. He'd stir every time Grace came in during the middle of the night. She'd get him off to bed by lying next to him and singing a song." Donovan closed his eyes as his chin wobbled.

"Did Grace have any enemies?" Karen asked. Though she wanted to leave Donovan to grieve, time was of the essence for her. She had to crack this case before another woman met a brutal end.

"No. Not that I'm aware of," Donovan replied, opening his eyes.

"Do you know where her pitch was?"

Donovan couldn't be certain but rattled off a few streets that he recalled Grace mentioning in earlier conversations. She nodded at Ed, who left the room to make the call.

"Did she take any drugs?"

Donovan shook his head. "Grace said a lot of the girls took

stuff to block out what they were doing. But Grace said it was getting so dangerous on the streets that she needed to keep her wits about her."

Karen narrowed her eyes as she thought about that. That sounded promising. "What did she say specifically?"

Ed returned and took a seat.

"Grace told me stories that other girls had shared with her. She had a friend, Monica, Polish, who worked in the same areas as her. Monica was desperate to get away, but the gang who put her on the streets kept her passport. Every time she tried to get away, they tracked her down and beat her. If it wasn't the pimps causing her problems, then it was the customers." Donovan stared up at the ceiling, clutching at threads from his memory. "Monica told Grace about one particular time when a customer picked her up and drove her a few streets away, and then put on a weird Japanese mask and wanted oral sex."

Japanese mask. Another connection.

Donovan continued. "After they did the business, he tried to stop her from leaving. She put up a bit of a fight and got away before the customer raced away."

Karen turned to Ed. "Ed, can you pass that information on to the officers on the ground? See if they can ask around and locate Monica."

Ed pulled out his phone to text a message.

"Grace told me it was getting tough out there to earn a living." Donovan sighed. "There had been a recent influx of prostitutes from Poland, and criminal gangs were exploiting them. The gangs were putting pressure on

English girls to either conform or be *replaced*. Whatever that meant. I guess it doesn't take a genius to figure that out. I don't know the name of the girl, but Grace told me about a woman hospitalised when she had a run-in with a Polish prostitute. Some Eastern European men tracked her down and slashed her."

Donovan used his fingers to show how the victim had been cut from her ear to her collarbone. "She nearly bled to death. It was a warning to others. Next time, they would cut off her arms."

"Thank you, Donovan. We really appreciate your help. I'm sorry about your loss. I know it's a difficult time for you. But here's my card," Karen said, taking one from her purse and passing it to him. "If you think of anything else, then you have my number. I'll also arrange for a family liaison officer to get in touch with you. If there are any major developments in the case, they will be your contact. I'll also contact social services and see if they can offer you extra help or support if you like?"

"Thank you. Will I be able to see Grace now?" Donovan asked.

Karen nodded. "The family liaison officer can sort that out for you."

Just before leaving, Karen spotted a hairbrush on a table in the hallway. "Is this Grace's?"

Donovan nodded. "Yes, she'd always used it before heading out."

"May we take it?"

Donovan narrowed his eyes, confused by the strange request, before he shrugged his approval.

Karen scooped it up and placed it in an evidence bag in case she needed any extra DNA identification. "Once again, we're sorry for your loss."

50

KAREN DROPPED ED off at the police station and picked up Jade before swinging by the second crime scene again. With a significant police presence, the investigation saw a stream of inquisitive spectators arriving. Karen imagined this lane had never been busier as cars were turned away. Extra PCSOs were positioned to intercept people traipsing on foot across the fields to *encourage* them to turn around and retrace their steps.

"I feel really sorry for Donovan," Jade said, stepping from the car. "From what you've said, he seems a pretty decent bloke to be fair, and now the little boy Charlie has lost his mum."

Karen understood the sentiment. Not every prostitute came from a drug-ridden cesspit they called home. She'd known prostitutes who sofa surfed between friends for years. Others who'd been in and out of rehab and temporary accommodation offered by charities, and yet still found themselves back on the street. The temptation and lure of drugs and easy money was often too irresistible and a necessity just to survive.

Grace was different. Perhaps she didn't believe she could make it as a cashier in a supermarket or as a commercial cleaner in an office block. Maybe she doubted people would trust her enough. Or perhaps she was worried that she could never shake off the stigma of being a prostitute. Either way, Grace was earning money to feed her child.

"Yeah, it sucks. I hope Donovan can deal with his grief and care for their child. If he can get enough support, then they have a slim chance of making it."

Jade followed Karen as they dipped under the cordon tape and made their way back towards the site. An extensive search of the adjoining fields was now underway, with a line of officers in overalls holding long sticks as they walked in a systematic sequence covering every square inch. Each time they found something of interest, an officer would raise their hand and the PolSA team leader would make their way towards that point to decide if there was anything of significance. Slow and arduous, but necessary as part of the evidence gathering process.

A tent remained where Grace's body once lay.

Karen took a few moments to catch up with the PolSA team leader only to find that they had come up empty-handed so far. It wasn't the news Karen hoped for, but she only needed one small lead or breakthrough.

Having spent the next thirty minutes discussing the case, they made their way back towards the cordon where several reporters and photographers remained camped out, hoping to get the first scoop on any developments.

"Brace yourself…" Karen uttered.

"Anything new to report?" one reporter shouted, thrusting her phone in Karen's direction.

"We'll be releasing updates to all the media outlets as the case progresses."

"Is this linked to the murder of Sallyanne Faulkner?" another butted in.

Karen pursed her lips. This wasn't a conversation she wanted to get into.

"Should the public be concerned?" the reporter pressed.

Karen narrowed her eyes; she'd seen this reporter around. Sam Peters, a dogged and persistent woman with a habit of popping up at serious crime scenes. It was common knowledge that she wasn't a fan of the police. Karen had been warned about Sam Peters by the press liaison officer not long after she had started. The officer had told Karen about the number of scalps Sam Peters held to her name and was advised to give her a wide berth.

Karen and Jade dipped under the cordon tape and made their way back towards Karen's car, with several of the reporters and their photographers hot on their tail.

"Is it safe for women to walk the streets at night? Why is the killer targeting street girls? Does the killer have a personal vendetta against prostitutes? Is it true that the killer is carving up his victims? Is he a Jack the Ripper copycat? Is the killer a vigilante police officer? Does he torture his victims first?"

The questions hit Karen from all angles as she closed the door.

"Blimey, they're like vultures. Vigilante police officer? Where did they get that from?" Karen whispered, aware that the reporters were still watching her.

"No idea," Jade said beneath her hand covering her mouth.

Karen pulled away from the scene and instructed Jade to get on to the press team to put out a follow-up statement.

51

BONES STRIPPED BARE OF FLESH. Cleaned and dried, ready for assembly. Each little bone offered little insight into its use, but once assembled would show the hand that always reached out for money.

Many hours of slow boil had left his house smelling like a pork pie factory. A musty and earthy smell. It resembled the aroma you'd have midway through cooking a delicious casserole just before adding the salt, pepper and herbs to bring depth to the gravy.

His intention was never to go that far, but it didn't stop his mind from thinking and entertaining the idea of what it would take to create a thick stew made from the flesh of one of his victims. *How weird would that be?* Probably no weirder than the situation he found himself in now.

He sat tucked into his table, his lamp stretched to cast a light on the sheet of velvet he had laid out in front of him. He'd watched the lunchtime press coverage of the second crime scene and had nodded his approval. The police were clutching at straws. He knew that. To make their job harder, he'd left little in the way of evidence.

One bone at a time, he delicately threaded them together using a small 0.3mm drill bit and low-powered drill to create an anchor point at both ends of each bone, before looping them to the next with 0.22mm fine copper wire. It was a delicate process. He did it by looking through a free-standing desktop magnifying glass with a built-in light, which left both hands free.

He paused every fifteen minutes to stretch his neck and roll his shoulders. With his laptop open beside him, he scanned the classifieds looking for his next victim. It wouldn't be something he normally did but he was determined to mix it up a little to confuse the police. In York, he'd picked his first two victims off the street. If he picked his third through a classified, it would throw them off his scent.

It wasn't as much fun as cruising the streets, but the girls on this site feared working the streets. Though their identities were disguised in the classifieds, there was enough information to decide who to choose and who to contact.

"The Slasher…" he whispered. That was a name given to him in some threads that he'd seen on several social media sites. Theories were rife as to who The Slasher was, the motive, and where he would strike next. Sites like this were doing his job for him. Online gossip whipped up fear and panic. Other madcap and frankly ridiculous theories suggested it was an ancient swordsman who had been resurrected from the grave to rid the planet of whores. There was even speculation that a modern-day relative of Jack the Ripper had taken over where Jack had stopped. He was happy with all of those assessments. He would let the public form their own conclusions. His motive was plain. Killing women who acted out of greed and desperation.

He returned to his work, hunching over his desk for another hour before it was done. Placing the hand on the velvet pad within its box, he carried it down to the basement and placed it in the cabinet along with the others.

He stepped back, pleased with his efforts, before turning to stare at the wall which housed his collection of gleaming swords. Which should he use next?

The desire to kill beckoned him on.

52

"I'M SO BLOODY HUNGRY," Karen said as she took another bite of her sandwich. They had pulled up in a parking bay outside the main entrance to the University of York. As she inspected the old structure, it reminded Karen of the impressive buildings associated with an elite boarding school with an imposing façade. But from her research she'd learned that they had initially constructed the Grade II listed building as a country house with the pendant stucco ceiling of the great hall, elegant staircases and land-scaped gardens consisting of a gazebo and yew trees.

"Me too," Jade added, stabbing her fork into her chicken pasta salad.

They took a few moments to catch up over a bite to eat before wrapping up and heading over towards a different part of the campus surrounded by a plethora of modern buildings. They headed into the main reception from which they were sent to the second floor to meet Jennifer Reid, course director of Japanese studies.

Jennifer walked them the short distance to her office and offered them a seat and refreshments, which Karen declined as she did her hardest to stifle a burp that threatened to escape, the pain from which sat in the back of her throat.

Karen introduced herself and Jade before taking a quick look around the room. Documents and leaflets sat in piles around them, confined to the edges of the room. Jennifer's desk appeared to be overflowing with even more paper and a stack of books. From where Karen sat, most of the titles carried a Japanese theme.

"Thank you for taking the time to see us. We are investigating a series of what we believe to be connected murders."

Jennifer gasped and sat wide-eyed.

"We believe they may be connected to an incident in Dorset where a female was attacked by a male claiming to be a lecturer at the university. We don't know if he was a former or current lecturer, but from the list of names your office provided us with and descriptions from the university website, I'm not sure that this individual is part of your teaching staff."

The news alarmed Jennifer as she swallowed hard and took a sip from her water bottle to compose herself. "That's dreadful. I would hope that none of our teaching staff would be involved in such a heinous act. You say that your initial investigations couldn't find a match with our current teaching faculty?"

Karen nodded. "That's correct. We can't even be certain if he was telling the truth." Karen gave a brief description of the suspect that Nugent had given her.

Jennifer shook her head and racked her brain for a few moments. "It doesn't sound like someone who is part of our teaching staff."

"What about former?"

"Again, it doesn't ring a bell. I've been here for ten years and interviewed every member of our teaching staff. I can't recall everyone, but I could have a look for you?"

"That would be helpful. I'll get one of my team to contact you. From those that you can remember, do most former members of staff just resign and move on to different posts elsewhere? Or retire?"

Jennifer nodded and agreed it was one or the other, but also confirmed that their staff turnover was very low because the university was part of the Russell Group. The group represented twenty-four of the leading universities in the country and was known for outstanding research and teaching, with unrivalled links to the business and public sectors. For that reason, many members of staff remained at the university for much of their teaching career. It was a prestigious notch on their belt.

Jennifer paused. Karen noticed the woman's frown.

"Is there something else?" Karen probed.

Jennifer hesitated and cleared her throat. "It's only just sprung to mind, but we had a dreadful situation back during the 2018/2019 academic year. The university dealt with it quickly, but we were only made aware of the incidents a few weeks after they'd happened. Following an internal investigation, we were able to identify an individual back to our teaching staff."

Karen was interested now as she looked across to Jade who

sat closer to the edge of her seat, pen hovering above her notepad.

Karen sensed the woman found it difficult to carry on.

"One of our former lecturers, Adrian Wells, was sacked for inappropriate conduct with several female students." Jennifer pulled up a picture of him from her records and swivelled her screen around for the officers to see.

The picture showed Wells with long dark brown hair tied at the back in a ponytail. His eyes were beady and deep-set. He carried an untidy beard.

The photo bore striking similarities to the description given by Nugent, in particular angular features and beady eyes.

Jennifer explained that several complaints had been lodged for inappropriate behaviour by a male member of staff towards their female students in some of the city bars. The enquiries led back to Adrian.

"When you say inappropriate behaviour, what do you mean?" Karen asked.

"Oh, dear, this is very unpleasant," Jennifer replied, feeling flustered. "He was accused of groping a female's breasts while drunk. Apparently, he tried to spike her drink but was caught in the act by the student's friend. And when confronted, Mr Wells hurried off. There was another incident where he tried to befriend a female student in a city bar, which didn't end pleasantly."

Karen understood how difficult this was for Jennifer by the pained expression on her face. "I appreciate it's uncomfortable. Anything you can tell us will remain confidential."

"Very well," Jennifer replied, her eyes flickering with

concern. "The account given by the second female student was that when she rejected Mr Wells's drunken advances, he became verbally aggressive to her. She felt frightened and feared for her safety."

The information was helpful in Karen's mind, but the Dorset E-fit presented to Jennifer cast further doubt whether they were looking at the same person. Karen made a mental note to get a copy of Wells's university picture for Nugent to show Denise Carr.

"I'm afraid that's not the worst of it," Jennifer said, her voice trailing off. "He sexually assaulted and tried to abduct a female student. It only came to light when the victim called our confidential and anonymous student helpline."

"Student helpline?" Karen enquired.

"I guess it's a bit like the Samaritans helpline." Jennifer explained how all staff and volunteers underwent thirty hours of specialist training, including specialist modules on managing mental health conditions such as suicidal thoughts, anxiety, depression and self-harm. Only then were they allowed to man the phones. "We informed the police as a standard protocol because of the serious nature of the allegation and that she wanted to take her own life."

"Was a name put for the assailant?"

Jennifer nodded. "Mr Wells. The police tried to locate him but were unable to trace him. His office remained untouched. Emails and phone calls weren't being answered. He just vanished."

Karen shook her head. "Do you have a name for this potential victim?"

"I'm afraid not. It was an anonymous female caller."

"Are the calls recorded?"

"Sadly not. But the student mentioned that Mr Wells had plied her with drink and then she couldn't remember much until she woke to find Mr Wells attempting to rape her. When she tried to fight him off, he tried to drag her to a vehicle close by. Her screams forced him to flee."

"Thank you, Jennifer. Your insights and information have been very helpful." Karen and Jade stood and saw themselves out.

53

THE MINUTE KAREN got back she made a beeline for Superintendent Kelly's office. She outlined the conversation with Jennifer Reid.

"And you think Wells is a likely suspect in both cases?" Kelly questioned.

"I do, ma'am. A lot of it fits. There are similar features between the Dorset E-fit and Wells's photo from his university personnel records. I'm going to get the facial imaging officer to strip out features from the university photo to compare it against the E-fit before getting it over to Dorset for an ID. Wells was a former lecturer of Japanese studies. There's evidence of him being a sexual predator towards other female students. He boasted about his collection of Japanese memorabilia, including swords. And he lived in York and perhaps still does."

"But he didn't kill?"

"Not as far as we know, ma'am."

"And what about the other persons of interest?"

Karen explained that Grant Rowling was still unaccounted for, and his whereabouts were unknown. Roberto Joseph had been eliminated from their enquiries. Warnock was still a suspect for Sallyanne's murder, but they'd been unable to link him to the second crime scene or victim so far.

"Okay, so locate Adrian Wells. What's your theory behind Grace Abbott being whipped repeatedly when Sallyanne Faulkner wasn't?"

"I'm not sure, ma'am. Either Grace Abbott put up more of a struggle which angered her killer, or he's escalated his propensity for violence. Perhaps he wasn't getting enough of a kick from just beating his victim and then cutting off her hand." Karen shrugged.

She left Kelly promising to update her later and returned to her team. Jade had already updated all available officers on the outcome of the conversation with Jennifer Reid.

Karen darted through the desks towards the incident board. "I want everything we have on Adrian Wells, a former lecturer." Karen said, outlining the importance of this new lead.

The incident board had filled up with more information as the investigation had proceeded. Karen stared at the image of Sallyanne taken when she was at university. A fuller figure, trendy clothes, dark hair, rounded face and an attractive smile. It certainly was in marked contrast to the image of her face taken at the crime scene.

Karen pulled out her phone and called Zac.

"Hey, how's the investigation going?" he asked.

"I think we've had a fresh development. At first, I wasn't sure if we were dealing with the fallout from rival gangs, or a new firm trying to muscle in. But the more I think about it, the more I believe this is a lone wolf operation and we have a likely suspect." Karen recapped on the visit to the University of York and the reasons behind her thinking.

"That sounds promising. What's the plan of action?"

Karen had already thought about her next step while talking to Kelly. Between them, they had sketched out a plan of action.

"We are pulling up all the information we can on Wells. If it is him, then he is in the York area. We still don't have a current description to put out, nor the vehicle he's driving, but the plan is to get as many officers as possible to flood the most common spots this evening. I'm just about to organise an operation, and Kelly has put in a request for extra resources and surveillance units. It will help keep the girls safer, calm local concerns and hopefully stop another killing."

Karen heard Zac take a sharp intake of breath. "What?"

"Your favourite person isn't going to like this. Flooding the area with officers is only going to put a spanner in his operations."

"That's fine. The super is going to have a word with him. If there is a likelihood that it's Wells, then he could be out there right now cruising the streets looking for another victim."

"Is he linked to Warnock?" Zac asked.

"I don't think so. But we are cross-referencing the database now. Maybe Wells had been a former patient of our pervy

GP, and their interests had crossed paths, but I doubt it. I'll let you know how we get on."

Karen hung up. With a surveillance operation to organise, there was just enough time for her to dash back home for a change of clothes and to feed Manky.

54

CHANGED AND READY TO GO, Karen assembled her team of officers in an adjacent building which normally served as the press briefing venue. It was large enough to seat over fifty people, and more than adequate for her needs. Kelly had come through with the goods and had delivered another dozen bodies which swelled the team.

A ripple of muted conversations echoed around the large space. Karen took her place at the front and cast her eye around the assembled officers. A sense of pride and excitement sent shivers through her. It reminded her of the large-scale operations she'd conducted while in the Met. Karen hadn't thought for a moment that she'd be doing another op so soon after coming to York.

"Okay, if I can have your attention. I'll keep this brief," Karen shouted. The pockets of conversation petered out as officers turned in their seats to face her.

Karen's closest team members sat at the front of the crowd, including the newest recruits, Ned and Preet.

"This evening we're going to be conducting a small pre-emptive operation that serves several purposes. To begin with, in response to growing concerns from members of the public, we need to increase our visible and covert presence on the streets."

"Our uniformed colleagues have increased patrols in the area which have gone some way towards reassuring local concerns, and we're thankful for that. Tonight is about ramping up our covert presence. We want to try to protect the safety of the girls who work the streets. And we want to try and spot Adrian Wells. You have an old picture of him in your pack. It's not his most recent, so his appearance may have changed."

Papers being rustled filled the silence.

"We don't know what he looks like and don't know what he drives?" asked an officer towards the back of the crowd.

Karen didn't know the officer and judging by the hint of flippancy in his tone, he wasn't keen about being there. "No. If we did, the information would be in the pack, wouldn't it?" she replied sternly. "This is about policing and finding the missing parts."

Karen was just about to continue when the door opened, and Karen's number one fan appeared. "Why wasn't I called to this briefing?" Shield demanded. "If you're running an op against the OCGs, then my team needs to be involved," he growled.

"Excuse me. Talk among yourselves," she said to her assembled team as she marched towards the door and pushed past Shield. "Outside, now," Karen hissed.

The door closed behind them, and Karen faced her nemesis

once again in the quiet corridor. She'd had enough of the man. The olive branch had been short-lived. "Don't you ever talk to me like that again in front of other officers," Karen said through gritted teeth, jabbing a finger in his direction. "Who do you think you are? I've tried to be nice. I've tried to mend bridges with you. I've even agreed to work with you to share intelligence and findings from my investigation. And this is the way you thank me? Barging into my briefing and throwing your *substantial* weight around in front of those officers," she said, pointing back towards the door.

"If you're doing an op that jeopardises my investigation, and the OCG gets wind of it, they'll slip away and move their operations elsewhere," he fired back.

"I'm not looking for your OCG. They may have nothing to do with the deaths of two street girls, so I won't be interfering with your investigation. I have a new suspect, and we've no intelligence to suggest he is part of any organisation… at all!"

Karen took a step back to control her breathing as her heart hammered in her chest. Kelly's chat with Shield had infuriated the man further. "Now back off. I'm warning you." Karen didn't hang around to wait for an answer as she turned her back on him and disappeared through the door.

The raised conversations petered out the minute Karen walked back in. With all eyes on her, many of the officers had not only been surprised, but amused to have had front row seats between the two duelling officers.

Karen shrugged it off, not wishing to give them anything else to gossip about. "As I was saying, look out for anyone matching Wells's description." Karen picked up her own folder and pulled out mugshots of several unsavoury looking characters. "I also need you to keep an eye out for these individuals." Karen ran through their names. "They are known associates and members of the Polish organised crime group who are bringing their girls in and scaring off the local street workers with threats of intimidation and violence. We are not interested in them tonight, but I want you to keep an eye out for them for your own safety. They are dangerous and not to be approached unless there's a threat to life, and even then, you need backup in place first. Understand?"

A sea of nodding faces.

"The attacks are becoming more violent and aggressive. Whether that's out of frustration or excitement, we're unsure. That's why we need to stop him before he gets another chance to escalate even further."

Finally, Karen went through the most recent images of Warnock and instructed her team to be on the lookout for him or his grey BMW 3 Series as well.

She fielded the final few questions before they set off.

55

THE CONVOY of unmarked police cars left the compound and splintered off in different directions, making their way towards the key hotspots for prostitution activity.

Fifteen minutes later, Karen parked close to a set of cross-roads, where she and Jade would have the perfect vantage point. Karen tucked in between two cars to keep her presence discreet. The spot was less than five minutes away from where Sallyanne had been picked up, and less than a mile from where Grace was last seen.

Even though it sounded glamorous to be on covert surveillance, the reality was far from it. Boredom, desperation for the loo, hunger and tiredness all added to the frustration of being cooped up in a car for hours. It wasn't so bad now with milder temperatures, but during winter, it was punishing.

Karen spent a few minutes checking in with her teams. Many were parked at key locations, but she had four pairs of mixed officers on foot casually walking the streets.

"Ed, anything at your location?" Karen asked, pressing the mic button.

"Negative. There are a couple of girls about twenty yards behind us. A few cars have passed, but nothing so far."

"Okay, stay alert."

"Do you think we'll get lucky?" Jade asked, sipping from her insulated mug of coffee.

"I hope so. I can feel it in my waters," Karen replied.

Jade laughed. "You sure that's not you wanting to go for a piss?"

"Don't start talking about going to the toilet. Once I get an idea in my head like that, it's game over."

Jade teased her, pretending to be a young child desperate for a wee and begging her teacher to go to the toilet before she wet her knickers.

"Enough," Karen said, turning to look out of her side of the car, desperate to push away the thought forming in her mind.

They spent the next half an hour talking about the case and Adrian Wells. They weren't sure of Wells's current connection with Sallyanne. Karen wondered if he knew Grace too, or whether he was a frequent visitor to the area and Grace had been in the wrong place at the wrong time.

As the hours ticked by, Karen noticed the frustration her officers felt as she radioed them. Most surveillance operations would often end without an outcome or conclusion. With that in mind, Karen and Jade set off on foot to stretch their legs. As they walked around, they glanced up and down the side roads looking for Warnock's car, as well as closely scrutinising cars that cruised past, hoping to glimpse someone resembling Wells.

Karen's phone rang. The illuminated screen identified Belinda, who had been at the post-mortem for Grace Abbott.

"Belinda, how are you getting on?"

"It was a late one. Izzy has just finished. There were twenty-seven markings across her back and buttocks. A few were deep and raw. Izzy believes Grace would probably have passed out from the pain within the first dozen strokes. Grace had a cracked cheekbone and bruising to the side of her face from repeated blows. She'd also suffered a severe laceration to the front of her throat and the severing of an artery. I don't understand what kind of animal could have done this. Grace bled out."

Karen grimaced as she thought about Grace's last moments. "What about her hand being severed."

"Little to no damage to the surrounding tissue. It was a clean cut done with force. Izzy believes the same weapon was used. She's taken detailed photographs and also cut away the lower section of ulna and radius and sent them away for detailed microscopic analysis. She is expecting the same results found in Sallyanne's bones."

"Okay, Bel. That's helpful. Cause of death?"

"Stress induced heart attack and blood loss."

"Not good," Karen sighed. She told Bel to call it a night and head home before hanging up. Karen updated Jade as they continued to walk.

Two women leaning against a fence panel saw Karen and

Jade approach. They viewed them with suspicion, their conversation coming to an abrupt halt.

"Ladies," Karen said, holding up her warrant card.

The women rolled their eyes and glanced at each other. "We've not done anything wrong. We're chatting," one replied.

"Of course you are. We're out here trying to make sure you're safe. That's all. You know about the murder of two street workers?" Karen gave a brief description of Warnock and Wells. "Have you seen anyone matching the descriptions?"

Both women shrugged, unwilling to answer. Despite Karen's best efforts to reassure them she wasn't about to pull them in, their reluctance did little to help Karen. The harder she pushed, the less cooperative they became before both scurried off into the dark night.

"This is going well..." Karen sighed as they headed off again.

56

THE CLASSIFIEDS WERE PROVING HARDER than he'd imagined. Too many details to sort out, far too many questions, and a few no-shows. Getting frustrated with the wait, he'd returned to the streets. Excitement coursed through his veins, tingling his skin.

The dark streets had become his second home, a playground of entertainment and a place that delivered his ultimate satisfaction. He figured it was no different than strolling along a food aisle in a supermarket looking for a delicacy to grab his eye.

It felt like a normal weekday night. Cars navigated the narrow streets, dog owners stopped at every streetlight as their dogs sniffed and did their business. Some streets were darker than others. Fewer streetlights. A chance to blend into the shadows. Hide from prying eyes.

He cruised slowly and watched as street girls stepped forward, leaning in to see if they could catch the eye of an interested punter. He laughed at those who thrust out their chests, as if that was going to draw him in.

Oh, no.

He had a particular taste in women. And not the finer ones, either. He wanted the street rats. The ones who hung around in pure desperation and would take any punter regardless of whether they were fat or thin, black or white, rich or poor. It didn't matter to them. All they were interested in was an exchange of services. His thoughts turned to his swords.

The swords made the difference.

He could have used a small knife. For crying out loud, he had plenty of them in his kitchen drawer. But every gang member, every street robber, every juvenile seemed to carry one. He needed to make an impact.

The swords gave him indestructible power.

He spent hours polishing them. Sharpening their blades until they could slice through paper with the smallest of effort. He'd lost count of the number of times he'd nicked his fingers on their razor-sharp edges.

The swords made the statement.

Perhaps he should keep his next victim alive. He wondered if he'd see terror etched in her eyes as the blade neared her throat. What would go through her mind? Would she pray and beg for her life? He laughed. It would be too late for that. God or no other divine intervention would save her.

He'd been driving round for ages. There were plenty of women out this evening. But most didn't deserve a second look and he was in no hurry until he found the right one. But as the hours passed, frustration crept in. He cursed under his breath, ready to give up, when he spotted a lone female hovering on the fringes. Most hung about near streetlights, the sodium yellow glow casting shadows across their faces. This one was different. She hung back in obscurity. He found a convenient place to stop close to her. He killed his ignition and sat in the darkness. She was too busy looking up and down the street to notice him.

He dared not blink. Too scared he would miss something. He ran his tongue along his dry lips. He wanted her. He wanted her now. He imagined running the blade across her neck. Seeing the helplessness and confusion in her eyes.

She disappeared out of view and walked along the street. It was a while before she reappeared beneath a streetlight as another car approached. She took a few steps forward and rested one hand on her hip before taking a puff on her cigarette. She shook her head as the car passed her, the driver not bothering to look.

He glanced in his rear-view mirror. No one behind. No one in front. Perfect.

He started his car and pulled away from the kerb, heading towards her before coming to an abrupt halt.

Another tom appeared from nowhere, followed by another. *Act like a normal punter*, he thought, so continued forward, throwing them a quick glance as he passed.

Too many witnesses.

He needed to find someone else as he slapped a hand on the steering wheel, annoyed for taking too long. Dithering had spoilt the moment.

57

THE STREETS HELD a distinct energy this evening. He couldn't quite figure out why. A heightened tension in the air. Maybe he was just imagining in it.

Could any of this be down to him? Had his brief reign of terror already changed the dynamics on the streets? Whichever road he drove down, he sensed the same sensation. Tension prickled in the air. The hairs on the back of his neck stood on end. His hands felt clammy and sweaty.

Was he imagining it? Had the excitement got to him? Or was it the frustration of not finding someone yet?

His suspicions grew as he turned down another road and saw women disappearing. Scattering in all directions. As if spooked by a ghostly apparition. A few disappeared down "Condom Alley", a notorious haunt where prostitutes did the business when the punter didn't have a car.

Then he realised it could only mean one thing.

Police.

He scoured the darkness, his eyes darting from left to right. Oddly, there were no cars on the move, no punters cruising past with dipped headlights.

Yes, this has to be down to the police.

Not what he needed right now. He needed to stay alert. He'd seen their tactics before from afar. Undercover officers posing as a couple, holding hands, while they listened in on their earpieces for any information.

This is turning in to a nightmare.

Without drawing attention to himself, he increased his speed, travelling to the end of the road before taking a sharp left. It was a further ten minutes before he slowed again in a different neighbourhood with a different feel. Almost soulless. A rougher part, where feral youths on bikes roamed the streets, performing wheelies in the face of oncoming traffic in their own twisted version of chicken. Litter bins overflowed and the local independent supermarket didn't bother removing graffiti sprawled across its glass frontage, knowing it would be back hours later under the cover of darkness. Terrified locals refused to leave their homes after dark as the tentacles of violent crime continued to creep across this once safe place.

He didn't travel to this area often. He preferred his regular haunts, the streets that he knew so well. But from his research, he knew it was another, lesser-known spot where prostitutes gathered. Pulling up to the side, he killed the ignition and took a few deep breaths to control the hammering in his chest.

Stay calm. Breathe slowly. Remember the way of the warrior.

A few minutes passed before he brought the turbulence under control to restore an equilibrium.

After starting the car, he pulled away again, turning his attention to another street close by. A narrow street double-parked with traffic. Families tucked away in safety behind closed doors.

Only the desperate would be out now. The punters and the prostitutes. Both were desperate, but for different reasons.

Braking hard, he almost missed her. A lone female. She was definitely the one.

He reversed a few feet until he was parallel to her, lowering his window as he did. First impressions were promising. Dark hair. Jeans. Ankle boots. Black denim jacket. He couldn't tell whether she had tattoos but remained optimistic.

"You looking for business?" she asked, her voice gravelly and hard.

"Definitely. You're my type," he replied, offering his broadest smile as he adjusted his glasses and tipped the edge of his baseball cap lower to shield his face.

"Well, you're in luck then, because I'm ready if you are? We can do it around the corner if you like? Quick and easy," she said, nodding towards a side turning near to them. "A tenner," she added, poking her tongue into her cheek.

He glanced up and down the street. *Still clear.*

"I had something more in mind. We can take a drive and I'll pay you more for extras."

"Nah, I've not got the time to piss off from my pitch. Someone else will nick it."

"Come on. You'll make a ton more in thirty minutes with me than you will all night…" he suggested, hoping the offer would tempt her.

She shook her head. "Nah, you're wasting my time, luv. Do one, alright," she said, tutting, before giving him the finger and walking off.

Incensed, he pushed open his door and raced around to the pavement, grabbing her from behind as he threw his arm around her neck.

A scream tore from her throat as she gripped his arm, desperate to pull away from his hold.

"Don't fight it, bitch," he hissed into her ear as he dragged her back to his car.

She screamed louder, thrusting her hands back towards his face, grabbing for skin, or hair, anything that would give her a hold. Her fingertips met his cheeks, raking her nails down his face. He yelled and released her, clutching at his face.

That gave the woman enough of a reprieve to put some space between them as she staggered and screamed, hammering on the nearest door.

His burning cheeks stung as he snarled, spittle erupting from his lips as panic washed over him. He needed to get away…fast!

58

KAREN AND JADE returned to the car after walking the streets for an hour. The outcome had been less than promising, which doused Karen's spirits. Her misery only worsened while checking in with her teams. Their efforts had proved just as unsuccessful. A few teams had spotted punters picking up street workers and passed the information to patrol cars in the area who put in stops.

"When do you think we should call it an evening?" Jade asked, letting out an almighty yawn and slapping her cheeks to wake herself up.

"I think we're done here to be fair," Karen replied, noticing the despondency in Jade's voice. She felt the same too. It hadn't been a great night. A few prostitutes begging for money because business was slow and no sign of the hostile welcome the last time she'd hit the streets alone. The cases were a *slow burn,* little in the way of forensics, no CCTV breakthroughs and a potential suspect who may have changed his appearance.

Karen started her car and headed off, asking her teams to stand down and return to the station. She drove in silence, making her way towards Jade's apartment to drop her off. Thoughts rushed through her mind. Had she got it wrong? Was she missing something? Were they concentrating their efforts in the wrong places? And what would Kelly have to say? Karen slumped in her seat at the prospect.

Jade's radio crackled to life, breaking the silence in the car and making them both jump.

Control had taken an emergency call about the attempted violent abduction of a lone female. A street worker.

Karen glanced at Jade and furrowed her brow. "Could that be our man?"

Jade shrugged. "Abduction isn't his MO?"

"Worth a look, since it's close to our op area," Karen replied, executing a sharp U-turn.

By the time they turned up, other patrol cars and an ambulance were on scene. Officers and paramedics huddled around a woman wrapped in a red blanket in an open doorstep.

"What do we have?" Karen asked an officer who stood by his car as he provided an update over his radio to the control room.

"Vicky… won't give us her surname. Street worker. Tried to pick up a punter, but she picked up a bad vibe off him so walked away. He came after her, made a grab and tried to pull her into a car."

"Description of her assailant?"

The officer checked his notes. "Tall, about my height and

I'm five feet ten, short, light-coloured hair, clean-shaven, cigarette breath. He wore glasses and a baseball cap."

"Anything on the vehicle he was driving?" Karen asked.

"The victim can't be certain. All she could give us was a white, four-door saloon."

"Who found her?"

The officer nodded towards a woman standing on the pavement. "Angie. A local prostitute. She came running when she heard Vicky screaming."

"Thanks. Can you start knocking on doors to see if anyone heard or saw anything? Also check to see if there are any residential CCTV cameras along here. We may get an image of the car and even a reg."

"Will do," he replied.

Karen thanked the officer before making her way towards the paramedics tending to the victim. Angie stood close by, her arms folded across her chest, a handbag looped through one of her arms, and a look of concern on her face.

Karen flashed a warrant card in Angie's direction. "I understand you found Vicky? Did you see what happened?"

Angie shook her head. "All over by the time I got here. I was only around the corner. Vicky was slumped across that doorway. I got here just as they opened the door. They called for an ambulance straight away."

"Did you see anyone driving away?"

"Nah. I heard tyres screeching. But that was it. Then I heard screams. I thought a girl had been knocked over."

Karen studied the woman for a minute. "Do you know Vicky well?"

Angie shrugged. "Sort of. We keep an eye out for each other around here. It can get rough on the streets. We get spat on by residents, slapped about or robbed by the punters, and the dealers are always chasing some of these girls for money. I don't do drugs myself."

"There's been more attacks on street workers. Have you heard of any other girls being attacked in this way in neighbouring streets?" Karen asked, casting a glance up and down the road.

"A couple. Those murders have made me a bit more wary about getting into cars, but I have to work because I need the money."

"Are you happy to make a statement?"

Angie's eyes widened as she shook her head. "No way. I was just here to help. I'm glad she's gonna be okay. There's no way I'm putting my name on anything," she said, waving a hand. Angie took a few steps back and turned on her heels.

Karen shouted after Angie. "You won't get into trouble for it. It's just to help us with our enquiries. Anything you tell us might help towards finding who did this to her?" But it was no good. Angie was insistent that she had done her good deed for the evening and scurried off.

Jade joined her a few moments later. "It looks like Vicky is going to be okay, though she's had a knock to the head. Paramedics are going to take her to hospital to give her the once-over in case of concussion. She scratched his face, so I've placed evidence bags over her hands and put in a call to forensics to send someone over to the hospital to take nail scrapings."

The description Vicky had given Jade left Karen more certain than ever that a man closely resembling Wells had been in the area. Vicky's lasting impression of him was his square jaw and cold, beady eyes.

The vehicle description given by Vicky didn't help Karen, a white, four-door saloon. With thousands of them on the roads, Karen could hardly put out an alert for patrols to be on the lookout for such a vehicle. They'd be pulling one over every few minutes at that rate. But she hoped that at least one resident had CCTV or a Ring doorbell cam that might have picked up any passing cars.

A search by officers of neighbouring streets had yielded no further sightings, but door-to-door enquiries would continue for the next hour or so. Frustrated and impatient, Karen headed back to the car.

They'd been so close, only to have him slip away.

59

"WELL, that didn't turn out how I'd planned," Karen said, taking a sip of her morning coffee.

She'd met Jade at a local café for breakfast. Between them, they had ordered scrambled eggs on toast, along with black coffees. Karen was already on her third cup and waiting for the caffeine to kick in.

"No, it certainly didn't. Mind you, at least we know we were that close to tracking down a suspect, possibly Wells," Jade replied, bringing her thumb and index finger to within a hair's breadth of each other.

"True. Even with a hundred officers, we still wouldn't have had the resources to cover all the hotspots. He was lucky," Karen replied.

Karen's mind buzzed as she finished her breakfast. She wasn't sure if it was from the caffeine hit, or from the many ideas tumbling through her mind about her next step in both cases.

Today was supposed to have been her day off with Zac, but with an active case, her plans took a back seat. They had decided on a day out to get away from everyone. A walk along the river, a spot of lunch and then a lazy afternoon in bed. Her mind flitted between the sordid thoughts and work. She shook her head in disbelief.

"What?" Jade said, having noticed Karen shaking her head.

Karen smirked. "Nothing. Just a few bits I had planned for my day off today."

"Jade…" came a voice from behind them.

Jade's eyes widened in surprise, her fork hovering just centimetres from her mouth. "Oh, James. Hi," Jade replied, having fallen mute for the first few seconds.

James was dressed the way Jade remembered him. Almost identical in fact, and she wondered if he had much else in his wardrobe. Drainpipe black jeans, white trainers, electric guitar T-shirt, with his trademark floppy brown hair parted in the middle, hanging over his forehead like a set of curtains.

"How are you doing?" Jade asked, unsure of what to say.

"All good, thanks. I've grabbed a latte before shooting off to work," James replied, looking across to Karen and offering her a warm, friendly smile.

Karen looked back as Jade raised a brow.

Jade cleared her throat. "Oh, sorry. Karen, this is James from the outreach charity that I visited. James, this is my boss, Karen… DCI Karen Heath."

James straightened up as if on parade. "Oh… so this is your boss, right. Nice to meet you."

Karen narrowed her eyes in Jade's direction and viewed her with suspicion.

James turned his attention back to Jade. "Did you get my text about meeting for a drink?"

Jade nodded as her cheeks blushed red with embarrassment. "Oh, sorry, I completely forgot to reply. Yes, I mean no, um... We have a case on at the moment, so I didn't want to commit to meeting up and letting you down at the last minute."

"That's fine. But how about the next time you're passing you pop in for coffee? It'll be nice to see you again."

Jade shrunk into her seat, hoping the ground would swallow her up. She didn't want to be having this conversation in front of Karen, knowing the ribbing she'd get the minute James left.

"That sounds great, but only if you have..."

"Jammie Dodgers," he replied, finishing her sentence.

"Yes. That's my only condition."

"Great. Okay, I must dash. Nice meeting you too, Karen."

They both watched James leave before Karen leant on her elbows across the table and stared at Jade. "What did you say to him about me?"

Jade shrugged innocently. "Nothing why?"

"There's no nothing about it, you cheeky mare. What was the 'oh so this is your boss, right' stuff? You been bad-mouthing me?" Karen threw a scrunched-up napkin in Jade's direction.

Jade laughed. "It was all complimentary."

"Yeah, right. I know exactly what you're like."

They sat in silence for a few moments. "I think he has a soft spot for you," Karen teased.

"Shut up. He's just being friendly. We got on well when I popped in for coffee. And it's nice of him to suggest it again."

"Well, it sounds like he's keener than you are," Karen said, finishing the last of her coffee. "Give me enough time to find a decent hat for the wedding," Karen added, rising sharply from her chair to pay the bill before Jade could come back at her.

"Karen!" Jade yelled as she tossed her napkin on to her plate and chased after her.

60

"ENOUGH, KAREN," Jade said in a hushed tone as they entered the station. Karen had wound up Jade for the entire journey, much to Jade's frustration. "There's nothing in it. Drop it for Christ's sake."

Karen threw her a smile. "You're so easy to wind up. I won't say another word," Karen replied, pretending to zip her mouth. "But I reckon he does like you," she added, before marching ahead, leaving Jade speechless in the middle of the corridor.

"He does not!" Jade protested.

"Come on, Jade, live a little. You need a bit of action." Karen teased.

Jade stopped in her tracks and stared at Karen. "Seriously, you need your head examined. How can you say that!?" Jade protested. "I didn't blow him out, did I?"

"True, but I reckon you're not that interested."

"Give me a break, Karen. I've only met him once, and that

was on police business. I have no idea what he'd be like outside of work. We may have completely different interests."

"Well, there's only one way to find out. Don't keep him hanging too long." Karen shrugged.

They strolled through the corridors towards the SCU. Karen smiled as a few officers passed, nodding in her direction. Jade splintered off towards her desk when Karen dipped into her own office.

Karen grabbed her mobile and dialled Nugent.

"Karen," came the reply.

"Tommy. How's tricks with you?"

"All good here, mate. Dealing with an armed robbery on a small post office out of town. So bloody remote that it took officers twenty minutes to get there."

They discussed his case for a few minutes and the challenges of policing in rural areas before returning to the reason for Karen's call.

"Tommy, I think your man is on our patch. There was an attempted abduction and violent assault on a street girl last night."

"You reckon it's him?" Nugent replied.

"I think so. The description is a bit vague, but it does closely match the one given by Denise Carr. We have a name, Adrian Wells. Former lecturer of Japanese Studies at the University of York. I'm going to send over a revised image that officers are working up for me. Your E-fit and his university picture are different, but certain features match. And if you close one eye and roll your head to one side, they look alike." Karen laughed.

"I suspect he's changed his appearance." Nugent replied.

Karen filled Nugent in on her discoveries following her visit to the university.

"Sounds like it could be him based on that. When did he disappear?"

Karen checked her notes. "February 2019. I can't tie him to either of our two victims at the moment as we're short on forensics and CCTV, but his profile, interests and background put him at the top of my hit list."

"That's a month before he could have ended up down here. And seven months before the attack on Denise Carr, and then Raduca's death a few weeks after that," Nugent added. "The timeline fits."

"For sure, and our vic from last night might have grabbed his DNA after scratching his face. SOCO has taken nail scrapings. She's been kept in hospital for a slight concussion after receiving a heavy blow to the head. I'm heading there for a chat with her. I'll also arrange for a composite E-fit to be done with her help and I'll send that over to you too. Can you show them to Denise?"

"Sounds good, Kaz. Let me know how it goes at the hospital?"

"Of course," Karen said, and then offered Nugent a quick goodbye as Kelly appeared in her doorway.

"Ma'am."

"Karen, we need to do a press briefing later this afternoon. I have the press team putting in the calls and making the arrangements. We have two victims, and the attempted abduction last night. I'll need you there as lead SIO. Okay?"

Karen sighed inwardly; she hated them at the best of times. With so many unanswered questions, she expected a less than warm reception from the assembled press. That Kelly was springing this on her at the eleventh hour only added to the ball of anxiety that swirled within her chest.

"Of course, ma'am. I'm heading off to see the victim from last night. I'm hoping she can give us a description we can use in the briefing?"

Kelly offered one of her thin smiles before disappearing.

61

"DON'T you think we should have a small office here?" Jade said as she paid for two coffees from the small booth in the hospital foyer. "We're here often enough."

Karen welcomed the cup offered to her and brought it to her lips, before blowing away the hot steam and taking a tentative sip. "If you love it here that much, you can be based here. I think my office is probably the best I've ever had. I'm not swapping it for anything."

They carried on their idle chit-chat as they snaked their way through the hospital, scanning the signs overhead and looking for the right ward. The silence of the corridor was soon replaced by the tinny sound of trolleys being pushed around in between beds, and nurses discussing individual patients at the nurses' station. The ward was a hive of activity as Karen led the way looking for Vicky.

They found her towards the far end of the ward, propped up in bed, her head tipped back on her pillow.

"Vicky," Karen said as she came alongside, with Jade

walking around to the other side. They both offered her a warm smile.

Vicky lifted her head off the pillow and glanced at the two women. Her eyes were sunken, lifeless pits of misery. She looked tired.

"How are you doing?"

Vicky shrugged. "A bit shaken up. I've got a banging headache. The doctor said it's a mild concussion. With a bit of luck, I might leave tomorrow morning. Maybe even tonight," she said with hope in her voice.

"The man who attacked you last night. Had you seen him before? Perhaps even driving around the area on previous occasions?" Karen asked.

Vicky shook her head. "No. I took him as being another punter."

"The description you gave to our colleagues, if you saw him again, would you recognise him?"

Vicky pondered the question for a moment and pursed her lips in reflection. "Possibly. I didn't see his features properly when he was in the car. It was dark. He also had a baseball cap on and glasses. But he had short, light hair. He wasn't overweight or anything like that. And he had stinking cigarette breath. I remember that bit when he grabbed me and was shouting in my ear."

"You said you picked up a bad vibe, which made you walk away. What was it about him that troubled you?"

Vicky shrugged. "It's hard to say. Gut instinct, maybe. I've been doing this since I was sixteen. I'm thirty-eight now. I'm a mother of three. My kids live with their grandmother.

It's a better life than I could give them. I've had sex with more men than you've had hot dinners. Yeah, gut instinct."

The woman's revelations shocked and saddened Karen. Jade grimaced.

"I really want to get this toerag off the streets. We've taken nail scrapings, so hopefully we'll be able to build up a DNA profile. Can I arrange for an officer to visit? With your help, we'd like to make up an E-fit profile?"

Vicky nodded before she dropped her head back into her pillow and gazed at the ceiling.

Karen was about to say her goodbyes and leave Vicky in peace before she stepped in closer and lowered her voice. "Why do you do this?"

Vicky continued to stare up at the ceiling. "I wish I knew. Growing up, I was a promising athlete. Fastest one hundred metres runner for the under fourteens in the district. By the time I was sixteen it was all over. A friend introduced me to crack cocaine and heroin. She injected me straight away and said I would feel amazing. I had bruises up and down my arms. By the time my mum and dad found out, it was too late. They went ape. I just cried." A tear squeezed from the corner of one eye and rolled down her face.

Karen squeezed the woman's arm. She had heard so many stories like this during her career, but each new one was as heart breaking as the first.

"My mum broke down when she saw me with no clothes on. It was like I'd aged fifty years. I looked like an old woman. Don't get me wrong, my parents tried everything they could to help me. They'd take it in turns to stay with me twenty-four hours a day. I remember my mum holding my hair while I was throwing up. I knew I was ripping their world apart, but I was hooked."

The heart-breaking story continued as Karen and Jade listened in silence. Vicky needed to get her story out, and they were in no hurry to cut her short. They listened as Vicky talked about her three beautiful children and how she couldn't look after them because of the drugs. With a £120 a day habit, she couldn't afford to not sell her body for sex.

"One day my parents took me to hospital because I was so bad. From there I was admitted into a rehab place. A place where I was supposed to be safe but I kept escaping to fix my need and ended up around the wrong people who drugged and abused me. I guess it made prostitution *easier*." Vicky turned and stared at Karen. Her eyes were wet and red as further tears flowed. "I remember breaking down in tears after having sex with my first punter. Another girl took me under her wing. She came with me to my first client. It was awful. She had to get in the back of the car with me because I didn't know what to do. She gave me this gear, which sent me off my head a bit, but it helped me to cope with it."

"I'm sorry the system let you down."

Vicky smiled. A smile of despair. "It's let down so many kids over the years. It's a broken system. Do you know that after my first few clients, I went home and scrubbed myself with bleach? Scrubbed myself so hard that I gave myself a skin infection? That's how disgusting I felt. They watched me cry, but the dirty bastards just kept violating me. To them, I was nothing more than a piece of meat. And you know what's worse? Things haven't changed. We all feel like this. I've been raped, attacked, and robbed while standing in these streets. I'll be back out there as soon as

I'm released. I need the money," she said, holding out her right hand.

Karen thanked her for her time and for sharing her painful story. Before leaving, Karen made a mental note to contact a support group to see if they could help Vicky.

Vicky shrugged and closed her eyes.

62

KAREN FLOPPED into her chair and let out an almighty yawn. It was the first opportunity for her to catch her breath and take stock of where they were in their investigation. Having returned from the hospital, she'd hurried straight into the press briefing, one of the force's press officers updating her along the way. Over twenty journalists and broadcasters from local and national networks had attended, with Karen, Kelly, and the press officer sat behind a desk with the force's press banner in shot behind them.

As expected, Kelly, *the Terminator,* led the show with her request for help from the public. Karen closed her eyes as she recalled Shield bagging himself a seat in the front row, a faint hint of a smirk pinned on his face as his eyes travelled between Karen, Kelly and the press officer. *What is it about him that annoys me so much?* One minute he was nice and cooperative, and the next, throwing words at her that were sharper than barbed wire. He was being ratty and irrational with his behaviour. *Is it down to malice, or does he see me as a threat?* She considered that last thought.

If he was expecting her to roll over and crumble with his veiled threats and intimidation, he'd picked the wrong woman. She was a good copper, and though she'd been a bit more blasé and risqué in her early career and personal life, something had changed in her in recent months. *Maybe it's an age thing? Older and wiser?* She chuckled to herself remembering one of her birthday cards. *"To be old and wise, you must first have to be young and stupid."*

Her eyes drifted off into the distance as her thoughts took her on a whistle-stop tour of everything that had happened. Losing her sister. The truth behind DCI Skelton. Meeting and falling for a man she cared for. A new job away from London.

Maybe my days of being young and stupid are over.

Karen thought about Wells. Her checks had revealed a student population fast approaching twenty thousand, so the opportunity to prey on young female students had proved irresistible. It would also explain why his behaviours hadn't been reported at once. With the dozens of bars and pubs in the city centre, he could have blended in as any other reveller and befriended women without them knowing anything about his background. It was a perfect environment for a sexual predator. Drinks were cheap and plentiful, bar crawls were commonplace, and drugs were freely available.

Other than the link that Sallyanne Faulkner and Wells were both at the University of York, nothing else tied him to the other victims. But the question still niggled in her mind. Why prostitutes? Was it easier to pick them up? Did he have to do less to persuade them to get in his car? Was it too easy to get caught on security cameras if he continued to trawl the bars?

She wasn't sure about Warnock now. Yes, he had a thing for prostitutes, and he wasn't a friendly character, but she doubted whether he could kill. All their searches hadn't revealed swords, a baseball cap, or dark thick-rimmed glasses. Cell site data didn't correlate with movements of Grace Abbott, and Courtney, the deaf and loud-mouthed Scottish prostitute, believed she'd seen Sallyanne being dropped off by Warnock. So unless he'd tracked her down after that, she couldn't forensically link him to the crime scene.

Karen picked up her phone and called Bart Lynch, the CSI manager.

"Bart, any news on the green suede skirt?"

"Hi, Karen. I'm still chasing it. I'll try again. We had to request a different analysis to be done on it because of the time frame involving years."

Karen scrunched up her nose. Again, it was a long shot, but advances in detailed forensic analysis had come a long way in recent years, and even cold cases dating back decades were being re-examined in the light of new technology available to them, and convictions were forthcoming.

Bart continued, "We can find forensically valuable DNA on evidence that's decades old. But several factors can affect the DNA left at a crime scene or on items recovered, including environmental factors such as heat, sunlight, moisture, bacteria and mould." He sighed. "Not all DNA evidence would offer a usable DNA profile."

"Are you laying the groundwork to let me down gently?" Karen sighed.

Bart laughed. "Not at all, Karen. There's plenty of research showing that even two seconds of contact with clothing can leave enough DNA for scientists to obtain a person's full profile."

"Seriously?"

"Yep. It's really helpful where the perp left no other sources of DNA like blood or semen behind. But they'll check that in full anyway. Stay positive!"

Karen rubbed her eyes and stifled another yawn. "I am. I have faith in you. I know it's a long shot, but I need a breakthrough."

"Leave it with me. I'll bell you as soon as I know anything."

Karen thanked him before hanging up and checked the time on her phone. She'd had enough today and decided it was time to knock off early and head to Zac's for dinner.

63

A WARMTH BATHED her face as Zac greeted her at the front door with a smile and a hug. He took her jacket and embraced her again in the hallway.

She kissed him deeply and ran her hands up and down his back.

Zac pulled away and smiled. "Hold on, tiger. Summer is in the kitchen. We don't want to embarrass her."

"I heard that, Dad!" Summer shouted.

Karen pinched his waist before heading into the kitchen. "Hi, Summer. You okay?" she asked, heading over to where Summer was standing to give her a hug. She peered over the girl's shoulder to see an array of salad finely chopped and thrown on to a plate. "Good start. Presentation needs more effort," she teased.

"Yeah, Dad roped me into helping him," she moaned.

"Well, it doesn't harm for you to learn new skills in the

kitchen. When I'm old and grey, you'll be cooking my meals."

Summer looked at her dad and pulled a face. "You'll be in a home. They'll cook for you."

Karen burst out laughing as shock creased Zac's face. He flapped his hands.

"I spent all these years bringing you up, and this is how you repay me? Sticking me in an old folks' home? Charming!" Zac said, shaking his head in mock sadness.

Karen rushed over to him and mopped his brow in jest. "You poor thing. Don't worry. I'll look after you. I'll make sure I visit you in the care home once a week…"

Summer cheered and laughed along with Karen as Zac stomped off towards the fridge to grab a bottle of wine.

"That's it. I'm going to drown my sorrows."

For a moment Karen felt overwhelmed, pushing away the moisture in her eyes. She wasn't sad. It was this. Whatever *this* was. Shaking her head in consternation, she accepted a glass of wine from Zac. For the first time in her life, she felt part of a unit, a family unit. Was it weird? It should have been. But it didn't feel that way.

"What's for dinner then?" she asked.

"Something cheap and simple. Barbecued spare ribs from a packet and sweet potato fries," Zac replied, rushing towards the oven to make sure nothing was burning.

"Don't forget my salad!" Summer shouted.

"How could we?" Karen and Zac replied in unison. They

shot each other a smile before a soothing and warm silence settled in the room.

As the evening went on, the warmth and humour continued as they tucked into their food. Karen commented that the salad was a perfect palette cleanser for the sticky, sweet barbecue ribs. Time ran away with them, and it was a few hours before they rose from the table to clear up.

A ring at the front door interrupted family time. Zac threw the tea towel over one shoulder as he went to answer the door. The hushed conversation in the hallway filtered through to where Karen and Summer were loading the dishwasher.

Karen froze when she recognised the voice. She hadn't had a moment to prepare herself before the whirlwind that was Zac's ex breezed through and into the kitchen.

Michelle and Karen locked eyes for a brief second before Michelle averted her gaze and headed straight towards Summer.

"There you are my gorgeous!" Michelle bellowed, thrusting her arms forward and pulling Summer into a tight embrace. She planted a big kiss on her daughter's forehead before hugging her again. Michelle glanced in Karen's direction, her face taut, smile now a sharp frown. "Here again!"

"Michelle," Karen replied, choosing not to rise to the bait.

Zac followed Michelle in and crossed his arms. "Make this quick. We're having a quiet night in."

Michelle raised a brow at Zac. "How cosy. Where was my invite?"

Zac remained stone-faced, holding his ground.

Michelle sighed, reached into her handbag and pulled out a form. "One of the savings plans we set up for Summer has reached maturity. I want to withdraw the money, but the form needs both of our signatures. If you can sign it, I'll be on my way. I don't want to stand here any longer than I need to," she said, casting a glance in Karen's direction.

Zac furrowed his brow as confusion spread across his face. "You want to withdraw the money? Why?"

Michelle shrugged. "Summer doesn't need it at the moment. It's four grand. She has another bonds that will mature later. They'll be of more value to her then. I thought I would use this money to get my bathroom remodelled. Summer would benefit from it anyway."

Zac ran a hand through his hair in disbelief. "Are you for real? This is money that we are saving for Summer, and you want to blow it on a new bathroom?"

Michelle glared at Zac, her facial features twitching. "Don't be an idiot all your life, Zac. I'll set up another bond in a year or two and put the money back in there. I'm not a thief. This is no different to me having four grand in my bank account and paying for the bathroom refit."

"Well, when you have four grand in your bank account, you *can* pay for it. I'm not signing. This is Summer's money for her future. We agreed to that from the beginning. For her university, car, or her own place. Not yours!"

"You can be such a fucking idiot sometimes. I don't know what I saw in you," Michelle spat.

Karen was about to intervene when Summer stepped forward.

"Enough. Please stop fighting. Please." Summer looked to her parents, tears welling in her eyes. "If you want the money, then Dad can sign it. I've had enough. If this is how you want to be, Mum, then don't expect me to come round as much. If it's not your drinking that puts you in a foul mood, then it's your fighting with Dad. The only sensible person here is Karen!" she shouted, casting a glance in Karen's direction.

Karen's eyes widened as her cheeks reddened.

Michelle stood open-mouthed, stunned at her daughter's outburst. Her eyes darted between Summer and Karen before she drew her lips into a thin line and nodded, glaring in Karen's direction.

"Just leave," Zac said, his voice soft and dejected.

Michelle let out an angry sigh before storming from the kitchen, the front door slamming behind.

The three of them stood for a few moments staring at one another, no one knowing what to say.

Zac stepped forward and beckoned to Karen and Summer to join him as he placed his arms around both of their shoulders and pulled them into a tight hug. The three of them embraced for what felt like ages. Just the occasional sniff from Summer breaking the silence.

"We are okay. We're more than okay," he whispered. "I'm sorry, Summer. I'm sorry you got caught up in that. You shouldn't be forced to choose between any of us. I'll talk to Mum, and I promise I won't shout. How about we have dessert and the three of us can curl up on the sofa and watch a movie?"

Summer didn't reply but nodded into Zac's chest.

"Sounds like a great idea," Karen replied as she stared into Zac's eyes feeling a sense of pride that he'd stood up to Michelle, but also a deep sadness for both Zac and Summer.

64

THE SOUND of Karen's phone vibrating on the bedside table woke her from a deep sleep. She opened and closed her eyes a few times, rubbed the sleep from them, and cleared her throat. Too much wine last night had left her brain feeling hazy and sluggish. She glanced across to see Zac fast asleep.

She reached for her phone, silently praying it wasn't another dead body.

"Tyler, what's up?"

"We had a call from a local college towards the west of the city. They didn't catch the televised version of our press briefing but saw it online this morning. The principal of Pendleton Cross FE College recognised the description and pictures released during the briefing. Adrian Wells is one of their tutors, but he goes under the name of Chris Dobbs."

Karen bolted upright, her sudden movements jerking Zac from his sleep as he too sat upright. Karen placed a finger on her lips while she listened.

"Can they be sure it's definitely him?"

"Pretty much. The E-fit release alarmed the principal enough for him to call. If you check your emails, you'll see that one came in last night from the facial imaging officer regarding your request. He stripped out the beard from Wells's university photograph and replaced the dark hair and ponytail with short, highlighted hair. The resemblance is uncanny, especially when you compare it with Vicky's version from the hospital."

Karen kept Tyler on the line while she dipped back into her phone and searched for the email. She opened the image and gasped. "No way," was all she could offer. The imaging officer had carried out facial mapping. The shape and size of his face carried a close correlation between all the different sources. Each feature like Wells's nose, ears, eyes, and jawbone had been cross-mapped and highlighted. The imaging officer believed that there was at least an eighty-seven per cent chance that it was the same individual in the E-fits provided by Nugent and Vicky, and the university photograph.

"Shit," she said, jumping out of bed.

"Yep."

Karen raced around the room, gathering up her clothes. With one hand on the phone, she tugged on her trousers as she wiggled them up her thighs. She glanced across at Zac as he buried his head under the duvet.

"Send me the address and the principal's name. Tell them I'll be there in half an hour. Are they expecting Wells in today even though it's a Saturday?" she asked.

"No. The principal, Barry Cruickshank, had come in to catch up on paperwork ahead of their summer exams."

"Right, tell Mr Cruickshank to not go into Wells's office. Are any other members of staff due in today?"

"I don't know, Karen. I didn't ask."

"Well, get back on the phone to him. If anyone else turns up, then no one is to go into Wells's office."

"Understood."

"And if for any reason Wells turns up before I get there, tell Mr Cruickshank to leave the building and to wait for me outside."

"Do you want me to meet you there?" Tyler asked.

Karen thought about it for a minute. Even though Wells wasn't expected in today, having an extra officer with her for backup and safety wouldn't be a bad call. "Yes, meet me outside in thirty minutes."

Karen hung up and rushed into the bathroom to brush her teeth and wash her face before returning to the bedroom. Zac hadn't moved much other than to pop his head above the duvet to offer her a small smile.

"Sounds like good news then?"

"It's great news. I think we may be closing in on him. He is a slippery bastard." Karen said as she scrambled across the bed towards Zac. She kissed him and felt her skin tingle as his hands reached for her waist. "God, I fancy you so much. You're too much of a bloody distraction."

"Hey, I'd be doing my hardest to pull you back into bed,

but I know this is important to you. Go on. You shoot off and let me know how you get on later."

Karen kissed him again. "I'm sorry. I promise I'll make it up to you."

Zac groaned and slid down beneath the duvet. "That's what I'm hoping for. Now bugger off and let me get some sleep."

65

As she made her journey across town, Karen's mind teemed with thoughts. After what felt like an eternity of chasing their tails, Kelly's gamble on an extensive press briefing had paid off. The drive gave her the opportunity to check in with the rest of the team. Officers had taken a steady stream of phone calls from members of the public and additional press outlets who had shown an interest in the case, and the unusual nature of the attacks.

All of it was good in Karen's opinion. The more eyes they had out there looking for their suspect, the easier it made her job. She hoped with a bit of luck that it would cause the killer to make a mistake which would lead to his downfall. In previous homicide cases that she had dealt with, killers often slipped up not long after a press release as pressure mounted. Friends, neighbours, and even members of the public were quick to report sightings or the whereabouts of suspects as soon as the information came into the public domain.

This could be it! Karen thought as waves of excitement rippled through her body, and nerves tensed her muscles.

The college loomed into view ahead of her. She spotted Tyler leaning against his car, his hands stuffed in his trouser pockets.

Having pulled up a few cars behind Tyler, she covered the remaining distance on foot and stopped beside him. "Anything to report?"

"Nothing. Quiet as a church mouse. I looked at their website and the pictures of their teaching staff. This is Chris Dobbs." Tyler turned his phone screen towards Karen.

"That's him." Karen nodded. "Let's go."

They swung through the revolving doors to be met by a man in an open-necked shirt, brown tweed jacket, and dark blue jeans. He pushed his glasses up his nose, and hurried towards them, hand extended.

"Barry Cruickshank, principal of Pendleton FE College," he offered, his voice jittery and nervous.

Karen shook his hand and introduced herself and Tyler. She noticed Barry's sweaty palm. *Nerves.* The second thing was how terrified the man looked. Fixed eyes, restless hands, and a heaving chest.

"This is very worrying," he began. "I couldn't believe it when I read the online news. The photofit, mugshot, or whatever you call it bore a striking resemblance to Chris. But then when the article mentioned the police were keen to speak to him... Well, that sent shivers through me."

"What can you tell us about him?" Karen asked.

Cruickshank shrugged one shoulder. "He's been with us since September 2020. Quiet and keeps himself to himself. He gets on fine with the other lecturers, but he's not one to attend many of our social gatherings."

"What does he teach?"

"English."

Interesting. "Any cause for concern about his interaction with students?"

Cruickshank furrowed a brow. "I'm not sure what you mean. Do you mean favouritism? Or how strict he is?"

"Have there been any complaints about him?"

"No, detective chief inspector. He is well-liked among the student population."

"Any reports of inappropriate behaviour towards female students?"

"Oh, my Lord!" Cruickshank threw his hand over his mouth as his eyes widened. "You don't think…?"

Karen cut him off before speculation sent him into overdrive. She asked to be shown to Wells's office.

Cruickshank hurried along the corridor and up a flight of stairs before marching along the full length of the first floor, arriving at one of the last few offices before the door to the fire escape. A plaque on the door confirmed that Chris Dobbs occupied the room.

"Mr Cruickshank, do you mind waiting outside?" Karen asked as her and Tyler snapped on a pair of latex gloves.

Cruickshank nodded and unlocked the door before taking a few steps back, folding his arms across his chest.

Karen and Tyler stepped in and closed the door behind them.

"The poor bloke is very concerned," Tyler whispered.

Karen nodded as she cast her gaze round the room. Pokey, cluttered, untidy. A large bundle of papers teetered on the edge of the desk. Rows of books sat on a bookshelf on one wall. Karen took a quick glance. English related topics. There were also teaching manuals and folders of past exam papers.

Above the desk was a calendar, a lecture timetable, and a list of contact numbers of other staff members.

"His teaching certificates look legit," Tyler observed as he glanced at the wall behind the door. Several framed certificates hung in a row.

Karen opened each of the drawers beneath the desk and rummaged through the contents. Stationery, notepads, cereal bars. Nothing that set alarm bells ringing.

Karen grabbed an evidence bag from Tyler and placed a few pens she'd retrieved from a penholder on the desk. A used mug with dried tea stains at the bottom was added to another bag before Karen leant towards the chair and picked off a few hair fibres.

"I can't find anything else incriminating," Tyler reported as he searched a metal filing cabinet beside the desk. He pulled it forward and double-checked the space behind.

Satisfied they had recovered everything they needed, Karen and Tyler stepped out into the corridor where they were met by a nervous Cruickshank pacing up and down.

"When was Chris Dobbs last here?" Karen asked.

"Yesterday morning. He had two lectures back-to-back. He would have been free after lunch."

"Okay. One more thing, Mr Cruickshank. We'll need his address and any other contact details that you have for him."

Cruickshank escorted them to his office where he pulled off all the details he had on Chris Dobbs.

"Thank you, Mr Cruickshank. You've been very helpful. We'll be in touch if we need anything further," Karen said as they walked back towards the main entrance. Just as she was about to leave the building, she stopped and turned towards the principal. "Out of interest, did you do thorough checks on his background? References? All that kind of stuff?"

Cruickshank nodded. "Of course. We took up references which came back good. DBS cleared. Excellent presentation skills."

Karen thanked him again as she left.

66

WITHIN MINUTES of arriving back at the station, Karen dropped off the items seized from Wells's office with the forensic team. She stressed the urgency in fast-tracking the items as a priority. Before leaving forensics, Karen told the officer to contact her if she hit any obstacles. She prayed Shield wouldn't get in the way and hold her up. The last thing she wanted was another fall out with the man.

Grabbing her phone from her bag, she dialled Nugent's number. Everything was moving so quickly now; she only had a few minutes to spare before gathering the team together to visit Dobbs's address.

"Tommy, it's me."

"Your parents didn't like you then? That's a shit name. Might as well have gone the whole hog and called you Meh!" He laughed at his own joke.

"Haha, hilarious… not! Lucky you're not here now or I'd be stapling your dumbo cars to the nearest corkboard."

"Oooh. Getting personal now? Well, I've seen a better-looking face on a crash test dummy." Nugent fired back.

Karen loved the banter. After all these years, they still had the connection that had bonded them as mates in Hendon.

"Kaz, I'm happy to hear from you for another reason. I have good news. Denise Carr positively ID'd your E-fits. We're looking for the same person."

Karen nodded. Though she'd been expecting the news, it was good to have it confirmed. "Great. I have good news too. Adrian Wells is a primary suspect. He's living and working in York under a false name of Chris Dobbs, a college lecturer in English."

"Hold on. How did he pick up another teaching job? If they had taken up references with the University of York, they would have found out that he'd left under a cloud of allegations."

"I don't know. I imagine he's falsified his documents. But I'm not worried about that at the moment. We have an address for him and I'm heading there now. I'll give you an update once I know more." Karen hung up and dashed off to the main floor.

"Okay, team. Gather round." Karen scanned the faces to see who was present. "Where is Ed?" she asked.

"I sent him to forensics to get an update for us," Jade replied.

"I've just been there and didn't see him." Karen turned towards Belinda. "Bel, can you and Preet go to this address right away? Observe from a distance. Let me know if you spot any movement. We believe that Adrian Wells lives at this address. I don't want to scare him off. I'll be there not long after you."

Belinda nodded and grabbed her jacket before shooting through the doors, Preet hot on her heels.

Karen turned and faced the rest of the team before giving them an account of their visit to Pendleton College. She jabbed Wells's picture on the incident board. "He's our number one suspect. Jade and I will visit the address. Where are we with any updates?"

"Vicky discharged herself from hospital first thing this morning," Jade began, rolling her eyes.

Karen wasn't surprised. It was clear from her conversation that Vicky needed to earn money. "Anything on the streets last night?"

A sea of shaking heads came back at her. That had to be a blessing as far as Karen was concerned.

Another officer chipped in. "We have a partial index on the white saloon used in the attempted abduction of Vicky. It was caught on a ring doorbell cam. Just a few seconds mind you." The officer shrugged and checked his notes. "Starts with P and ends with D. It might be PE, but that's all we could see."

Karen added those details to the incident board. "Not great, but it's a start. Run that through the DVLA and cross-reference for any that are registered in York. It's a long shot, but you never know. I'd also contact second-hand car dealers in York. Find out if they've sold any white saloons with that partial plate in recent weeks."

Ed burst through the doors, causing everyone to crane their necks in his direction. He waved a sheet of paper as he darted in between the desks towards the team. "I think we've had a breakthrough!" He dropped into a seat and scanned the information. "Forensics have received the results back on the green suede skirt that you prioritised for analysis. They found a strand of human hair that wasn't Sallyanne's. There's no DNA profile match on a database. But they also found semen stains from which they could extract a partial DNA profile. Again, there was no match on the database."

"That's fine. We have lots of cross-referencing to do." Karen interrupted. "I believe the skirt contains vital evidence on it. Esme, Sallyanne's sister, confirmed that Sallyanne wore it all the time. Following the incident in her final year, she never saw her wear it again. I find that odd, and my copper nose tells me to look at it a bit closer."

Ed continued. "Forensics also confirmed that a print recovered from Sallyanne's lipstick matches one of the partial prints discovered on her pendant."

Karen slowly paced up and down in front of her team, occasionally glancing at the whiteboards, deep in thought. "While some of us visit the address, I want the rest of you to build up a profile of Adrian Wells aka Chris Dobbs. I want to know everything about him, right down to shoe size. We need phone records, banking details, medical records. Out of interest, find out if he's got any connections with Warnock. I doubt it, but for completeness let's play safe."

———

KAREN AND JADE arrived at the address given by Cruickshank. A small semi in Skelton, on the north-west fringes of the city. Belinda and Preet left their car to meet Karen at the front gate of the address.

"Anything?" Karen asked, taking a step back to look up towards the first-floor windows, before pushing through the gate and peering in through the front window. The lounge appeared functional. Two sofas, TV, a coffee table, and a couple of prints on the wall. With it being a semi-detached address, Karen noticed a path that led along the side of the property. She instructed Belinda and Preet to have a nose down there while she knocked on the front door. When no one answered, she knocked again, forcefully this time. "Anything?" Karen asked, looking in Jade's direction.

Jade peered in through the lounge window, looking for any signs of movement. She shook her head. "Do you think he's still here? He could be staying somewhere else? It might be a rental property with new tenants?"

Karen reached for her phone and called control. While they checked for ownership of this property, Karen also asked them to search for drivers' details linked to either Adrian Wells or Chris Dobbs at this address. It took a few minutes for them to get back to her, but officers back in control couldn't find any driving licence details linked to the address. In fact, they said that there were no driving licences in the name of Chris Dobbs within York, but there were for Adrian Wells. Karen asked control to send a unit to the address given for Adrian Wells but advised them to approach with caution and with backup from a firearms unit.

The development only confused Karen further. Wells had probably used false documents to secure employment in York, so he must've had some form of identification to buy or rent a property. Further searches back at control confirmed that the property was rented to Geoff Mead and there was nothing on the PNC in that name. Whether or not it was a coincidence, the first name corresponded with the alias used in Dorset. Karen wasn't comfortable with that information and requested that further searches were carried out on everything to do with Geoff Mead, including any other properties or vehicles in that name.

67

HE THOUGHT he'd been clever using multiple disguises, aliases, and changes in his appearance to throw the police off his scent. It had brought him time and space to continue his path of punishing women, but the events of last night and what he'd seen on TV had set alarm bells ringing. The clever police had managed to join the dots together. He should have known that the technology available to police could have manipulated his photographs to reveal his identity.

With the help of some hair dye, he'd changed his appearance again overnight. His hair was now jet black, and he hadn't shaved this morning, which left him with a five o'clock shadow.

He gripped the steering wheel and gritted his teeth in frustration. It wouldn't be long until they managed to piece it all together. But he wanted one more victim. *Needed* one more victim. He'd already put plans in place to leave the country next week. A B&B booked for a few days close to Manchester airport. A one-way ticket to Japan with an overnight stop off in Istanbul. With his credentials, back-ground, and experience, he could pick up a teaching post and start again. His friends in Turkey could knock up another set of false documents for him.

With the walls closing in, there was an urgency in his efforts. He hated being out at this time of the day. What were the chances of picking up the right kind of woman at lunchtime on Saturday? Families with children would be out, streets would be busy, and working girls would be in short supply.

Not good.

The location he'd chosen for his next kill wouldn't work because of the time of day and the risk of being seen. He needed a change of plan.

He'd already trawled two areas without success. A couple of girls hung around, but not the kind he needed.

A further hour passed as his anxiety levels grew. He wanted to work under the cloak of darkness. He felt so exposed in broad daylight. Frustration gnawed away at him. Perhaps he was better off trying again tonight. "Yes. That's what I'll do," he whispered. He turned his car around and followed the road out of town.

After only a few minutes into the journey, he spotted a soli-tary female leaning up against the side of a house at a set of crossroads. She piqued his interest. Asian. Attractive. Big hoop earrings, nose piercing, long black flowing hair. A white vest top revealed a few tattoos down the length of her right arm. He slowed and studied her for a few moments.

It surprised him that no one had picked her up. From where

he hovered, she had a great figure, looked good, and dressed provocatively, showing off her shapely brown legs.

He waited for the traffic to die down before he moved off in her direction, slowing as he reached the woman. With his window down, he flashed her a smile.

She chewed her gum and stood rooted to the spot. "You want business, gorgeous?"

"Definitely. I like what I see."

She pushed herself off the wall and walked towards him. "What are you looking for?"

"It depends what you offer," he replied.

She tossed back a slight smile. "Everything. Everything for a price."

"How much for full sex?"

"Thirty quid."

"Sounds good. Get in," he replied, glancing up and down the street from beneath the rim of his baseball cap.

The woman didn't need asking twice as she came around towards the passenger door, opened it and slid in, before closing it behind her. "There's a place two streets away. It will be quiet at this time of the day. I'll show you the way."

He studied her for a moment. She was even more good-looking close up. She had a natural beauty. *What a waste*, he thought.

"I'd prefer to go somewhere quieter. I'm happy to pay more. I want to take my time and have some proper fun."

"I haven't got time for that, luv. I'm here to make quick money. You've got ten minutes, and that's it."

He gritted his teeth as the muscles in his jaws flexed. "I make the rules. Not you," he muttered.

The woman glanced at him. "Sorry? What are you on about? You either want business or not? I don't need time-wasters like you. You bloody weirdo," she shouted, reaching for the door handle.

Just as she went to push the door, he curled his hand into a fist and launched it towards her face. The first impact struck her right temple, forcing her head towards the side window. The double impact made her scream as she clutched her forehead. Several blows followed in succession, each one pulverising her face. With blood streaming from a split lip, she screamed again, grabbing for the door handle, desperate to get away. But the blows kept coming until he beat her into submission.

He glanced up and down the street, his heart pounding in his chest, his mouth bone dry. *It's not supposed to go like this!* He glanced across at her. She'd sunken into her seat. Unconscious. Blood streaming from her mouth. Right cheekbone swollen and bruised.

"Stupid bitch. Stupid, stupid bitch!" he hissed, before accelerating away.

68

KAREN WAS MAKING her way back to the station when the call came in. A concerned resident had witnessed what appeared to be the violent abduction of an Asian female on a quiet residential street. With Belinda following in her pool car, they raced towards the location as further details filtered through.

By the time Karen arrived, several police cars were already on the scene. Residents milled about on the pavements outside their houses, a few having hushed conversations while they pointed and gesticulated at the police presence.

Having left the car, Karen made her way to the nearest police officer. "What do we have?"

"Ma'am, a resident was putting out her rubbish. She saw an Asian female loitering further up the street. A white car approached and stopped by the female. They talked for a brief moment before the female got in. There appeared to follow an argument between them before the driver attacked the female and drove off."

"Do we have a description of the female?"

"Yes, ma'am. Asian. Twenty to thirty years old. Long black hair. White vest top, short black skirt, knee-length black boots."

"And the car?"

"We've spoken to a few residents up and down the street. A white car. Small. Saloon. Partial plate, PE1. That's it."

Karen sighed. "Not much to go on then but that's looking like the car used in a prior attempted abduction."

"Agreed, ma'am. But having spoken to the resident who called it in, and several other residents in the street, the Asian female may have been a street worker who frequented that corner for the last few weeks."

"Description of the driver?"

The officer glanced at his notepad. "White male, baseball cap. That's it. The resident only caught a fleeting glance as the car sped away."

Karen's immediate risk analysis indicated a threat to life, which meant that all resources would be called upon to find the occupants of the car.

Jade joined Karen a few minutes later. "I've been talking to Irene, the lady who called it in. She's pretty upset. Bel is making her a cuppa. Irene didn't approve of the girl standing on the corner all the time, but she was no harm to anyone."

"Jade, get on to control. Get them to check all available street CCTV that is run by the council. Give them the partial plate. We are on the lookout for this white, small car with two occupants, one white male and one Asian female.

Let's see if we can locate a general direction it headed off in."

"On it now," Jade replied, stepping away and talking into her radio.

Karen turned towards the officer she had been speaking to. "Any CCTV down this road?"

"Not much, ma'am. We've started doing the checks. There are a few Ring doorbells. We might have picked up movement? There is one house about a hundred yards down the road which has CCTV. John... PC John Travers is checking now."

Karen nodded her approval. She glanced up and down the street, deep in reflection. *This isn't his MO. He targets women at night. Why broad daylight? Was it even him? Could it have been a violent argument with her pimp or boyfriend instead?*

Karen wandered up and down the street getting her bearings. Concerned residents stopped her every few yards. This was turning into a PR exercise for her as she did whatever she could to calm their nerves and concerns. With Preet taking witness statements, council CCTV footage being scanned, and officers making door-to-door enquiries, they were doing everything they could.

Torn from her thoughts yet again, Karen's radio crackled into life with reports of a minor collision between a white Toyota and a blue Peugeot 308 north of the city. It wasn't the collision that bothered Karen. RTAs happened all the time. But the scene following it had Karen and Jade racing back towards the car.

69

KAREN SPED north out of the city, her fingers tingling with excitement as adrenaline coursed through her. Though she couldn't be certain that this was her man, and it wasn't fitting Wells's MO, it was possible that he'd mixed up his routine through boredom or to confuse the police. Jade sat with her radio close to her ear while she listened for further updates.

After reports of a minor collision between two vehicles, they'd been notified the white Toyota didn't stop as required by law, leaving the lady owner of the blue Peugeot 308 both dazed and confused. The statement from the Peugeot driver set alarm bells ringing for Karen. The driver of the white Toyota was a white male wearing a baseball cap. His occupant appeared to be a female with her head lowered.

"Get out of the way," Karen hissed. Despite her unmarked pool car fitted with sirens and blue flashing lights, the traffic was slow to part for her as she weaved among the vehicles. "Why do drivers freeze when we approach? Surely when you hear a siren, the first thing you do is check your surroundings and see where you could manoeuvre to create space?" It was logical in her mind. But when caught unawares, logic seemed to go out of the window.

"Take your next left," Jade said, checking the directions on her phone.

Karen screeched round the corner, narrowly missing an oblivious pedestrian wearing earbuds in both ears.

"Idiot."

Jade gripped the overhead grab handle. She swayed from left to right. "This is why I drive, and you don't. Thank God I've not eaten."

"Oh, shut up. You're just as bad."

"Don't get all defensive on me, Karen. Everyone back in London moaned about your driving."

Karen shot her a glance in disbelief. "No, they didn't!"

Jade laughed. "Of course they did. They discussed it in dark corners with hushed tones and said it behind your back to not offend you."

Karen shook her head in disbelief and swore as she slowed. Stationary traffic ahead signalled the aftermath of the accident. Karen scooted to the right, travelling along the opposite side of the road until she spotted the flashing lights of a patrol car and an ambulance.

"Is the situation under control?" Karen asked through her open window, holding up her ID.

An officer diverting traffic towards a neighbouring street nodded as he took a quick glance at Karen's credentials. "Yes, ma'am. There's nothing more we can do here. I've put in a call for a recovery truck."

"The driver?" Karen asked, flicking her head towards the ambulance.

"I think she's going to be okay. Paramedics are giving her the once-over. Shocked more than anything. Potential signs of slight whiplash."

"Any other information on the white Toyota?"

The officer pointed in the direction ahead of them. "Last seen speeding off in that direction. It happened so quickly that it's all a blur to the other driver." The officer explained that the lady of the Peugeot was turning right when the Toyota struck her front nearside, which sent her car into a one-hundred-and-eighty-degree spin.

As the officer updated Karen, further information came over the airway. A white Toyota with front impact damage was reported driving erratically, last seen heading north on Wigginton Road.

"Received," Jade replied. "That's him."

Karen thanked the officer before she drove away from the scene. "Get units to the area and put in a request for NPAS. We have a high-risk situation with a threat to life," Karen barked as she put her foot down and raced towards Wigginton.

They continued to receive a running commentary as the driver performed reckless manoeuvres to pass slow-moving vehicles in the face of oncoming traffic. A secondary report came in of another vehicle leaving the road and crashing after swerving to avoid a vehicle driving on the wrong side of the road.

"He's going to bloody kill someone at this rate!" Jade shouted over the roar of Karen's engine.

Karen didn't reply as she stared ahead. The tight B road had opened up with low hedgerows and open fields replacing residential streets. Further slowing vehicles ahead of her impeded her journey. She passed the cause of it, a vehicle with its nose tipped down into a ditch, a local traffic unit in attendance. Further police vehicles had joined the pursuit. Karen spotted one behind her, and a further two units, several hundred yards ahead of her which provided a running commentary. The Toyota was last reported speeding through Sutton-on-the-Forest before officers lost sight of it.

Karen blew out her cheeks as she finally caught up with them a few minutes later. Two patrol cars had slowed while waiting for further sightings.

"There isn't an available NPAS unit," one officer replied as he stepped from his vehicle and came over to Karen's door. "We have a unit positioned at Easingwold and another at Brandsby in case the vehicle is spotted further out."

Karen tapped her fingers on the steering wheel while she thought this through. He couldn't be far away. There weren't many places to hide out here. Flat, open agricultural land stretched to the horizon. "I don't know this area as well as you. Is there anywhere else he could go which would allow him to slip past us unnoticed?"

"Take your pick. There are so many little B roads that

branch off. We have the main road into Easingwold covered. If he was hoping to hide out in some of the residential streets, we should be able to spot him before he gets a chance." The officer looked round and grimaced as he weighed up the options. "There are a couple of tiny little hamlets and villages between our position and Easingwold. It's a big area to cover on the ground. We could have done with a pair of eyes in the sky."

Karen shrugged. "Yeah, well we don't have that luxury today."

Karen didn't see the point in turning back towards the city, so parked up with the other officers, waiting for further updates.

"How long do you want to stay here?" Jade asked, checking the time on her phone. They'd been there for nearly fifteen minutes, and no further sightings had been reported. "He might have gone to ground?"

"I hope not. We were this close to catching him," Karen said, holding her forefinger and thumb just millimetres apart. "This close."

Just as Karen was about to accept defeat, a new report came in. Returning from a walk to a local beauty spot, a driver reported being attacked and dragged from his vehicle before it was stolen. He was thrown to the ground, sustaining bruising on his back and arm. The attacker dragged a female from a white car to the victim's vehicle and made off. A white Toyota Avensis had been left behind at the scene. Registration PE13 LLD.

This was reckless and dangerous in Karen's eyes, and she needed more boots on the ground. She instructed Jade to put in a request for extra resources as she started the car. The grey Mazda 3 was last seen travelling south on the A19. She needed an alert set up on every roadside camera and ANPR camera between her position and the city centre.

"He's mine!" Karen said as she sped off.

70

HE HAD BEEN an idiot this time. Too hasty. He hadn't thought it through or put a plan B in place. This wasn't the way it should have been. As he pulled up towards the rear of his property, he paused for a second, a flashback from his childhood puncturing his thoughts. Every time he'd got something wrong, his dad would always cite one of the many Japanese proverbs that flowed so eloquently off his tongue.

Even a fool has at least one talent.

His dad had said that frequently. If he'd uttered those words to inspire him, it had made him feel worse. He tried so hard to emulate his dad. To be worldly. Wise. Knowledgeable. But as hard as he tried, he could never hold on to the amount of information and knowledge that his dad knew about the Japanese way of life. His early life at home had such strong Japanese influences. His father listened to Japanese music. Immersed himself in their traditions and ancient ways. Many of their meals came from a Japanese cookbook. Most of his father's books and magazines centred on Japanese topics.

His father's first wife was Japanese. When he'd got bored with her, he'd sent her packing. A one-way ticket back to Japan. His father's second wife, his mother, had lasted longer. Obedient, quiet, house-proud and caring. But with their marriage void of any emotion and his father too wrapped up in his own world, her life had ebbed away as cancer had ravaged her body. It was just him and his dad until he too had succumbed to ill health.

Now it was just him.

To continue and persevere is power.

Another saying that his father had drummed into him. But those words held meaning as he stepped from the car and came around to the passenger seat. He checked to make sure that no one was peering through the back windows of the neighbouring houses. Grabbing hold of the woman, he pulled her from the car and dragged her through the garden gate towards the rear of his property. Her feet scraped along the ground, her black boots dirty and scuffed. Her limp body was heavier than he imagined as he hauled her through the kitchen and towards the hallway before opening the door beneath the stairs and dragging her into the basement.

Sweat beaded on his forehead. His heart pounded in his chest as he gasped for breath. He stood in the darkened space, allowing the sound from his inhalations to subside until silence returned. Composing himself, he switched on the light and placed a wooden chair in the centre of the room beside a small table. He spent a few moments positioning everything how we wanted it to be before he lifted the woman and placed her in the chair, securing her body to the frame with cable ties.

As he slapped her around the face a few times to awaken her, she groaned as a stinging pain penetrated the deepest parts of her mind. Her eyes flickered before closing again.

"Wake up." He grabbed her cheeks between his fingers and shook her face. The effect was almost immediate as her eyes opened and adjusted to the gloom.

"Good. You had me worried in the car. I thought I'd killed you. That would have been a pity."

Her eyes widened as she groaned again. She winced opening her mouth, the scab on her split lip parting to reveal a fresh trickle of blood. Her breath caught in her throat as she tried to free herself. She tossed her head from side to side, taking in the surrounding space. Her chest heaved as she fought for breath.

He smiled at her before bending down and picking up a large object hidden beneath the red cloth which he'd placed on the table. She glared at it, scared of what it might be. He pulled the cloth away to reveal a large oblong piece of wood with a smooth groove carved out in the middle, a few inches wide. He turned to face away from her, taking a few strides to the wall.

The woman flinched in her chair and craned her neck to follow him with her gaze. She gasped. "No. No," she mouthed.

He stared up at his collection of silver gleaming blades, the light bouncing off them. Perfectly polished, precision engineered, and sharp enough to slice a human in half. He nodded as one particular sword drew his attention. Lifting it off its storage handles, he brought it around to the table and placed it beside the block.

"Please. Please don't hurt me!" the woman cried as rivulets of tears chased one another down her cheeks. Her voice was small and soft.

He grabbed her right arm and pulled it across the table, resting her wrist in the block's groove. She tried to pull away, but he was too strong for her. She thrashed, tugging her shoulder to escape. The harder she tried, the tighter the grip became around her wrist as he pinned her hand down to the table, securing it with rope.

"No!" she screamed, finding her voice. The sound reverberated around the room.

A high-pitched scream that hurt his eardrums. He raised his hand above his shoulder and brought it down, striking the side of her face with the back of his hand. Her head jerked in one fluid motion, the sound of skin-on-skin contact cutting through the room.

He stepped away from her, ignoring her pleas. Switching on his music, he allowed the subtle sound of Japanese stringed instruments to filter through his awareness. He paused and closed his eyes, letting the music soothe him, compose him, and calm him. At that moment, it felt like he was the only one in the room.

Vision without action is a dream. Action without vision is a nightmare.

As he moved across towards a different display, his eyes widened in anticipation. He reached out and lifted the samurai helmet from its mount. It was a magnificent piece, handcrafted by the metalsmiths of Hanwei with exacting attention to detail to replicate the original helm and mask of the great samurai warlord Oda Nobunaga. He stared in wonderment at the craftsmanship and marvelled at the sheer terror it would have created in his adversaries. A small smile broke on his face as he placed it on his head and secured the structure beneath his chin.

He turned and faced her. "As long as your greed is stronger than compassion, there will always be suffering in your life," he recited. "It was always about greed with you. With all of you."

The woman shrunk into the chair and screamed, as terror pricked her skin like a thousand needles. A warm trickle of piss spread between her legs and collected in a pool on the floor.

71

KAREN RACED BACK towards the city centre followed by three police cars. The cacophony of noise from the sirens startled passers-by who stopped and gawked as cars whizzed past them. An ANPR camera had already pinged on the A19 and then moments later a traffic camera had picked up the Mazda 3 approaching the roundabout at Rawcliffe before heading south towards Poppleton.

"Where is he going?" Karen asked as she focused on the road ahead. Fifteen minutes had passed since the last sighting of his stolen car. With more than a dozen police vehicles now searching for the Mazda, and further units being deployed, the net had to be closing in on him.

"He's trying to give us the run around. Or he's trying to buy time."

"I don't think it's either, Jade. He's gone to ground. We have every single officer searching. Nothing is coming up on the cameras." Frustration tinged her voice as she cruised the streets close to the last reported sighting. Moments earlier, the police cars trailing her had branched off in different directions to expand their area of search.

The reports coming in through the radio were less than encouraging. Other officers had drawn a blank as well. They had extended the area of search to Earswick in the north, Bootham in the south, and Knapton in the west. It was like finding a needle in a haystack and something that Karen dreaded. She was almost certain that if he had headed towards the centre of York, he would have been picked up on several cameras, and he would have cornered himself. This meant that he still had to be on the periphery.

"We have a sighting. A grey Mazda turned off next to the Red Lion Inn on Roman Road about twenty minutes ago," came an officer's voice over Jade's radio.

Karen fixed Jade with a stare before shaking her head as if to suggest, "where's that?" She pulled her phone out and pulled up Google Maps. It was a few seconds before she figured it out. "He's gone back to his address. I want all officers converging on the location but to stay out of sight. Silent approach. Request armed officers."

Karen picked up the speed as Jade gave her directions. Moments later, she made a sharp right beside the Red Lion Inn. Two other police cars turned in just seconds behind her and followed, as the mini convoy raced along the quiet country road before entering the outskirts of Nether Popple-ton. Ivy-clad houses framed by black ornate dwarf railings and wide grassy verges soon replaced the bleak agricultural landscape.

They paused for a few seconds when they hit a junction where four roads converged, with Karen checking to make sure that an armed unit had been dispatched. Though they hadn't had a confirmed sighting of him in this case, the assault and abduction of this street worker so close to the attempted abduction of Vicky, only consolidated in her mind that it had to be the work of the same person, Adrian Wells.

A few tense moments passed before control confirmed an ETA of three minutes. That was good enough. Karen gave instructions to move forward and park up one street away until everyone was ready. While officers remained in that holding position, Karen used the opportunity to drive past Wells's address. There was no sign of the Mazda or Wells. She turned off and spotted a grassy access that led along the rear of the properties. Karen paused for a second. "Bingo!"

"That's the one," Jade said, confirming the registration. "He's inside."

Karen returned to her position as lead car before stepping out and gathering the surrounding officers.

"The stolen Mazda is towards the rear of the property. I want four officers to be positioned at the rear in case he makes a run for it. The rest of you," Karen said, turning to the other six officers, "are going through the front door with me. Who's going to use the big red key?"

One officer raised a finger as he picked it off the ground.

Karen turned towards the three armed officers. "I want you to go in as soon as we are through the door. He's violent and we know he's been using weapons. I believe that he's holding a young female within the property. We have permission to use lethal force, but our priority has to be the safety of the female. Is everyone okay with that?"

The three officers nodded in unison.

Karen gave the command to move forward. They converged on the property, keeping single file. The armed officers trained their sights on the windows, searching for any movement. The officer towards the front positioned himself by the door and gently pressed his hand on the door, assessing how much movement and play it had, and where would be the best position to hit it. Confident with his assessment, he nodded in Karen's direction before pulling the ram back and swinging it towards the door. The door shuddered but held firm. He pulled back and hit it again. Cracks appeared. The third strike pushed the door open, the latch splintering the door frame.

"Police! Stay where you are!" an armed officer shouted as he and his two colleagues trained their sights down the hallway, moving systematically. The second officer trained his weapon towards the top of the stairs in case there was any movement, while the third darted in and out of the rooms. "Clear," came the response.

Karen, Jade and the remaining officers followed, searching for any signs of the female or Adrian Wells. There was nothing. Once the shouting died down, Karen heard something. The faint sound of music. She looked bemused as she searched the faces of the other officers. Then she looked down at her feet and felt the faint vibration coming through her feet. "Downstairs!" she shouted. "Did you check all the doors?" she asked the assembled officers. A sea of nodding faces was her reply. Karen glanced around and narrowed her eyes before she moved towards the doorway beneath the stairs. She turned the handle, but it was locked. Resting a hand on the door, the vibration of the music crept through the wood.

"Police, open up!" Karen shouted as she thumped a fist on the door. A scream sent a chill through her. She took a step back. "Get that door open, now."

The officer with the big red key slammed it into the door. It shuddered and splintered. His second attempt left the door in tatters, allowing the armed officers to pull the pieces apart and train their weapons as they crept down the stairs.

Karen held back and looked across at Jade, who stood beside her with arms folded across her chest, chewing on her bottom lip.

72

HER SCREAMS WENT UNANSWERED as he picked up his gleaming sword and marvelled at the craftsmanship. The cold steel glinted in the light, its beauty masking its deadliness.

He lifted the blade above his head in readiness as he shouted "TENNOHEIKA BANZAI", the Japanese battle cry for "long live the Emperor".

Screams tore around him. Hers, his, theirs, every voice blending into one to create a melting pot of hysteria.

"Ei! Ei!" he screamed, the battle cry for "glory, glory" as he brought the sword down.

The first bullet struck his shoulder.

He reeled back, his face contorted in a mixture of anger and surprise. The sword never reached its target as he stumbled. Incensed with vengeance, he raised the blade again and charged towards the armed officer. "Ei! Ei!" he screamed, his sword held aloft, ready to deliver a deadly blow.

The second bullet struck him in the chest, sending him backwards and crashing to the floor. The sword fell to the floor with a metallic clang as officers rushed forward, the sights from their weapons trained on him.

"Don't move! Don't fucking move!" officers screamed, their guns trained on the man, ready to shoot again if necessary.

An armed officer rushed forward and knelt, checking for a pulse while ripping open the first-aid bag strapped to his thigh. Plasters, pads, airway tubes, and scissors spilled out on to the floor. "He's alive. Get the big medical bag," he barked to his colleague, who charged back up the stairs to retrieve their kit from the car. As he rushed past Karen in the hallway, he gave the nod to confirm it was safe for her to continue.

Karen and Jade rushed down the stairs followed by the remaining officers. Carnage greeted her. One officer had a bundle of gauze pressed against the man's entry wounds attempting to stop the blood loss, while another officer freed the female victim who sat shocked and motionless, as if she was an innocent bystander who'd stumbled across this chaotic scene.

Karen removed the man's helmet to check his identity. It was Adrian Wells.

She sat back on her heels while the other officers worked to stabilise Wells as he clung to life. "Jade, take her upstairs and put in a call for paramedics to attend. And it might be quicker to get an air ambulance for him," Karen said, staring at Wells being treated in front of her, piles of blood-soaked gauze and lint pads scattered around the floor.

Karen stood and took in the scene. She counted more than a

dozen samurai swords pinned to the surrounding walls. The instruments of war and ceremonial duties now bore witness to the death and destruction they had caused in the hands of this lunatic. "Someone switch off the bloody music," Karen shouted. She continued to stare in bewilderment. Samurai body armour and another helmet hung from a mannequin in one corner. The bookshelf was crammed with books on Japanese culture, lifestyle, famous battles, and the warrior way of life.

She stopped by a glass cabinet and noticed six identical small boxes, each one sitting on its own individual shelf. Snapping on a pair of latex gloves, she retrieved one box and prised open the lid. Her eyes widened in surprise and shock. Karen replaced the lid before sliding the box back on to the shelf. She took out another box and looked inside. Another bony hand. She guessed what would be in the others.

Karen left the armed officers attending to Wells while she headed back upstairs to where Jade sat beside the victim. Karen took the space on the other side and rubbed the woman's back. "What's your name, love?"

Even though Jade had thrown an insulation blanket over the woman's shoulders, she trembled. "Seema. Seema Panchal."

Karen gave her a reassuring smile. "You're safe now"

Seema shook her head. "Why me? Why did he pick me?"

Karen didn't have an answer for her.

"I thought I was going to die down there." She slumped forward as sobs racked her body. "I wet myself. I couldn't help it."

Karen rested a hand on Seema's arm. "Hey, it's fine. Please don't worry. We'll need all your clothes for forensic evidence, so you can change into a paper suit. The paramedics are only a few minutes away. They'll check you over. Once we have you away from here, we'll need to take a statement. Is that okay?"

Seema stared ahead as involuntary spasms jerked her shoulders.

"Seema?"

The woman nodded.

"Jade, can you see if you can rustle up a sweet cup of tea?"

"Yep, will do," Jade replied, rising and leaving the room.

The sound of approaching sirens heralded the paramedics and police backup, followed not long after by the whipping sound of blades as an air ambulance landed in a field close by.

Karen left Seema in the capable hands of a female police officer, while she stepped out to get a breath of fresh air. The street had been empty when they'd first arrived, but now a sea of concerned faces hovered on the grass verge opposite the house.

Karen pulled out her phone and made a call to forensics. The house was an Aladdin's cave of evidence and enough to put Wells away for a very long time.

73

ONE WEEK LATER...

Karen made her way through the hospital towards a small wing where Adrian Wells was being treated under the watchful eye of an armed guard. She quickened her pace as the excitement built in her. There was always a buzz with closing a case, especially one with overwhelming evidence. Since the shooting, Wells's doctors had kept him sedated. The intervention by armed officers had saved his life. Many would argue why? Why save the life of a killer? Some would say an eye for an eye. But her job involved catching those responsible and seeing justice served. Only then could the loved ones of those killed be left to grieve in peace.

Karen flashed her warrant card to the officers on guard who allowed her to pass. Wells was being held in a separate room away from prying eyes and other patients. His sedation had benefited her. The bones discovered in the basement needed extensive analysis to extract working DNA profiles. The work was a time-consuming process and if

Wells had been held in custody; she doubted if the results would have got to her in time to form part of the interview process. The best profiling results were often obtained using demineralization protocols that aimed to dissolve the bone matrix to release the DNA, which often took as long as twenty-four to thirty-six hours.

She entered the room and saw another police officer sitting on a chair in one corner of the room, flicking through a magazine. On seeing Karen, the officer jumped to his feet, looking sheepish.

"Sorry, ma'am."

Karen smiled at him and waved off his apology. "Don't worry. I don't imagine you signed up to be sitting in a hospital room for your entire shift being bored out of your skull. Why don't you grab yourself a cup of tea and stretch your legs?"

The officer hesitated, unsure what to do. "You sure?"

Karen nodded. "Go. Before I change my mind."

The officer darted out the door in a blur, making Karen laugh. She turned her attention towards Wells who was propped up on a few pillows, his right wrist handcuffed to the bed. He looked a dishevelled figure, the evidence of a small scruffy beard showing, his face looking weary with hanging jowls. A part of her wanted to go over and push the heel from her shoe into his eyeballs… just a small part of her mind you. The rest of her couldn't stand the sight of him.

She stood at the bottom of his bed, staring at him. He in return stared back at her, not blinking once.

"You're probably disappointed that we saved your life. I

guess you wanted to go out in a blaze of glory wearing a tin hat and waving your Captain Pugwash sword." Karen smiled. "You got too cocky for your own good. You'll be interviewed later on today, but you haven't got a leg to stand on. While you've been away with the fairies, it's given us time to build an overwhelming amount of forensic evidence to put you away for life."

"It doesn't matter. You can throw everything at me. It's just a shame that you caught up with me so soon."

Karen raised a brow. "Oh, you mean that one-way ticket to Japan? Did you think that leaving the country would stop us from catching up with you? Yes, we checked your laptop. Bit sloppy on your part."

When Wells remained stoic, Karen continued.

"We have enough evidence to charge you with three counts of murder. DNA analysis of the bones recovered from your basement confirmed they belonged to Sallyanne Faulkner, Grace Abbott, both from York, and Raduca Bogdan from Dorset." Karen paused to study Wells. He showed little emotion or concern. "We haven't been able to confirm the identity of the other two hands yet. Why don't you give the victims' families a break and tell me who they belong to?"

"No comment."

"There are also three counts of assault, one count of abduction, and one count of attempted abduction to add to the list. It's looking good, hey?"

"I said no comment."

Karen walked over to the window and looked out for a few moments before returning to the bed. "One of the hair fibres recovered from your office chair had the same DNA composition as Sallyanne Faulkner's. Your prints match those found on Sallyanne's pendant and lipstick. We also found one of your hair fibres and your DNA sample from semen traces that were recovered from a green suede skirt belonging to Sallyanne Faulkner. So we believe it was you that spiked her drink and tried to rape her during her final year at university."

Karen stiffened as she thought about what Sallyanne had endured. A member of the teaching staff whom she'd trusted had taken advantage of her for his own twisted and deviant means.

"That was enough to destroy her life. She was never the same again. Her parents lost a daughter; her sister lost her best friend. And for what? To satisfy your twisted needs."

Wells fidgeted in his bed and winced with pain.

"Why the right hand?" Karen said, folding her arms across her chest and raising a brow in his direction. This unanswered question had bothered her the most throughout the whole investigation.

Wells sniffed. "What hand do you always think they put out when touting for business and wanting payment?"

That made sense to Karen now. "So that's why you chopped them off?"

Wells shook his head. "I said nothing about chopping off their hands. I'm saying that from observation that whenever a prostitute wants payment, she puts out her hand ready to take the money. Don't put words in my mouth."

Karen laughed. "It doesn't matter. I don't care about motives. I'm interested in facts. The facts that will put you away in prison until they take you out in a body bag." She headed for the door and paused before looking back at Wells. "You should look after your swords a lot better. You thought you'd cleaned them very well. But we found a small fleck of blood on one of your swords. DNA analysis confirmed that it belonged to Grace Abbott. You messed up, mate."

Karen yanked open the door and walked out without looking back.

74

"TOMMY, IT'S KAREN HERE," she said, putting her phone on speakerphone in the car.

"Hi there," he shouted, his voice drowned out by the background noise.

"Bad time?"

Nugent laughed. "You could say that. I'm being dragged around the shops looking for a prom dress."

Karen laughed in reply. "I hate to say this, but I think you'd look scary and weird in one. Especially with your hairy legs. I know your dress sense was shit back then. What did we call you…? Oh, that's it… Mr Top Man."

"Haha, bloody hilarious. I can't see you getting many bookings for bar mitzvahs or weddings!"

"How is everyone, by the way?"

"They were my favourite two people, until Erin and Rosie dragged me around far too many shops while Rosie tried on dresses costing more than my car. Now she's giving me an earache about needing Louboutin shoes, whatever they are. What's wrong with a bloody pair of Clarks!"

"She has expensive taste! I can't believe it's prom time for her already. Where has the time gone?"

"I wish I knew. It doesn't feel that long ago when I held her in my arms smitten by this little bundle that smelt so cute."

It was so strange for Karen to hear him talking like this. He had always been the loud one. Always up for a laugh. Always had a pint in his hand. Now he was a happily married man with a daughter that was about to fleece him.

"Hang on to those memories, mate. I envy you sometimes. A lovely family, good job, and you live in a nice part of the country."

"Yeah, I guess. It's been so long since I've seen you. Why don't you come down here for a bit? Take a day or two off. We have a spare room. We're holding a delayed 16th birthday bash for Rosie soon. Come down? We can catch up like old times. Bring your fella?"

The question took her by surprise. She'd mentioned Zac on one of their earlier calls. Trust Tommy to remember that. "Yeah, that sounds good. As long as I'm not wrapped up in the case. A break on the coast would be perfect," she replied.

"I'm still on the phone. I won't be a minute," Tommy said in a hushed tone before returning to the conversation. "Sorry, Erin is giving me one of those looks. I'll have to head off. Great result on your case, mate. Thanks for passing the information through to me. It's good to know that we can get a conviction for Raduca. The family can come to terms with their loss."

"Definitely. Thanks for your help as well. And Tommy, thanks for everything, mate. And hope to see you soon."

"My pleasure. By the way, I forgot to ask. Have you stopped wetting your knickers every time you laugh?"

"Piss off, Tommy," Karen said before hanging up, his laughter ringing in her ears.

75

KAREN STOPPED off at the house where Sallyanne had last lived to pick up a few items before heading off again. With Jade visiting Donovan Jacobs, Grace's boyfriend, to break the news of charges being brought against Adrian Wells, Karen had the unenviable task of visiting Ted and Helen Faulkner.

She paused at the doorstep and took in a few deep lungfuls of air to prepare herself before ringing the doorbell. Ted Faulkner came to the door moments later and offered her a weak smile before inviting her in.

Karen joined Ted, Helen, and their daughter Esme in the lounge. She spent a few minutes updating them on the case and the charges being brought against Adrian Wells. All three sat in silence while they listened to Karen, with Ted and Helen exchanging the briefest of glances. Esme sat on the edge of the sofa with her hands balled into a fist in her lap.

Ted still appeared to show more emotion than his wife

Helen, who remained stoical, as he rubbed his eyes and took deep breaths. The pain of losing his daughter still appeared raw in Karen's eyes.

Karen reached for the carrier bag beside her and pulled out a shoebox before handing it to Helen. "This was under Sallyanne's bed. I thought it was only right that you had it. Of course, all her other personal possessions are still in her room, including her clothes, and I can arrange for an officer to go with you should you wish to go through the things one last time."

Ted nodded and thanked her.

Helen held the box like a foreign object she'd never seen before.

"Mum, I think we need to look, don't you?" Esme said, trying to encourage her mum.

Helen removed the lid, a swell of emotion stirring her chest as it rose. She pushed a finger among the items, picking up a small bracelet and staring at it for what seemed an eternity before she passed it to her husband. Ted held it and sniffed as his eyes welled up.

Helen continued to sift through the other items, pulling out the envelope of photos and passing them to Esme. She then picked up several other envelopes and flicked through them until she came to one which was sealed and addressed to Mum, Dad and Esme. Her fingers trembled as she picked it up and turned it over before unsealing it. She pulled out the single sheet of paper from inside it and unfolded it before pushing the tears away from her eyes.

"Do you want me to read it?" Karen asked.

With reluctance, Helen nodded and passed the letter to Karen.

Karen scanned the first few lines and felt a wave of deep sadness and emotion wash through her body. Her eyes moistened. Karen wasn't sure she could read it out aloud but she needed to be strong for the family.

Dear Mum, Dad, and Esme.

If you're reading this, then it's probably too late for me. I'm so sorry that I let you down. I tried to be strong, but life has a way of throwing us a curveball every so often, which just kept knocking me back down again. I know I'm a disap-pointment in your eyes. I know I had so much going for me. So many hopes and dreams. I really wanted you to be proud of me. But I didn't turn out the way you or I hoped I would.

Mum and Dad, I'm sorry that our relationship soured. Even though I'm gone, I hope you hold close those sweet memo-ries and photos of me growing up and us being a family in happier times.

Dad, I'll always remember the times when I rode around on your back and pretended you were my horse… remember? The one I begged you to buy for me every Christmas.

Mum, you are a proud and strong woman, but a real softy inside. I only wish I could draw on your special strength to fight the demons that poison my thoughts and rob me of my sanity. But I just can't any more. Please don't hate me for being weak.

Karen stopped as a soft cry filtered across the room. She looked up to see tears chasing one another down Helen's cheeks. She clutched Ted's hand so tightly that her knuckles turned white. Karen swallowed hard and returned to the letter.

Esme, my little shadow. Though you thought I didn't, I always knew that you were the one stealing my eyeliner pens LOL. Thank you for trying so hard to rescue me. You did more than any big sis could have asked for. You said you admired me and looked up to me as your big sister. In reality, I'm the one who carries huge admiration for you, and if anything, I look up to you. You'll have me by your side watching over you. Always, now and forever. Live life and keep that beautiful smile. Don't make the mistakes I made and look after Mum and Dad. You know what they're like when they can't open a fresh jar of pickled beetroot? All hell breaks loose!

Esme let out a strained squeal as she began to cry, her hands plastered over her eyes as her shoulders shook.

Please don't ever forget how much I love you all. I'm sorry to have to leave you in so much pain, and I hope one day that you will find it in your hearts to forgive me for choosing the wrong path. I'll be waiting up there for you with a kettle on the boil and your favourite biscuits.

Love you forever,

Sal

xxx

Karen looked up and choked as she watched all three family members sobbing. It felt as if she was intruding on their personal moment of grief.

After expressing her condolences, she saw herself out.

Standing on the pavement, Karen dabbed her eyes, keen to

wipe away the tears. Loss and grief were never easy for anyone to experience, especially parents. The grief of losing a child carried a lifetime of great courage. She hoped the Faulkners had the strength to endure that storm of emotions. Though drained after the visit, Karen would visit them again in a few days, not on police business as such, but out of compassion for their loss.

Grabbing her keys from her bag, she left to head home for a few rest days.

CURRENT BOOK LIST

Hop over to my website for a current list of books:

http://jaynadal.com/current-books/

OTHER WAYS TO STAY IN TOUCH

Other ways you can connect with me:

Like my page on Facebook: Jay Nadal

Email jay@jaynadal.com with any questions, ideas or interesting story suggestions. Hey, even if you spot a typo that we've missed, then drop me a line!

ABOUT THE AUTHOR

I've always had a strong passion for whodunnits, crime series and books. The more I immersed myself in it, the stronger the fascination grew.

In my spare time you'll find me in the gym, trying to squeeze in a read or enjoying walks in the forest…It's amazing what you think of when you give yourself some space.

Oh, and I'm an avid people-watcher. I just love to watch the interaction between people, their mannerisms, their way of expressing their thoughts…Weird I know.

I hope you enjoy the stories that I craft for you.

Author of:

The DI Scott Baker Crime Series

The DI Karen Heath Crime Series

The Thomas Cade PI Series

Printed in Great Britain
by Amazon